2ND WANNASEA TALE

POLITIZATION OF BETHANY STOLZ

By
NG Rippel

Table of Contents

RESTORATION

Wednesday 2:15PM. Beth, Marie and Sallie are seated at a picnic table on the rear patio of 'The Place" near the backside of the kitchen area. Beth and Marie have just completed a planning session with a representative of the Swansea Kitchen Supply company. Sallie has just returned from finalizing plans for tomorrow's delivery of a mobile kitchen unit with that firm's delivery specialist.

The mobile kitchen unit will be leased for one year. Additionally, Beth has arranged to purchase two new permanent ovens, two new espresso machines, and two large industrial microwave ovens from the firm.

The plan is to reopen 'The Place' one week from Thursday with Zack Tillerman headlining a three-day set of performances. A new order window has just been installed facing the patio area to allow customers to do walk up purchases of the entire menu as well as 'The Place' paraphernalia. Behind this area a storage room is in the process of being built out to replace the storage shed. This new area has been made possible by extending the kitchen rear wall area out five feet.

"What's the plan for Abe's old room?" Sallie asks in reference to the upstairs area over the restroom where Abe used to reside. Prior to the fire, this area was being converted into storage space as well as a small shop. The heat from the fire had damaged the construction which had been taking place in that area so that the area must be reworked.

"We are going to split it between a small office area on the left-hand side and a slightly bigger 'storage area," Beth says.

"It won't be ready until Jan. 15th however," Marie injects. "The shelving we want will take two weeks to produce."

"Your plan is for Zack is going to play the first 3 nights of the reopening?" Sallie asks.

"I certainly hope, so," Beth replies. "He seems to be in some kind of funk right now, so I'm not 100% certain.

"Funk about what?" Sallie asks.

"Zack is going through a bout of depression," Beth replies. "When Saanvi first contacted me about hiring Zack, she warned me that Zack has been diagnosed as a manic depressive to go with the PTSD which he acquired from his military service. Seems what we have seen of Zack so far is the manic side. He started slipping into depression last Thursday. Zack's not been working with Abe on songwriting. He's also not much interested in what's going on with that little company, he, Abe, and Molly have got going. Which is odd because they've been selling songs off their website like crazy."

"I didn't know Zack was in the Army," Sallie says.

"He went in the day after he finished Secondary school over in Halifax," Beth relates. "Nine months later he was in Iraq in the infantry. Zack doesn't talk about his time in the Army. Saanvi told me that Zack was involved in a bad incident in Iraq which killed two of his best Army buddies. Zack was riding with them in an APV, when he had asked him to get out of the vehicle and scout a small stream that they were about to cross. Once Zack was about 50 yards from the APV, an explosive blew up and killing his two buddies. Shrapnel from the explosion tore up Zack's back. He began having trouble coping. Zack was brought back to Hanover Army Hospital for treatment. He remained in the Hanover facility for almost a year until it was time for him to be permanently discharged from the Army. Saanvi says, when he's in the depression part of the cycle, he takes medication. Sometimes his medication works, sometimes it doesn't. Right now, it doesn't seem to be working."

"What will you do if he can't play?" Sallie asks.

"Beyond apologizing to two hundred or so of his fans," Beth says. "All I can offer is a rain check whenever Zack returns to playing. I've lined up the Wannasea Boys to front him, so if Zack can't come on, at least there will be some music. Though I'm not so sure I want to hear any damned Reggie Revival songs at this point."

"Has Zack been at the studio with Abe and Molly at all this week?" Sallie asks.

"No," Beth says, "he's been down at his grandma's playing his guitar for her. His grandma's condition is worsening. Saanvi thinks our being closed and his grandma's failing health, has triggered Zack's depression. Other than the party, playing guitar for his grandmother is pretty much all Zack has been doing since last Thursday.

"I've seen a lot of people coming and going up at the house," Sallie said. "I figured that had something to do with Zack's music business."

"All of that activity is the result of Abe's civil lawsuit against the Sylvester brothers and Reggie," Beth relates. "Cousin Herbert is pushing our civil suit against them as far and as fast as he can. He's got his youngest daughter, Olivia, working on it. She's got Abe hopping around like he hasn't for ages. Abe calls her 'the shark'."

"So how long do you think, we can operate out of this 'Mobile Kitchen' thingy?" Sallie asks.

"Depends," Beth says. "If we can buy the old government center, we'll be using it down here for as long as it takes to get everything going up there. If we can't buy the old government center, then we will use it for as long as it takes to build out a full kitchen here. I've committed to lease it for a year, but we can always have it pulled out the garage doors of the kitchen and use it somewhere else."

The trio sit in silence for a minute or so enjoying the winter sun.

"I was talking earlier this morning with Angelique," Beth relates in reference to her lawyer third cousin, "and the architect, who has been hired to come up with our plan for building out the old Government Zent Center. The space up there is going to be at least four times the area that we have down here. Angelique made an off-hand suggestion that front area with all the glass facing the parking lot would be a terrific place for a restaurant."

"You are thinking of doing a restaurant, up there?" Sallie asks.

"If I'm being honest with myself," Beth says, "I'm not all that interested in the food business. What's made food sales take off here, is that I turned the whole menu over to you. What has started me thinking is that it is probably time for us to have a serious talk. I've heard you talking about you and your boyfriend having an interest in starting up a restaurant. Would you consider doing it up there?"

Sallie looks at Beth slightly perplexed. "Sam and I were thinking about opening a little seafood place on the west end," Sallie finally says, "Based on what I remember last time that I was in the old gov center to renew my driver's license, that's a pretty good-sized area that you are talking about."

"About 4500 square feet," Beth says. "I'd be willing to have it build out to your specification and then lease it out to you. I'm also game to help with financing or being a silent partner if you'd like."

"This is kind of sudden," Sallie says.

"They aren't going to close off the bidding process until Jan.21st," Beth relates. "We are being told that it very likely will be the end of February at the earliest before the island finalizes their decision. Likely will take another 2 or 3 months to complete the property transfers. The reality is that we would be unlikely to get the facility much before August or September to start having it built out. Optimistically, if the place would be ready by the first of next year, it would be a minor miracle."

"Let me talk with Sam," Sallie says. "How soon will you need an answer?"

"Right after the island would select us as the winning proposal," Beth says. "If we don't win the bid, I still might be interested in doing something a little different here."

"What are you planning to do if you aren't in the food business? Sallie asks.

"I'm going to focus on building a retreat which cannot not only house more kids, but provide a lower cost resort experience," Beth says. "If we manage to get the old government center that likely will be done there near the quarry. If our bid isn't selected, I'm hoping that I can talk to whoever gets that property to sell me some of the land which runs from the parking lot down to our current properties. We could use the land to expand the venue here as well as possibly building the retreat."

"Beth and I also have some other plans which we are hoping to start taking action on shortly," Marie adds.

SEA CHANGE

Thursday 7:55AM. Beth has just come out of the in-suite bathroom of her bedroom and is in the process of pulling on a fresh pair of jeans.

"How are you going to tell Abe?" Marie asks sitting up in bed.

Beth buttons the top of her jeans, then walks to the mirror on the bureau which used to belong to her grandmother Jane and begins brushing her hair, before answering, "I'm just going to tell him matter-of-factly. That's how he always springs things on me."

"But this is a big thing," Marie says. "The biggest thing that I can imagine."

"Bigger than telling me Reggie Reginald is my biological father or that the Sylvester Brothers killed my mother and grandmother?"

"It's a different kind of big thing," Marie says. "Why don't you let me come with you?"

"No," Beth says, "at this point, what I have to tell Abe has to be between just Abe and I. Abe needs to be free to react without any outside influence."

"Okay, but I'm nervous."

"So am I," Beth says, "but the time has come."

Beth slides on a pair of canvas slip-ons which are beside the bureau and walks to the door at the front of the bedroom.

"Good luck," Marie says not moving from the bed.

Beth goes out the door, closing it gently before turning right and heading toward the empty studio. She goes into the studio, walks through the sliding glass door and exits onto the patio. Beth can see Abe sitting at his kitchen table looking at one of his green journals.

She walks across the patio and knocks on the window of the sliding glass door of Abe's in-law suite.

"It's open," Abe says without looking up from his journal.

"Morning, Gramps," Beth says as she walks inside.

"The water in the kettle is still hot, if you want to make yourself a cup of tea."

Beth walks past where Abe sits and fixes herself a cup of Taylors of Harrogate Lemon-Orange tea. She returns with her mug to Abe's kitchen table and sits down to Abe's left.

"I have a couple important things to tell you," Beth advises.

"Okay," Abe says putting his journal down, "is it about 'The Place' or our bid on the old government center?"

"Neither" Beth says dunking the teabag into the hot water. "On Monday, Marie and I are going to go to Hanover and get married."

Abe's eyes widen momentarily, before he says, "Married?"

"Yes, married." Beth says. "There is quite a bit more to it, but let's deal with that first. How do you feel about it?"

"I really like Marie," Abe says, 'but I had no idea that you and Marie were a thing."

'Maybe because you weren't paying attention?" Beth says impetuously.

Abe thinks for a moment, then takes a sip from his mug before saying, "No, I probably wasn't. I had no idea that you are lesbian."

"Does that bother you" Beth asks.

Abe looks away from Beth and out toward the patio for a long minute.

"You are the most important thing in my life," Abe says. "You know that I've been worried that you've tied yourself down to this place. My hope was that you would get yourself set on your path for the future while I'm still around."

"Being gay didn't factor into those calculations, I take it?"

"No Beth," Abe says, "it didn't cross my mind."

"Now that it has, how do you feel about it."

Abe takes a long sip of his tea.

"I can't tell you that I'm able to fully process what you've just told me," Abe said, "but the reality is that I love you more than anything on this planet, I will continue to love you and support you no matter what you are or decide to do."

"My being gay and married to Marie is not going to bother you in the least?"

Abe puts the mug down, rests his right elbow on the table and places his hand on his chin. He pauses for another long minute before saying, "I will learn to accept it. I will fully support it. It is just going to take me a little getting used to."

"Does it bother you that Marie and I are gay?"

"I don't think so," Abe says earnestly. "I have nothing against anyone who is gay, transgender or any other sexual persuasion. It is simply that it is going to take me some time to process the situation."

"What part of Marie and I being married will you have to start getting used to first?"

Abe takes a sip from his tea mug, then looks off into space for a long moment before saying, "The first thing will probably be adjusting to the idea that there aren't going to be any great grandkids."

'Then your first thing is dead wrong," Beth says, "because having kids is exactly why Marie and I have decided to get married."

Abe gives Beth a quizzical look.

"In addition to getting married on Monday," Beth says. "Marie and I are going to a fertility clinic in Hanover and hopefully begin the process of my becoming pregnant."

"How's that work?" Abe says somewhat incredulously.

"Marie's brother, Josh, has agreed to go with us to be the sperm donor," Marie says. "His sperm will be used to fertilize my eggs. Every Monday, Marie and I will be going back to Hanover for whatever treatments are required. Hopefully, it will result in a clean pregnancy."

"I see," Abe says rising from his chair. He walks over to Beth, leans down, and hugs her, before continuing, "Let me know what I can do to help. Both with this marriage thing and the trips to Hanover."

Beth hugs him back.

"Why can't you do all this on the island?" Abe asks. "Isn't there a fertility clinic down on the east end of the island?"

"Same sex marriage isn't recognized on the island," Beth replies. "The fertility clinic on the island isn't allowed to deal with same sex couples."

"Didn't know that" Abe muses as he goes back to his chair and sits down. "Can I go over to Hanover with you and Marie on Monday to be part of the marriage process?"

"We are only going to do a civil ceremony at the Hanover Courthouse," Beth advises. "We went over on Tuesday and got all the paperwork and tests done. There won't be anything to this other than getting a signed piece of paper. I appreciate your offer to come with us, but with all the running around we are going to need to do with the fertility clinic process, I think it would be better if you stay here to hold down the fort for whatever decisions need to be made about work down at 'The Place' or if Angelique needs something on our bid. We are going to have a little ceremony back here on Sunday on the patio. It's going to be officiated by Miss Vicky. I'd really appreciate it if you would be the one to give me away."

"I'll certainly give you my blessing and stand at your side," Abe says, "but I have no intention of giving you away. You are about all that I've got left."

"You know what I mean, Abe. Molly can help fill you in on the plans and details as she's arranging everything."

"Did everyone up here but me, not know about you Marie?"

"Marie and I don't go around advertising ourselves," Beth says. "We are what we are and hope that people will accept us for it. But yes, you are probably the only one up here, who didn't know Marie and I are a thing."

"I'm really happy for you, Kitten," Abe says after rising and giving his granddaughter a hug.

"I'm glad," Beth says with a smile. "Now, can you tell me if you have any idea what we can do about Zack?"

"If he doesn't show up today," Abe says, "Molly and I are planning on going down to his grandma's house and having a talk with him tomorrow."

Beth thinks for a few seconds before requesting, "Would you let me know your plans. If you are going to go down to see him, I'd like to come along. I'd also like Saanvi to be there, so it would be best to schedule any meeting after she is off work. Saanvi is usually home by quarter past five."

HANOVER PLANS

Friday 5:20PM. Beth is steering her VW Beetle out of the parking lot behind the house and heads toward the village of Wannasea for a 5:30 meeting with Saanvi and Zack. Abe is in the passenger seat. Molly is in the rear.

"Would you mind if we do some renovations to the upstairs area in your in-law suite?" Beth asks her grandfather. "For a week or so the construction people will need access through your suite to work up there. Once they have a direct outside entrance created, they likely will still need access to your plumbing for a few days to put in a bathroom on the second floor."

"Okay by me," Abe says. "Who are planning on putting up there?"

"Eventually Josh," Beth says. "Marie's mother kicked him out of her apartment when they found out that he is going to be a sperm donor for Marie and I."

Marie had not lived in her parents' house for over eight years. She had left to avoid abuse from her father.

"Josh says his mother went ballistic when she found out about our plans to get married," Beth continues. "I'm going to put him in Marie's room first, but eventually it will be better if he's got his own space."

Beth slows her vehicle a little as she enters the town. She completes the descent from the mountain, passes two side streets before entering the ferry dock and taking the third exit toward the west end of the village.

"How did Zack sound when you talked to him by phone yesterday?" Beth asks.

"Like he was stuck down a ten foot well in the middle of a snow fog," Abe says. "He seems disinterested in doing anything but playing his guitar for Emma."

'We've had two requests from music magazines wanting to do interviews," Molly says. "I've had to lie and tell them that he is out of town at the moment."

Sally swings left to go up West Road.

"We've also made enough money from our website," Molly continues, "that Zack could pay off all his debts and help get someone in to take care of his grandmother. Even that doesn't seem to interest him."

"Saanvi says this is the worse funk that she's seen him in since he got out of the Army," Beth relates. "During these first weeks out at 'The Place', she had never seen him as manic as he was. Saanvi thinks the sudden stop in being able to perform along with Emma's declining health is the trigger."

"The problem is that the only real option which Zack has for mental health treatment is at the military base in Hanover," Abe says.

"That's because all of Zack's mental issues are deemed to have originated in the Army," Beth says. "The Wannasea Healthcare System thinks that means the Army is who should be responsible for treating him."

Beth brings the car to a stop in front of Zack's grandmother's townhouse. Abe exits from the passenger side and helps Molly climb out of the back seat. As they walk to the cement steps, Beth has already used the metal wrapper to knock on the door.

"Come on in," Saanvi says. "Ralph is in the living room with grandma."

They walk through the open doorway into a room with two armchairs and a large couch. Zack is sitting on the couch with his grandmother. His guitar is between his legs but he's not playing it.

"You've got visitors," Saanvi announces. "Why don't you get them seated, while I go into the kitchen and grab another chair."

"Sit down wherever you'd like," Zack says his eyes avoiding theirs.

Emma, Zack's grandmother, seems to be dozing. Abe goes to the couch and sits on the other side of her thinking that any minute, Emma will be grabbing his hand. Beth and Molly take the armchairs as Saavi reenters with a wooden chair from the dining room which she places to the side of the couch then sits down on it.

The noise from Saanvi setting the chair down, wakes Emma.

"Who are these people?" the old lady says, turning toward Abe and looking as if she has never seen him before.

"These are folks from my work, grandma," Zack says.

"They don't belong here," Emma says.

"They've come for a visit," Saanvi says, "now you be nice."

"We have come to see when you might be thinking of coming back to the studio," Abe says to Zack.

"I don't feel up to it, right now," Zack replies. "Maybe next week."

"You know we are reopening next Thursday?" Beth says. "Do you think you will be able to play."

"Maybe," Zack says fiddling with the neck of his guitar.

"We've had two magazine writers call and ask if you'll do interviews with them," Molly says. "One is from 'The Scene'."

"Don't feel like talking with writers," Zack says.

"Are you taking any medication now, Zack?" Beth asks.

"He started taking Depakote again on Monday," Saanvi relates.

"When is the last time that he spoke directly with a doctor?" Abe asks.

"Monday, Ralph spoke to someone out in Hanover, who gave him a prescription renewal," Saanvi says. "They basically just confirmed that he is in the depression phase and issued a script. They keep telling Ralph that he needs to come in for evaluation, but he has only been out to Hanover once since he was officially discharged from the Army."

"I don't like leaving the island," Zack states firmly.

"I have a suggestion for you," Beth says. "Marie and I are going to be going to Hanover every Monday for at least the next few months. Where we are going goes right past the Hanover base. Why don't you see if you can schedule appointments for Monday and you can ride with us."

Zack looks at his guitar, his hand continuing to fiddle with the top tuner.

"I spoke to the facility yesterday," Saanvi says, "they say that they can set you up for a first appointment a week from this coming Monday."

"I'd also be willing to come," Molly offers. "I've arranged not to have any Monday classes next semester, so I'm free that entire day. I can help Zack take care of everything while Beth and Marie are in Hanover."

"Wouldn't you like to try to feel better?" Abe asks Zack.

"I'd like to get back to making music," Zack says.

"I think the only thing that is holding your back from that happening is you," Beth says. "Why don't you give these evaluations a try?"

Zack fiddles with the bottom tuner for a few seconds before saying, "I'll go once, and we'll see what happens."

"You promise?" Saanvi asks.

"I promise," Zack says his eyes still on tuner.

"No promises," Emma says loudly. "No promises."

"I think we need to make a toast to Beth and Marie getting married, Zack's decision and the New Year," Saanvi says. "I have a bottle of champagne in the kitchen."

Beth disappears with Saanvi into the kitchen to get the champagne as well as cheese platter which she had prepared earlier.

Emma has drifted off to sleep, her head now leaning on Zack's shoulder.

"Do you know Beth & Marie are getting married?" Abe asks Zack.

"Yes," Zack replies, "I've been trying to work out a song to play at the celebration next Sunday."

"Why don't you come out to the studio, and I'll work with you on it?" Abe suggests.

"Maybe I'll come out Sunday," Zack says. "I'll see how I feel."

Beth and Saanvi return with a bottle of champagne and sparkling cider. Everyone but Abe and Emma got a glass of champagne. Abe gets the sparkling cider. Emma continues to doze.

As everyone raises their glass, Saanvi says, "Here's to Marie and Beth and hope for a happy and fruitful union."

Everyone takes a sip.

"Here's to Zack getting back to his music," Beth offers raising her glass.

Everyone takes another small sip.

"Here's to a Happy New Year," Saanvi offers.

They all sip again.

While the cheese plate is being passed around, Abe asks Saanvi, "Is Emma doing okay?"

Saanvi shakes her head, "She has really been going downhill this past week. She's had increasing trouble walking. I'm afraid her memory is now completely gone. She doesn't really recognize anyone other than Ralph and I and that recognition is not very consistent."

"I'm really sorry to hear that," Abe says. "She seemed to enjoy herself at the holiday party."

"She did," Saanvi says, "but I have a feeling that might have been her last dance with reality so to speak. Dad and mom are starting to think that we are going to have to place her in a nursing facility soon. It's just become too much to try to care for her when she isn't mobile."

LEGAL UNION

Monday 10:18AM. Beth has just pulled into a coffee shop about five minutes from the courthouse in Hanover.

As Marie exits from the passenger side, she asks her brother Josh, who has been dozing in the rear seat, "You want us to bring you anything?"

"I'll take a Grande with two sugars," Josh says sleepily.

"Do you know what time he got in last night?" Marie asks Beth.

"Must have been after 1, because he wasn't in by the time I came to bed," Beth says holding open the door into the coffee shop for Marie.

The pair place their order for 3 coffees then carry them back out to the car. Their appointment at the courthouse to receive their marriage license is at 11. Marie hands a coffee to Josh in the back seat.

"Mom is going to force Randy to stop working at 'The Place'," Josh says offhandedly.

"Why?" Marie asks, "Randy needs the money he earns for clothes and school. Mom certainly isn't going to buy him those things."

Marie had left her parent's household going on seven years now due to abuse by her father. Abuse which Marie's mother refused to recognize. Marie's father has now become a more off again than on presence in that household. Josh has just been tossed out of his mother's apartment this past week for agreeing to be a sperm donor for Marie and Beth.

"She's started going to the New Jericho Temple," Josh says. "Mom now thinks that everything that goes on out at 'The Place' is some form of Satanic Ritual."

"When did this start?" Marie asks.

"She began going to the Temple around June," Josh says. "She's gone off the deep end since she heard that you and Beth are getting married."

"Is she getting this Satanic Ritual stuff from that Temple?" Beth asks.

"More or less," Josh says, "The Prophet Ainsley guy is a real hoot."

"How so?" Beth asks.

"He's got this whole spiel about how Satan has taken over the world with the exception of the island," Josh relates. "Say's the island is God's last stand. The only way God is going to triumph is if all the Satanists are run off this island. Then God's Army can be formed and the Mainland reclaimed."

"How many people go to this church?" Marie asks.

'Randy says at least 200," Josh says. "They've just taken over that big empty Hill's store out at the strip mall on the west end. They've got a big stage, sound system, the whole deal. Mom has dived headfirst into it."

"Do you know if this Ainsley guy is from the island?" Marie asks.

"Dunno," Josh says taking a sip of his coffee.

"I've never heard of him if he is," Beth says. "When I was in secondary school, I'm pretty sure I knew every family which were full time residents of the island."

Marie glances at her watch, before saying, "We'd better head to the courthouse. I don't know how easy it will be to get parking."

Beth places her cup of coffee in the center console holder before placing the Bug into reverse.

"So Randy is going to this church?" Marie asks.

"Yes," Josh says, "some of his friends from school go there. They have a lot of events and things, so Randy doesn't mind going."

"To each his own," Marie says.

"At least we hope so," Beth says she negotiates through the sparse leftover rush hour traffic.

Beth swings right at the town square, goes down two blocks and pulls into the courthouse parking garage.

Beth pulls a manilla folder containing the paperwork which they are going to need from the center console, then the trio exit the VW and make their way through security to the second floor of the courthouse, where the marriage license bureau resides. Beth and Marie walk to the counter where a young female clerk reviews their papers. After seeing everything is in order, she asks them to take a seat until the Magistrate is ready. There is no one else in the waiting area.

Beth and Marie take a seat beside Josh and begin checking messages on their cell phones.

"Molly says Zack has come out to the studio," Beth tells Marie. "She says he still seems kind of out of it, but he's started to work with Abe on a song, so things are looking up."

"That's good news," Marie says. "It's weird but I'm more nervous about getting 'The Place' up and going again than I am about us getting married."

"Whatever comes up," Beth says. "I think we can deal with it."

"Just hope we aren't taking on too much at one time," Marie says.

The clerk announces that the Magistrate is ready to see them. With Josh in tow, Beth and Marie walk into the Magistrates office with the clerk close behind them. A distinguished gentleman in a grey suit greets them from behind a large wooden desk.

"May I see your identification cards," the Magistrate requests.

Beth, Marie, and Josh take the cards out of the wallets and hand them to the man, who after matching the cards to the information on the marriage certificate, hands them back.

"So you, Bethany Alice Stolz," the Magistrate begins in a formal tone, "have come before me to ask to be joined in matrimony to Marie Ault?"

"I have," Beth states.

"And you, Marie Renee Ault, wish to be joined in matrimony to Bethany Alice Stolz?"

"I do," Marie answers.

"Please join hands," the Magistrate requests.

Beth and Marie move a little closer and hold each other's hands.

"Then by the powers vested in me by the County of Hanover," the magistrate proclaims, "I pronounce that you are now joined in matrimony. None other than the two of you have the power to undo this union. May your days together be filled with joy and prosperity."

Beth and Marie kiss.

"Please sign the certificate," the Magistrate requests.

First Beth, then Marie, signs the document.

"Young man,' the Magistrate instructs Josh, "would you sign on the line which says 'First Witness'?"

Josh complies.

"Ann?" The Magistrate motions to the clerk, who walks to the desk and signs as the second witness.

The Magistrate then signs the document after which he presses a seal into its lower right corner. He hands the document to the clerk, who walks the document out of the room and back to her station where she will scan and record it into the county records.

"I see you both live out on Wannasea Island," the Magistrate comments.

Marie, Beth, and Josh nod their heads.

"Bethany as your last name is Stolz," the Magistrate says, "I'm wondering if you might be related to Herbert Stolz, the attorney."

"He is my grandfather's cousin," Beth says.

"I went to school with him at Swansea," the Magistrate says. "Next time you see him, tell him Ben Bryant says hello."

"I will do that," Beth says.

"Tell him, good luck in taking apart that Halifax Sylvester mob too," the Magistrate says with a smile. "The sooner that group is completely out of business, the better."

The clerk returns with the recorded marriage certificate.

"Congratulations," the clerk says, "you are now officially married."

A DISTURBANCE

Thursday, 11:48AM. The reopening at the 'The Place' has gone slowly for the first two hours. A few former regulars have shown up but in general the morning thus far has been a little slower than normal.

Molly Peters comes in through the front entrance and walks over to Beth who is manning the new coffee machine.

"Who are those people picketing outside?" Molly asks. "I just watched them chase away two customers."

Beth gives Molly a quizzical look before saying, "What people?"

"Come out with me and see," Molly says heading toward the front entrance.

Molly finishes creating a cappuccino, puts it on a waiting tray and follows Molly out the front door.

A dozen protesters, led by a small man wearing a clerical collar and black duster marches right past the front entrance carrying signs which read, "Satan at work here", "God's Wrath is Coming", "This Business in an Ungodly Abomination", "Enter this facility and face eternal damnation", "Satan runs this Business".

"Evil sluts!" a sixty something woman carrying a sign which reads, "Marriage is between a Man & Woman", shouts at Molly and Beth.

"These are the Devil's spawn!" the small man at the front of the group calls through a bull horn.

Beth watches for a few moments, seeing an incoming car pull into the parking lot then turn around and pull back out.

"Let's go back in," Beth suggests to Molly heading through the door.

Beth begins walking among the wait staff and quietly telling them what is going on outside. "Just your best to ignore questions about it," she advises them before going into the kitchen to speak with Sallie.

"They showed up about ten minutes ago," Sallie relates. "There are three of them with signs on the back patio blocking access to the sales window."

Molly pulls her cell phone from her jacket pocket and calls Abe, who is in the studio with Zack. After Abe answers, Molly suggests that he come down to "The Place' to see what is going on.

Beth re-enters the dining room area and pulls her cell phone from her pocket. She calls Angelique, the Stolz firm lawyer who is working on the bid for the old government center. Over the past few weeks, Beth has developed an unexpectedly good relationship with Angelique.

"Hey Beth, what's up" comes from her cellphone's earpiece.

Beth describes what is going on outside 'The Place'.

"Do you have any idea who these people are?" Angelique asks.

"Guessing by the clerical collar on the little guy in the front," Beth responds, "they are likely members of the New Jericho Temple."

"Little guy with a trimmed beard with a wild look in his eye?"

"That's a fairly accurate description," Beth replies.

"He's become a real nuisance," Angelique says. "Here's the deal, if they aren't on your premise to purchase anything, they cannot be walking around your property picketing. If you have signed up saying your facility is only for the use of the customers, they are currently breaking the law. If you don't, you'll need to ask your grandfather to go out and tell them to leave and put up such signs. Abe will have to be the one to do it because he is the registered owner of the business. Additionally, if they have vehicles parked in your parking lot, those vehicles have no right to be there."

"Can't I go tell them?" Beth asks.

"No, it has to be the property owner."

"Thanks for the advice," Beth says. "How did I get by without you?"

"Keep me posted on what's going on with them," Angelique requests, "you might have to file an injunction against them. I heard one of the bars down on West Road has had to do that."

"Thanks again," Beth says before disconnecting the call.

"I asked Abe to come down," Molly tells Beth.

Beth goes back to her phone and rings Abe.

"I'm on my way, Kitten" Abe says through the phone.

"Would you take a picture of one of those signs which Uncle Hugh put up on your way down?" Beth asks.

"Sure," Abe replies, "see you in a few minutes."

Marie joins Molly and Beth at the bar.

"Did you notice if my mother is out there?" Marie asks Beth.

"I'm not sure if I would recognize her," Beth says.

"I'm going to go out and see," Marie says before she walks through the front door.

'What do you think brought this on?" Molly asks.

"Most likely Marie and I getting married," Beth replies. "I think Marie's mom belongs to the church that is out there protesting us."

Marie walks through the front door with Abe holding on to her right arm.

"My mom doesn't seem to be with them," Marie says. "She's usually working at the convenience store at this time."

Abe pulls up the photo which he has just taken with his cell phone and shows it to Beth before saying, "If those yahoos could read, they should already know what they are doing is illegal." Beth relates her conversation with Angelique.

"I'm going to go and formally tell them to leave our property," Abe says walking back through the front door with the three women following him.

"Satan's spawn. Satan's spawn must be gone from God's Island," comes through the leader's bullhorn.

Abe tries to shout over him but is unable to do so.

'You three stay here," Abe says as he walks toward the man with the megaphone. He still has a slight limp from his fractured lower right leg. The walking cast is due to come off next Wednesday.

Abe positions himself in front of the much smaller man and shouts, "Turn that damned thing off."

"Satan's   spawn…"
Abe jerks the device from the man's hands and throws it to the ground.

"If you could read," Abe shouts as he points to the two large signs, "you would already know by the signs at our parking lot entrance that you are breaking the law by being on my property!"

The picketers go silent.

"I'm giving you five minutes to vacate the premises," Abe continues. "If you aren't gone by then you will have to deal with the local Constabulary."

Abe moves around the protesters and gathers the three women before re-entering 'The Place'.

Once inside, Abe goes through his cell phone contacts to find the entry for the Defense One Security Service. He presses the call icon for that contact.

'Defense One," a voice answers after one ring.

Abe describes what is going on and asks whether it is possible to determine which of the protesters outside has parked their vehicle in Abe's parking lot.

"Give me a couple minutes," the responder on the other end of the call says.

"They are still chanting," Molly, who is peering through the partially open front door says, "but they have stopped marching."

'Have there ever been protesters here before?" Beth asks her grandfather.

He shakes his head before commenting, "Ben down at the bookseller's was telling me on Monday that little guy out there is a whole bunch of trouble. Seems he and his church are now running around the island calling for all the ungodly to forcefully be moved to the Mainland."

"Do you know if he is from Wannasea Island?" Marie asks.

"I think he's the grandson of those Ainsleys, who used to live out on the far end of West Road," Abe says, "but I don't believe that he was raised on the island."

"Mr. Stolz," the voice from his cell phone calls out to him, "we have completed the list. I am texting it to your cell phone. Please call back if you need anything else."

"Thanks," Abe says into the phone as he disconnects the call to go his text messages and find the one just sent by Defense One.

He clicks on the message and sees a list of eight vehicle types with license plates numbers.

"You think it's been five minutes?" Abe asks.

Beth nods her head.

Abe goes back out the entrance doors and into the parking lot. The protesters are gathered at the corner of the building in discussion.

Abe walks up to them and shouts, "You were given instructions to leave my property, I have no choice but to call the Constabulary." "We still have 30 seconds," the little man with the beard says angrily.

"Then in those 30 seconds, let me read to you the vehicles which need to be removed from my parking lot as well," Abe states loudly, "Vauxhall Corsa – placard WI-62-SMB. Ford Fiesta placard WI-53-LAQ, Ford Fiesta – placard WI-66-TXW …"

DIFFERENT ARRANGEMENTS

Thursday, 6:58PM. 'The Place' is full as Beth walks to the stage to introduce the night's proceedings.

"Welcome to the reopening of 'The Place', ladies and gentlemen. Tonight, we begin a slightly different method of offering you entertainment. We will start off the evening with a historical reading, then the Wannasea Boys will entertain you with a short set until 8PM. At 8, the portion of tonight's entertainment provided by Zack Tillerman and requiring payment of a cover charge to participate will begin. At least for this first evening, I am sorry to inform you that all the tickets for Zack's performance have been purchased. If you don't have tickets, you may however go out to the rear patio to hear Zack's performance through the new audio system out there as well as enjoying refreshments. Now without further ado, my grandfather will give one of his historical readings."

Beth walks from the stage as Abe comes around the kitchen corner of the bar area toward the stage. The crowd is again somewhat younger than is the norm at 'The Place'. Molly and Marie have worked out a system of ticket sales along with colored dated wristbands which designate which customers have paid the evening's cover charge.

"For those of you who have been here before," Abe begins, "you will find what I am going to do tonight different from what I have done in the past. On these evenings, I will either read to you a brief passage or a poem about the history of the Island of Wannasea. At least for the time being, there will be no further readings of the Reggie Reginald songs which my wife and I wrote."

Abe turns and nods to the Wannasea Boys, who will not only be performing a brief opening segment but backing up Zack this evening.

"I wrote this particular poem 48 years ago when I was still a student at Swansea University. For any of university-level students who are out in the audience tonight, I will note that I spent 15 years as a student at that institution of higher learning, so don't give up hope," Abe relates. "For the parents of students such as me, you have my deepest sympathies."

Laughs come from various sections of the crowd. The Boys break into a light background melody in the key of D Major, at a tempo of 122BPM in 2 / 2 time.

WANNASEA ISLAND

from volcanic eruption
and lava filled destruction
an island arose
where only a sailor goes
Wannasea
where I ever long to be
Wannasea
so blue its sea
always home for me
in the sea birds flew
across a sky of swirling blue
building nests in cliffs
among the Island's lasting gifts
Wannasea
where I ever long to be
Wannasea
so blue its sea
always home for me
green, green and more green
greenery, all that's to be seen
where black lava had been
green arose in sea air so clean
Wannasea
where I ever long to be
Wannasea
so blue its sea
always home for me
midst the foaming waves
lie dark tidal caves
where lonely pirates hid
the evidence of what they did
Wannasea
where I ever long to be

Wannasea
so blue its sea
always home for me
many came and many went
as an island made an ascent
from remote farming nation
to preferred tourist destination
Wannasea
where I ever long to be
Wannasea
so blue its sea
always home for me

Abe moves from the microphone after one reading as the 'Wannasea Boys' break into "Fiddler's Green".

Abe walks across the dining room area and joins Zack and Beth, who are leaning on the far end of the bar.

"What do you think?" Abe whispers to Beth in reference to the move away from Reggie Reginald songs.

"It's likely going to be a month or so before we'll know," Beth whispers back. "There is also the issue of how the tourists will take to it."

The Wannasea boys play a variety of non-Reggie, mostly sea songs over the next 45 minutes.

Beth returns to the stage, "Those who do not have tickets should now exit the dining room area. I think you'll find that it will be comfortable out on the rear patio, if you'd like to stick around."

Beth walks off the stage and follows some of the crowd out the hallway past the restrooms which leads to the rear patio. Over the next ten minutes, a third of the dining room crowd exits the area. Most go to the patio. At five minutes before eight, Marie, who is tending a table at the front entrance, opens the doors to let the ticketed customers in.

"Would you introduce me?" Zack asks Abe.

"Sure, but no readings,"

"I'm okay with that," Zack replies.

Zack appears to be a little more nervous.

"Our friends from New Jericho are no longer out there," Beth says returning through the kitchen entrance.

After Abe had chased the New Jericho protesters off early in the day, they had set themselves up on the road leading up the mountain. This left the protesters more the fifty feet from the parking lot and greatly reduced their presence.

'Maybe Ainsley thinks Satan goes to bed at eight," Abe whispers to Beth.

Beth pats Zack on the arm as she moves behind him to return to working behind the counter.

Abe waits until the wall clock reads 7:59 before moving to the stage. The Wannasea Boys are back on the stage adjusting the instruments and sheet music for Zack's performance. Abe motions for Zack to come to the stage. Head down, Zack obliges. He walks to the rear of the stage and picks up his acoustical guitar.

"Ladies and gentlemen," Abe says into the microphone. "I believe that most of you know that you will now be in for a treat. Zack is going to start his performance tonight by singing a few sea songs for you. We encourage you to join in. Zack will then perform a selection of his own original recordings after which he will take a short break. If you have a request for a song which you'd like Zack to perform, please write it on a slip of paper from the pad which has been left on the table and pass it to one of our wait staff. Now with out and further ado, Zack Tillerman."

Zack breaks into 'The Place'. As Abe walks back behind the counter, the crowd begins to sing along. By the time Abe is standing beside Beth at the cash register, most of the crowd is singing along. Zack repeats the song, they break into 'Roll the Old Chariot Around'. Zack does two more sea songs before moving to the back of the stage and switching to his electric guitar. He begins the set of his recordings with 'Hard Case' then moves to 'Don't blame it on the alcohol'. It is 9:15 before Zack completes the first set.

"He's a different person when he's playing guitar on that stage," Beth whispers to Abe.

"It's like he feeds off of it," Abe says.

Marie walks to the stage and hands Zack a handful of written requests which the customers have made. Zack glances through the requests for a few moments before looking toward the bar and gesturing for Beth to come to the stage,

Beth narrows her eyes, and mouths "Me?" back to him.

Zack nods his head.

Beth goes around the counter, walks up to the stage.

"Would you help me do 'We didn't start the Fire'?" Zack asks.

Beth grimaces a little as Zack reaches out his hand to help her onto the stage and walks with her to the piano.

"Do you guys want to take a break for a couple of songs," Zack asks the Wannasea Boys.

The band nods, puts down their instruments and proceeds to go out the rear entrance.

Zack helps position two of their microphones near the piano and Beth before returning to the microphone. He turns around and waits until Beth nods to him before breaking into Billy Joel's 'We didn't start the Fire'.

Beth and Zack did not start the fire, but their performance metaphorically burnt 'The Place' down.

34

A CELEBRATION

Sunday, 12:08PM. Miss Vicky stands in the center of the stage at 'The Place' just a few inches back from the edge. She is dressed in a flowing white robe with a flowered garland around her Princess Diana hairstyle. Beth is in a white-on-blue flowered full-length dress. Marie in complementing blue-on-white dress of the same cut.

The original plan to hold the celebration of Marie and Beth's marriage on the patio had been scrubbed due to rain which had moved over the island late Saturday night. Sallie has been the primary force in getting everything needed for the celebration moved into dining room at 'The Place'. Now 22 other people, 15 of whom work at 'The Place', are seated at the tables closest to the stage. The table closest to the middle of the stage has been left open for Beth and Marie.

Holding a copy of the 'Tao Te Ching' out to Beth and Marie to place their hands upon, Miss Vicky says in her high firm voice, "We are gathered this morning to bless the union of Beth and Marie. Two of the brightest flowers ever brought forth upon our island. Love and positivity brought them together. Despite prevailing public rules and through the powers vested in me by the spirits of Wannasea and the surrounding seas, I proclaim that Marie and Beth are now united in matrimony."

Beth and Marie kiss as a string of confetti poppers are shot into the air by Sallie, Molly and two other girls from the wait staff. The others in the audience clap and cheer.

Beth and Marie in turn shake Miss Vicky's hand and tell her, "Thank you".

Sallie walks up to Beth and Marie with a bottle of Corbet in hand.

"You need to open this to start the proceedings," Sallie informs them.

Beth and Marie unwrap the gold foil, jointly remove the muselet, then with each of their thumbs on the same side of the cork pop it up toward the dining room ceiling.

Beth and Marie carry the bottle of champagne around to each of the tables and pour a little into each plastic glass, before going to the table in the middle and pouring the remainder into their own glasses.

"Thanks to all of you for making this day possible," Beth says and lifts her glass in toast.

Everyone lifts their glass in toast, then takes a small sip. Even Abe, though his sip is but a wetting of the lips.

"It's time to eat," Sallie informs the guests, "Everything has been laid out on the length of the bar between the coffee machine and cash register. There are bottles of red and white wines and champagne lined up in front of the tea making area.

Most in the dining area rise and head toward the food and drink.

"That was nice," says Hugh's wife Helen, who is seated at Abe's normal corner table by the far-left of the stage along with Hugh and Miss Vicky.

"It was," Abe says as he rises to walk toward the table where Beth and Marie now sit. Abe hugs Beth around the shoulders, then waits until Hugh and Helen have offered their congratulations before pulling out the chair to Beth's left.

"I know you said no presents," Abe says as he reaches inside of his coat and pulls out a sheaf of documents which transfers ownership of 'The Place' to Beth. Abe had worked out the production of the necessary documents with Olivia, his cousin Herbert's lawyer daughter on Tuesday.

Beth studies the documents for a few moments before tears begin to trickle down her cheek.

"I will put them into the safe," Abe says putting the documents back into his pocket then heading around the kitchen corner of the bar, where he slides back a panel to reveal a file drawer sized safe. He enters the code to open the safe, swings open the door and sets the documents under the deposit bags before closing the door to relock it.

Beth and Marie are the last to the counter to fill their plates, once they have returned to their table, Sallie goes to the stage.

"Most of you know that I've been at 'The Place' longer than anyone but Abe and Beth," Sallie begins. "What you don't know is how I came to be here. Seventeen years ago, Becca, Beth's great-grandmother, found me at the Wannasea market with two blackened eyes, bruises all over my body and a burning desire to be as far away from my then-husband as I could get. Becca brought me out here, nurtured me past both my husband and some of my own self-destructive activities and taught me everything she knew about running the kitchen. I've seen Beth grow from a precocious eight-year-old into the primary force which now keeps 'The Place' running. I've seen Beth's relationship with Marie grow from friends to true friendship then into love. From the almost seven years which I was blessed to spend with Becca, I know that she would be extremely pleased with what we witnessed this morning."

Sallie walks from the stage toward the table which she is sitting at with Saanvi, Molly, and Zack. As Sallie pulls out her chair, Saanvi rises and walks to the stage.

"I have been friends with Beth since we were ten years old," Saanvi says. "Beth and I worked together as waitresses here and shared all our secrets. My mother was the best friend of Beth's mother. I did not know Beth's mother but from what my mother has told me, I am certain that she would be very pleased that this day has come. I cannot begin to put into words how much my friendship with Beth means to me. I wish Beth and Marie all the happiness that their hearts can hold and look forward to many coming celebrations with them in the future."

As Saanvi exits the stage, Josh, Marie's brother, walks on to it.

"I cannot tell you how proud I am of my big sis," Josh says. "I watched her stand firm against my parents and learned from her that their actions are not justifiable. Ever since I became a teenager, Marie has been my rock. She is the person who I can go to whenever I'm confused or need a reasonable adult opinion. Working at 'The Place', I've learned how special Beth and the rest of you are. I'm so thankful Beth and Marie are here, not just for me, but for all of us."

Hugh follows Josh to the stage.

"My wife and I have not been able to spend nearly as much time as we would like out here," Hugh says. "We have however always felt that 'The Place' and everyone in it is part of our family. Beth has made certain that what my grandmother and mother have started here continues. We are so proud of you, Beth. We hope that Marie and you will continue in happiness, love and health."

Over the next twenty minutes, all the attendees but Abe and Zack, walk to the stage and make comments. When Ana, who has been working at 'The Place' less than eight months and is the most recent resident of the house, completes her well wishes. Zack rises from his chair and walks around the front edge of the stage to its rear. First, he turns on the audio system, takes a microphone by the piano to the front of the stage, then goes to the back wall and picks up his electric guitar.

"Most of you know that I would rather play music than talk," Zack says as he returns to the microphone. "I'm more into letting my music speak for me, so last week I asked Abe to help put something together for this occasion. Beth and Marie, I hope you know how much you mean to us."

Zack plays and sings,

<u>BEYOND TIME -</u>
99BPM KEY OF C 3 / 4 TIME

through hurried days
and worried nights
your love grows beyond time
time flows in many ways
up the valley and to the heights
hand in hand, you shall climb
ignoring meaningless talk
through this life you shall walk
forgetting the ticks of the clock
your love becoming solid as rock
eternity flows
around you, around she
binding your souls beyond time
the one you chose
to always be
truly and completely thine
ignoring meaningless talk
through this life you shall walk
forgetting the ticks of the clock
your love will become solid as rock
past the minutes
around the hours
beyond all time you will go
the future becoming witness
to this growing love of yours
and why you need each other so
ignoring meaningless talk
through this life you shall walk
forgetting the ticks of the clock
your love will become solid as rock
through hurried days

and worried nights
your love grows beyond time
time flows in many ways
up the valley and to the heights
hand in hand, you shall climb

Zack follows it up with Elvis Presley's 'Can't Help Falling in Love', Whitney Houston's 'I wanna dance with somebody', Ben E. King's 'Stand by Me' and The Temptation's 'My Girl'.

CALL TO BATTLE

Thursday, 2:12PM. Marie lays opens a copy of the weekly 'The Islander' newspaper to page 6. She places the open newspaper atop the table in the rear corner of 'The Place's' dining room near the stage. Beth, who has been reviewing documents for the bid on the old government center, sits in the chair closest to the stage.

"Look at this," Marie says pointing to the half page advertisement from the New Jericho Temple.

"I guess he didn't much like Abe chasing him off," Beth says.

"Is there anything which we can do about this," Marie asks.

"I doubt it," Beth says. "I'll give Angelique a call to see what she thinks as soon as I finish up answering these other items for the purchase of the government center which she sent to me this morning."

Marie returns to the bar area as Beth spends the next fifteen minutes reviewing the proposal Angelique has made about leasing most of the castle to the Historical society and what requests are to be made for tax breaks for that facility.   After completing the questionnaire and texting it back to Angelique, Beth takes a cell phone picture of the advertisement and sends it along with a query as to whether Angelique thinks anything can be done about Ainsley.

Beth picks up the newspaper from the table, rising from her chair as she calls out to Marie, who is now at the cash register, "I'm going up to the house to talk to Abe."

Beth slowly walks across the dining room area and out the heavy front entrance doors before taking a right to head up to the house. Beth has just had her second meeting at the fertility clinic in Hanover. She's been advised that everything appears to be going well but she must be certain to not overexert herself. She crosses the slight uphill slope and walks around the left side of the house, past the rear bathroom, onto the patio and then through the sliding glass door into the studio.

Abe and Zack are sitting at the piano looking over a musical score. Molly is at her desk printing out reports from the ZackTillerman website.

"You probably should take a look at page 6," Beth suggests, handing the newspaper over to her grandfather.

Abe takes the newspaper from Beth and opens it to the requested page. He studies the page a few moments before saying, "Seems we now have ourselves war with the Right Reverend Ainsley and his sheep."

"Let me see," Molly says rolling her desk chair over to where Abe is sitting.

Abe hands her the paper.

Beth waits until Zack finishes his writing on the score before asking Zack, "So you have agreed to begin going over to Hanover for treatment every other Monday?"

Zack and Molly had traveled with Beth and Marie to Hanover this past Monday. Zack had spent 90 minutes undergoing various evaluations before being assigned a staff psychiatrist named Schiller. Dr. Schiller, who vaguely reminds Zack of his base-playing uncle, the psychiatrist has switched Zack's medication to lamotrigine and developed the begins of a rapport based on service in Iraq. Zack is positive enough about the visit to agree to continue both the evaluations and bi-weekly sessions.

"Yeah," Zack says, "I like Doc Schiller."

"These people are out to wreck our business," Molly interrupts angrily, pointing to the New Jericho Temple advertisement.

"I wouldn't worry about it too much," Abe says. "I doubt people who frequent Ainsley's church would come out to 'The Place' to do anything other than protest anyway."

Zack takes the newspaper and studies the ad.

"I've decided to get a new car," Abe announces. "Zack's offered to take me out car shopping tomorrow."

Abe has had the walking cast removed from his right leg earlier in the week. Although the ankle area is still a bit stiff and tender, Abe is now trying to get back into his old routines.

"Going to buy that red convertible Grandma Jane wouldn't let you have?" Beth asks.

"Nope," Abe says. "I'm thinking of a station wagon or a van."

Beth crinkles her brow before saying, "What on earth for?"

'First, so you lot won't have to cram yourselves in like sardines into that little tin can when you go to Hanover," Abe replies. "Secondly I'm hoping on needing a rear car seat to drive my great-grandchild around in the near future."

JOINING THE BATTLE

Saturday, 6:52PM. Beth is standing at the kitchen end of the bar filling tea orders. Ana, the youngest waitress at 'The Place' walks around the that side the bar and says in a lowered voice, "Those two tables back in the far corner have been sitting there for more than twenty minutes without ordering anything but water," Ana says. "I've asked them twice for their orders and they have gotten rather snippy about my asking."

Beth looks out to the area which Ana is referencing. The two tables have a total of 7 people seated at them. All are well past forty.

"Just leave them alone unless they call you over to place their orders," Beth tells Ana. "I will handle them as soon as I introduce the band.

On Thursday, 'The Wannasea Boys' had asked Abe to allow them to get out of their three day per week commitment to play at 'The Place'. Abe tried to talk them out of it but the band members were insistent that they could no longer play at 'The Place'. Beth is uncertain whether 'The Wannasea Boys' asking out has been driven by the swing away from Reggie Reginald music or the efforts of the New Jericho Temple. In addition to 'The Islander' ad, the New Jericho Temple has plastered posters all over the village of Wannasea denouncing 'The Place' as well as handing out similar flyers in the afternoon at the ferry dock. '

Tonight, there will be a new band playing with Zack. Zack had begun to jam with a trio of students from Wannasea Extension called 'The Northenders' over the Christmas break. He liked their playing style well enough to ask Beth to try them out. Due to the cancellation, 'The Northenders' will be playing a 45-minute opening set and will then back up Zack during his sets.

Zack has also been petitioning Beth to let him do a session every night that 'The Place' is open. Beth is awaiting an answer from Doctor

Schiller as to whether he feels that this is a good idea before responding to Zack's request.

Beth and Marie have begun to notice that the food business seems to have dropped off a little, post-holidays, though this is a annual occurrence with so many turning to counting calories. She isn't all that concerned however, since reopening, 'The Place' has been filled every night that Zack has performed.

Abe is standing at the corner of the bar with Zack's father, Hank Jones, who is going to play fiddle with Zack on his opening sea songs. Hank has just told Abe that his mother's condition has worsened to the point that they are going to place her in an assisted living facility on Monday. Zack, who was beginning to gradually climb out of the depression at the end of the cycle, isn't handling Emma going into a facility particularly well. Zack is seated with his mother and sister at Abe's usual table.

As Beth exits her duties at the coffee machine, she goes behind Abe and Zack and walks toward the stage. The band is nervously making final adjustments to their musical instruments. 'The Northenders' consist of a tall, slim lead guitar/bass player, a keyboard player, and a drummer/percussionist. All three are descendants of the island's oldest black families. The drummer is the cousin of Annette, one of 'The Place's' longest serving waitresses.

Beth walks on stage, turns on the mic and says, "Good evening lad-"

Beth is cut short by shouting from the area of the two tables which Ana had just complained about.

"DEVIL'S SPAWN!!!"

'Satan is at work here!!!"

"This is an evil abomination growing on God's own island!!!"

"Vile slut!!!"

Abe with Hank Jones close at his heel hurries from the end of the bar to the source of the commotion.

"ENOUGH," Abe shouts as he gets to the tables, "You will leave this establishment immediately!"

"You will burn in hell," the large man just to the left of Abe shouts before he pushes Abe into the next table knocking water glasses sprawling and sending Abe to his knees behind the overturned table.

"Spawn of Satan defiling God's Island," a grey-haired woman shouts toward the stage as she spits on Abe.

Marie, Hank Jones, Ben, the bookseller, Zack, and the band plus an off-duty Wannasea patrolman come to the area of the disturbance.

"You will leave these premises immediately," Abe shouts after returning upright.

"I'm calling the Constabulary now," the off-duty policeman informs the disrupters.

With the protesters still shouting and screaming, Abe and his group manage to shepherd all seven protesters out into the parking lot. As Abe uses his cell phone to call Defense One, the seven disrupters quickly disperse into three vehicles and disappear into the night.

"Why don't you guys go back in and try to get everything back to normal," Abe suggests. "I'll wait out here for the Constabulary."

"I'll wait with you," the off-duty police officer says.

Marie leads everyone else back through the front entrance.

"Troublesome lot," the policeman tells Abe.

"As we are beginning to discover," Abe says. "I'm going to call our security company to see what they can provide us about what just occurred."

The off-duty officer nods his head in acknowledgement before saying, "There is more than enough trouble in this world. For the life of me, I can't figure out these people are so hellbent on stirring up trouble where none exists."

Back inside, Marie and the wait staff clean up the mess at the two tables, the band returns to the stage and after a full three minutes, Beth steps back up to the microphone.

"I'm very sorry folks," Beth says. "That wasn't part of tonight's planned entertainment. What is are 'The Northenders', a trio from Wannasea Extension. Zack likes their music. We hope you will too."

The trio breaks into Dylan's 'Hard Rain'. Zack has the presence of mind to pick up his electric guitar, seat himself on a stool in the rear of the stage and play along with the group. The result is a decent musical product. Zack switches to his acoustic guitar when the group does Cat Steven's 'Peace Train' next.

Beth moves to the end of bar and remains there unmoving until Abe returns from the parking lot. Abe starts to speak but Beth motions him to follow her. She moves around Abe and turns right at the outside corner of the kitchen. She then goes to the end of the hallway. Pulling a set of keys from her pocket, Beth unlocks the door to the covered stairway which was just recently built to provide access to Abe's old living area. The second reconstruction of this area, except for the arrival of new shelving, was completed earlier in the week. Beth unlocks the door at the top of the stairs, walks past the new counter area and goes to door leading into the office area which has just been built out on the left-hand side. Beth switches on the light and motions Abe inside. Beth takes a seat in the office chair in front of the new desk. Abe sits down on the small bench beside the desk.

"What did the Constabulary say?" Beth asks.

"They suggest we need to file an injunction against the New Jericho Temple," Abe says. "Defense One was able to establish that two of the vehicles the protesters got into were the same as two of the vehicles out here last week. They are still working on facial recognition to match it with those protesters. There isn't any question that we can file charges against the guy who pushed me into the table if he can be identified."

"I'm going to call Angelique," Beth says fishing her cell phone out of her apron pocket.

Angelique answers on the second ring.

"Hey Beth, what's up?

Beth describes to Angelique what has just occurred at 'The Place'.

"You need to file a cease-and-desist order against the New Jericho Temple," Angelique says. "Olivia is whiz at that sort of thing, so I'll get her on it. Will Monday be, okay?"

"We aren't open after tonight until Wednesday, so that will work," Beth says into her cell phone. "I'm off over to Hanover that day so it will be best to have Olivia call Abe. He knows more about the specifics of this recent incident than I do.

"Have Defense One pull together whatever evidence they have of the first protest and tonight," Angelique instructs.

"Will do," Beth says, "Sorry to bother you on a Saturday night."

"No problem," Angelique replies. "Let Abe know that Olivia will be calling him."

Beth puts her cell phone back into her apron pocket.

"Guess we are going to have to figure out how to make these people go away," Abe says.

"How does somebody get themselves that filled up with hate?" Beth asks.

"I don't know, Kitten," Abe says shaking his head sadly. "We can't waste time trying to psychoanalyze them. Best we can do is try to figure out how to make their nonsense irrelevant."

Abe glances at the clock over the desk which now shows 7:56PM.

"I'd better go downstairs to introduce Zack," Abe says.

"I'm going to stay here for a few minutes,' Beth says to Abe as he rises and walks out of the small office.

When she hears Abe going down the stairs, she begins crying. Beth has not shed these kinds of tears since Grandma Becca died. She is uncertain whether this is a result of the hormone treatments which she is receiving at the fertility clinic or whether the attacks from the Sylvester Brothers and now the New Jericho Temple have finally gotten to her.

A BATTLE HYMN

Tuesday, 11:03PM. Beth is seated on her piano bench scratching the head of a three-year-old Irish Setter, which Miss Vicky has talked her into adopting on Sunday. Miss Vicky said the setter was perfect for 'The Place'. The dog had been abandoned by a couple forced to move off the island by work requirements. Beth had decided to name the dog "Six".

After three days, Six had decided that the studio at the house was his favorite place. There were always humans around to take him outside and throw a ball or go for a hike. There was also usually plenty of company and the kitchen was just down the hallway. Now in addition to Beth, Molly sits at the desk, Abe is at the table and Zack is leaning back in the chair in front of the piano trying to pull together a new melody.

"We need a battle hymn," Zack says aloud to no one in particular.

"Who is we?" Abe asks.

"Us. 'The Place'. We need some kind of anthem to combat the stupidity of that New Jericho Temple crowd."

"You are hoping to rile them up even more?" Molly asks without looking up from her computer.

"I'm looking for something which makes them understand that they aren't the only ones who can get angry," Zack says as he plays around with a Dorian scale on his electric guitar.

Six doesn't seem to like the sound.

"What did Olivia decide to do about that incident on Saturday?" Molly asks.

"Defense One was able to identify three drivers of the cars, the big guy who pushed me and the lady, who spit," Abe relates. "Charges have been filed against all five of them. In addition, Olivia has sent a cease-and-desist order to the Right Reverend Ainsley."

"We are also going to have a new physical security guard from 6:30PM until closing," Beth adds.

"Does she think it will do any good?" Molly asks.

"We'll see," Abe says.

Zack returns to trying to find the right chords to express anger.

"I'm thinking about moving out of my grandma's house now that she is in the nursing home," Zack says apropos of nothing.

"Where are you planning on living?"

"There is a really nice holiday trailer for sale over on the Southwest Side which I think I'll take a look at tomorrow," Zack says.

"Does anyone live in those places full time?" Beth asks.

"A few retired people," Zack says. "The park this trailer is in, is nice. It's no more than a quarter mile walk to the Southwest beach. It's quiet there."

"What would this place cost you?" Molly asks.

"They want $55,000," Zack replies, "but I think that I may be able to get it for less."

"You don't think there's any chance Emma will improve at the nursing home?" Abe asks Zack.

Zack shakes his sadly before saying, "Grandma has reached the point where she doesn't recognize anyone. She doesn't even know who Eugene is any more. Besides, I think my parents could use the extra bedroom when guests come."

"How big is this trailer that you are looking at?" Molly asks.

"It's 920 square foot Willerby Double," Zack relates. "It has two bedrooms. It's eight years old but it's in very good shape. The price includes the lot. The park is a co-op. The maintenance charges are $285 per month."

"Seems you're serious about this," Molly says as she turns toward Zack.

"Don't know how long I can stand to be in Grandma's house without Grandma," Zack replies.

Beth rises from the piano bench and takes the retractable dog leash from atop the piano. Six has not yet learned the boundaries of the properties.

"I'm going to take Six for a walk around the Lakes," Beth announces before attaching the leash and walking the dog out the sliding glass door.

"Will you help me write our anthem?" Zack asks Abe after striking another dissonant chord on his guitar.

"You're certain that you want to do this?" Abe asks.

"I am," Zack says firmly. "I spent the better part of a year fighting people with martial arts. I figure that it is now time to learn how to do it with my guitar."

Abe rolls his chair over to where Zack sits, his tablet with the keyboard open and on his lap.

"Tell me some words that describe what you are feeling about this anger of yours," Abe says.

Zack thinks for a few long moments before saying, "Haters. Liars. Know-nothings. Small minded fear mongers…"

"Okay that's enough for a start," Abe says typing those words along with a few others of his own choosing into a new file on his laptop. After a few minutes, Abe shows Zack a couple of lines about small minds.

"Is that sort of what you are thinking?" Abe asks.

"Pretty close," Zack says.

Abe fiddles around for more than five minutes coming up with a first stanza behind which he adds the 3-line small minds stanza.

"What do you think of this?" Abe asks Zack.

"How about we make it insuatin' and perpetuatin'?" Zack asks, "I think that makes it easier to sing.

Abe changes the spelling of the words.

Abe prints out the 7 lines which he has. Goes to the printer, comes back with the printout and hands it to Zack.

"Why don't you play around with this and see if you can build some kind of melody around it," Abe says. "I'll fool around and see if I can get make a few more stanzas."

Abe and Zack go back and forth for the next 3 hours without even stopping to take a break for lunch. At 1:30 Molly told the pair that they were both have gone mental and goes off into the kitchen to make something to eat.

Just before 3PM Zack is finally satisfied with their product. He plays it through twice on his guitar before saying to Beth, who has returned from her walk with Six, "Would you mind playing me a little piano to see how it sounds?"

Beth humors Zack, playing along with him as he feverishly writes down notes on the print outs.

At 3:30, Zack picks up his cell phone and dials Clarence Cooper, the lead guitarist with 'The Northenders'. He asks the young man if he can come out to 'The Place' with his mates around 5PM after their classes are over. Zack explains that he wants to record a new song for his podcast. Zack offers Clarence and the drummer $100 each for their work.

Suddenly remembering that Molly is going to be going off to classes in half an hour, Zack calls Dave, the A/V guy, who he has been increasingly relying upon to make his recordings. Zack tells Dave about his new song and asks what he'll charge to make both a video and audio recording. They work out a deal for $125 for two hours. Dave agrees to be at 'The Place' by 5:30PM.

While Zack is doing the negotiating, Beth takes Abe into the kitchen to get him to eat the first food that he has had since breakfast at 9.

"You aren't 23 years old," Beth tells her grandfather as she prepares him a ham and swiss omelet with a small side salad. "Just because Zack goes into a musical frenzy doesn't mean that you have to."

"I do kind of like his battle hymn idea,' Abe admits as he sits down at the kitchen table.

"I think Zack is now formally out of his depression cycle," Beth says sitting down at the table and watching Abe eat. Six lays beside Beth's chair. "Unfortunately, the other side of Zack's equation is that he will now be manic for a while."

Molly pops her head into the kitchen and says, "I've got to run to school now. Please make sure Zack doesn't do anything too wild."

"We'll do our best," Beth promises.

Molly heads out the back kitchen door to her Vespa scooter.

Finished with the meal, Abe carries the dishes to the sink, rinses them off and places them in the dish washer.

"Are you going to come down to the place to see Zack's recording?" Abe asks.

"I'm not sure he needs me in on it anymore, since he's decided it doesn't work on a piano," Beth says. "Anyway, I promised Marie that we'd go to a movie when she gets back from taking Josh clothes shopping."

Abe rises and goes back into the studio. He helps Zack carry his guitars out to his VW.

"You want to ride down with me?" Zack asks.

"I need to stretch my legs a little," Abe says. "Been doing too much sitting today. I'll meet you at the front entrance."

Abe goes back into the studio and grabs his tablet. Passing the new ash gold metallic Volvo XC70 which he purchased last week, Abe goes the long way around his in-law suite to get to 'The Place'. Clarence and the drummer are parked outside 'The Place' in the front row. Abe nods a greeting to them before opening the front entrance and disarming the alarm. Abe then goes to his table at the rear stage corner and deposits both himself and the tablet. Zack and the two 'Northenders' go through Zack's new song multiple times until Dave arrives at twenty past five.

"I'd like to turn our recordings tonight into a podcast," Zack tells Dave. "It will give people a taste of how we get the songs out to them."

"How long do want the podcast?" Dave asks.

"Twenty-five minutes max," Zack says.

As soon as Dave has his equipment set up, Zack and the two 'Northenders' begin to play.

SMALL MINDS
TEMPO OF 120BPM KEY OF A MINOR IN 4 / 4 TIME)

always insinuatin'
things just aren't right
goin' round perpetuatin'
wholesale lies and fright
small minds
ain't got no time
for small minds
lurkin' in the shadows
pretendin' to know
tellin' us what goes
and it's them we really owe
small minds
ain't got no time
for small minds
screamin' bout evil
claimin' to hear God
with thinkin' pure medieval
backwards and flawed
small minds
ain't got no time
for small minds
to hate they cling
like dust to an empty shelf
complainin' about everything
but their own sad sorry selves
small minds
ain't got no time
for small minds
always insinuatin'
things just aren't right

goin' round perpetuatin'
wholesale lies and fright
small minds
ain't got no time
for small minds
lurkin' in the shadows
pretendin' to be in the know
tellin' us what goes
and it's them we somehow owe
small minds
ain't got no time
for small minds
screamin' bout evil
claimin' to hear God
with thinkin' pure medieval
backwards and flawed
small minds
ain't got no time
for small minds
ain't got no time for small minds

Over the next two hours, four recordings are made of 'small minds'. Zack thanks the two 'Northenders' and pays them. As they disappear into the night, Zack and Dave carry their equipment back up to the studio while Abe locks up 'The Place'.

By the time that Abe walks back into the studio, Dave and Zack have picked out the best recording and uploaded it to YouTube. The pair spend the next half-hour editing the video into an MP-4 file and upload it to Zack's podcast service. After this is complete, Dave happens to take a look at the YouTube statistics on 'small minds'. In a little over 30 minutes, the video has been played over 53,000 times. The count is increasing in fits and starts.

A HISTORY LESSON

Thursday, 8:00PM. Abe has walked to the stage and is adjusting the microphone. Beth is pleased that she has been able to talk Abe into giving a short speech and poem about how Wannasea Island came to acquire its name. From the time she was eight, it had been one of her favorites from her grandfather's writings.

"Good evening, ladies and gentlemen," Abe says sitting down on a stool in front of the microphone. "Before we get into the musical portion of tonight's proceedings, I would like to tell you a little story about how Tomas Wanna's Sea came to be called Wannasea."

Abe adjusts the microphone down a little before continuing, "In 1557, a whaling ship dropped a young, impressed sailor named Tomas Wanna off at the far west end of our island. Dropped may not be the appropriate term. Dumped might be better. Seemed this particular captain wanted Tomas off his boat. In 1557, this was not all that uncommon a practice. It was common for ships to drop off at deserted islands the sick, mentally ill or troublesome shipmates who they could no longer tolerate. Sometimes those ships even dropped off their captain.

When Tomas was dropped off on our island, his belongings contained a journal that he had been keeping while aboard 'The Bully Rider', a whaling vessel out of Borness, Tomas continued to add to that journal during his unscheduled visit. First Tomas wrote in pencil. Pencils were rare commodities in those days. Tomas, being in possession of one and being able to write, tells us that he was not your typical sailor from that time period. When Tomas's pencil gave out, he used burnt sticks to write in his journal.

Tomas Wanna was a sixteen year old student in Glasgow, who picked the wrong place and the wrong time to drink too much rum. A wrap upon the head with a leather-bound billy jack and Tomas was changed from student to apprentice sailor. For the following six months, Tomas made entries into his journal complaining about the food, sea sickness and most of all the first mate. The first mate had taken to calling Tomas, 'the bilge rat'. An untimely argument with the first mate on the return from an unsuccessful whaling run resulted in Tomas being dropped off at our island. It is unclear how long Tomas was able to survive alone on the island. It may have been twenty months. It may have been four years. Each day spent alone on the island clouded Tomas' mind. Once on our island, Tomas went from gathering greens, shellfish, and crabs, trying to catch fish, collecting flotsam which washed up on the beaches near him and building himself a shelter at the island's western end to believing that the island was a vessel which he was sailing to freedom. As each new day on our island came, Tomas' mind became more clouded.

2/3rds of a ship's wheel which Tomas had found washed up on the sands became Tomas' prized possession. As Tomas added to his shelter, he took to calling it his vessel. He placed the ship's wheel facing westward toward the open ocean and from a distance it may have looked as if Tomas had indeed turned that end of the island into his own sailing ship. Tomas named the waters surrounding his vessel, Wanna's Sea. The final five pages of Tomas' journal entries refer to captaining his ship over Wanna's Sea in pursuit of 'The Bully Rider'.

In 1665, when a group of farmers came out to the island to escape the Black Death running rampant on the Mainland, one of the first things that the stumbled upon was Tomas' structure which had been built around a small rock outcrop at the island's far west end. Inside they found Tomas' remains and his journal. After several readings of Tomas' journal by the new village's vicar, the farmers began calling the island Wannasea, after the stranded youth, who believed that he was sailing this island in pursuit of his tormentors.

That journal now resides at the Wannasea Historical Society.

Almost fifty years ago, in honor of Tomas, I wrote this poem:

TOMAS WANNA'S SEA

Tomas Wanna is what they call me

A clerk was I in trainin' to be

Til a billy to me head turned me to sailor

Toiling aboard a westbound whaler

The Bully Rider didn't like me words

Told me to save my talkin' for the birds

The cruel first mate and Captain loathed me

Dropped me off in the middle of the sea

On a deserted island far from shore

From which I would return no more

I spent me days gatherin' wood

Build me own sailin' vessel, I would

Off my lonely island I would sail

And chase that Bully Rider straight into hell

First made me a deck, solid and strong

Added a wheel so I wouldn't steer wrong

Sailed me vessel for many a long day

Keepin' me burnin' hunger for revenge at bay

Across the blue and bountiful waves

In hopes me own life I saves

Through sun-soaked day and stormy night

sailed me vessel on the only course that's right

Captained me ship over rising seas

Hoping that Bully Rider I'd someday seize

The winds blow strong on Tomas Wanna's Sea

Into oblivion those winds will blow thee

none do remember that Bully Rider crew

But history has learned what I knew

That Bully Rider floats no more

As me own vessel sails on full bore

Me journal tells what became of me
and how Tomas Wanna's Sea become Wannasea "

Abe pauses for a moment before saying, "Now here is Zack Tillerman with the 'Northenders'."

Zack and the group break into a sea song version of the poem which Abe has just read. The crowd gets into it enough that they play it through twice before switching to 'The Place' to formally start off the evening.

Beth smiles for a moment before following Marie into the kitchen.

"It's a little chilly outside," Beth tells Sallie. "Why don't we go up to the office to talk."

Marie had arranged for the three of them to meet after Zack's session to discuss their bid on the old government center. As the kitchen closes at 7:30, this is usually the time when Sallie is free.

The trio exits the kitchen, goes past the restroom hallway. Beth uses her key to unlock the doors. The storage area has now received the promised shelving. Goods are in the process of being moved on to those shelves. Part of those goods are t-shirts, hats and other memorabilia from 'The Place'. Marie is proud of the new t-shirts which she has designed. They come in two colors, dark blue with silver imprint and sea green with ivory piping. The front has a small picture of 'The Place' over the left breast. The back of the t-shirts has a modified version of the last stanza of Zack and Abe's song by the same name:

> "where musical threads are often sewed
> violins fiddles and strings are bowed
> where island song has always flowed
> we'll chart a course to sensory overload
> singing tunes which time will not erase
> be welcome now to our favorite place"

Marie grabs the stool from behind the counter as Beth unlocks the office area. Beth takes a seat in the office chair. Sallie sits in the chair beside the desk. Marie pulls the stool up just in front of Sallie and half leans, half sits upon it. "Have Sam and you decided what you'd like to do about the participating in the restaurant if we get the old government center?" Beth asks.

"We'd very much like to take a crack at it," Sallie says. "Unfortunately, we don't have enough funds to take on the build out of the restaurant. Between the two of us, we have about $90K saved up. That's probably enough to cover our living costs while we start but nowhere near enough to own the restaurant equipment and have a cushion. The other question is whether we may make use of your liquor license?"

"Using the liquor license can be arranged. As far as covering the build out and equipment purchases, we can pay those costs then lease them back to you," Beth says. "If you prefer, we can form a partnership where we would be you financiers and silent partners."

"Do you have any idea what the lease costs will be?" Sallie asks.

'The building lease will be between $5-6K month, then another $1-2 thousand per month depending on what type of equipment you put in," Marie says. "You could always lease equipment yourself if you want."

"What length of lease?" Sallie asks.

"We'll make it one year," Beth says, "then guaranteed month to month for the following two years."

"I know we want to do the building lease," Sallie says, "I'll have to work out the equipment part with Sam. How soon do you need to have everything finalized?"

"Tuesday at the latest," Beth says. "Final proposals are due now on Friday."

"If we give you a final commitment for the amount space that we want, will that work?" Sallie asks.

Beth nods her head.

"Then we'll go for 3500 square feet as you first suggested," Sallie says. "Are you still planning on having us operate the concessions in the theater?"

"We are," Marie replies.

"Sam had a thought," Sallie relates. "Maybe expand 'The Place's' menu right now to include fish, shrimp, oyster sandwiches plus the gumbos and stews that we are planning on having at restaurant to see how it plays with the existing customer base."

Marie and Beth look at each other for a moment, until Beth nods.

"Let's give it a try," Marie says, "How soon do you want to start?' "Maybe week after next?" Sallie replies.

"That should work," Marie confirms.

"What are you guys planning to do with this place if you get the old government center?"

"Still hoping to build it out into a hostel/resort," Beth says. "A place where staff can stay and a lower cost facility than most of the other places on the island. Right now, though, we don't know if we will have enough money to cover doing that build out. It probably depends on how much money we get back from the insurance companies and lawsuits from the damage which the Sylvesters did. To date, we haven't gotten a cent from either."

AN UNEXPECTED TURN

Tuesday, 11:24AM. Angelique and Olivia sit across from Beth at a table near the kitchen end of the bar. They are finalizing the final items for the bid on the old government center.

"That ought to do it," Angelique says after completing the electronic signature line. "I'll submit our package tomorrow."

"Guess all that's left now is the wait," Beth says.

"There will likely be quite a few questions coming back from the Government once they get started reviewing," Angelique says. "We can't get too comfortable."

"That's part of the reason I've come out here," Olivia injects." Angelique asked me to hold off on talking with you until your bid is submitted. As it soon will be there is something else that I'd like you to think about taking on."

Beth gives Olivia a curious look.

"Quite a few people on the island aren't happy with what the Right Reverend Ainsley has been trying to foment,' Olivia continues. "The island has been a live-and-let-live kind of place for as long as anyone remembers. What Ainsley is doing has given many on the Mainland the impression that this island is becoming a bastion for people like Ainsley."

"Ainsley's actions,' Angelique adds," already have started to have an economic impact. Since Ainsley started his crusade last May, tourists are deciding they don't want to bothered coming out here and being accosted by activists from Ainsley's church."

"I didn't know that the New Jericho Temple has that many church members,'" Beth says.

"They don't,' Olivia states. "There probably aren't 500 people total following Ainsley but those 500 people have proven themselves to be very disruptive."

"Okay,' Beth says, "but what does this have to do with me?"

""Last weekend there was an article printed in the Swansea Intelligencer bout Ainsley's New Jericho Church and their negative impact on the island," Olivia relates. " A group of islanders are now talking about forming some type of organization meant to counteract Ainsley."

"i haven't heard anything about it," Beth says. 'Guess there are just too many other things going on."

"Considering the amount of money which you are looking to put into the old government center," Olivia says, "I suggest paying attention to Ainsley. Otherwise, you may be looking at putting millions into an investment going nowhere.'

"Ainsley's efforts have already managed to close down Clyde's" Angelique notes. " Some of Ainsley's Christian church members made a habit of attacking people, who came out Clyde's bar. Clyde decided that he'd had enough and has closed and move over to Halifax.""

Clyde's' was a bar down on Main Street which most of the islanders and tourists know as a meeting place for the LGBTQ community.

"Something has to be done to thwart Ainsley,' Oliva says, "We hope that you are willing to join with us."

Beth decides that now isn't the time to tell her cousin that she had been planning on using these free months to concentrate on the start of her family with Marie.

"I'm interested," Beth finally says after a few moments' hesitation. "What can I do to help?"

'Might it be possible for you to host a meeting here at the place on one of the nights which you aren't open?" Olivia asks. "Monday might be a good day.'

"I can't do Monday," Beth says without providing explanation to her cousins. "How about Tuesday?"

"Could you do it at 7:30?" Olivia asks. "That will give people a chance to get home from work, grab a bite to eat then come out here."

"Sure," Beth says. "When do you want to start?"

"Next Tuesday/?" Olivia asks.

"Okay.'

"I'll add you to the email list," Olivia says. "Be on the lookout for messages from Wannasea Concerned Citizens," Olivia says.

As Angelique and Olivia put their tablets back into their attaches, Beth begins to wonder how she's going to explain to Marie why she has just given away their Tuesday nights out.

Beth walks her cousins to the front entrance of 'The Place' and holds open the door for them to exit.

'I'll let you know when something comes up with the bid," Angelique says.

"See you next Tuesday, if not before," Olivia adds.

Beth watches them walk to Angelique's car before returning inside 'The Place' and arming the alarm. She then exits through the front door and walks to the house, entering through the front door. She checks the kitchen but the only person there is Ana.

'Have you seen Marie?" Beth asks.

"She took Josh to the Vespa dealers," Ana says. "Josh is looking into buying a scooter to use to get back and forth to the classes which he started down at the Extension."

"Thanks,' Beth says before turning and walking down the hallway and into the studio.

Zack and Abe are in conversation in front of the piano. Molly isn't around.

"Hey guys," Beth says by way of greeting.

"You have completed the bid?" Abe, who is seated in his rolling chair, asks Beth.

"Angelique is turning it in tomorrow."

"Everything is worked out with the Historical Society?"

"They have agreed to provide us with $1 million toward the purchase," Beth states, "in return for a 100-year lease on all of the castle except the turret area. That will give me enough ready cash to purchase the quarry property. This is also going to give both us and the Historical Society a big break on taxes."

"Steven DeJean has been telling me that the only other bidders on property are from Qatar," Abe says. "Supposedly the governor will stand in the way of acceptance of any off-island bids. It seems your bid may be golden."

"We'll see,' Beth says, "Has Olivia mentioned anything to you about a group of islanders, who want to oppose Ainsley?"

"She hasn't," Abe says, "but Ben down at Island Booksellers told me about a group of business owners, who want to take some kind of action to counter Ainsley.'

"They will be having their first meeting down at 'The Place' next Tuesday night."

"Count me in,' Abe says.

"Me, too," Zack says without looking up from his work on a sheet of music.

Beth walks to the front of the piano and sits down on the bench.

"I've decided to buy that trailer out in Open Seas Park,' Zack says to Beth.

"That's great," Beth says without matching his enthusiasm. "Where's Molly?"

"She went into town with Marie and Josh," Zack says. 'Josh is buying a scooter or something."

"How are things going with 'small minds'?" Beth asks.

"Amazing,' Zack says. "The song has only been up on the website since Friday and it's already the top selling single. We are also getting a lot of positive commentary as well.".

"Do you think people are seeing it as the 'battle hymn' you wanted?"

Zack shrugs his shoulders, "I know it's a battle hymn against those New Jericho characters but I'm not so sure that's how people on the internet interpret it."

"Considering they asked for 'small minds' to be played three times," Abe suggests, "I think most of our customers at 'The Place' understand the message."

Zack played 'small minds' for the first time this past Wednesday evening.

"At least making the song helps get out my frustration about those New Jericho characters," Zack says, 'but it's probably going to take more than a song to stop those guys."

"Ben says,' Abe interjects, "that Ainsley has been recruiting over on the Mainland. He's trying to get people, who follow him there, to move out to the island."

"So how are they going to make a living," Beth asks, 'People, who are born here, have to move away because they can't find enough work to get by on."

"Seems Ainsley has gotten a group of Mainland donors and similar church organizations to underwrite the living costs for six months," Abe says. "Ainsley is also working on developing some type of business to sell New Jericho paraphernalia. HIs plan is to grow those sales into a vehicle to support the people, who he gets to move out here, as well as fund his political activism."

"Where are these new people living?" Beth asks.

"Ben thinks that it's in the basement of the building that Ainsley is using for his church," Abe explains.

"Is that legal? "Beth asks.

"Nobody is stopping them at this point." Abe says.

"What's happening with those charges you filed against Ainsley's people for that incident last week?" Beth asks Abe.

"Just heard from Herbert this morning," Abe relates, "that the big guy and one of the drivers, who we filed charges against, were on probation for beating some guy outside a bar down by the wharf. Their probation has been revoked and they are now serving their full one-year sentences. Ainsley supposedly is beside himself over it."

SEA SONG THROW DOWN

Friday, 8;24PM. Zack with Northenders had opened his set with 'The Place'. Followed it up with 'Roll the old Chariot around", then 'Shan't deceive her'. Before continuing, Zack nods to Dave, who will be live streaming this next song on the ZackTillerman website, then walks to the microphone.

"As some of you may know, "Zack says, "this establishment has recently had a couple run-ins with the New Jericho Temple. This next song, "New Jericho - same old hate" is a shout out to the people of New Jericho just to let them know, they won't be taking over our island any time soon."

Zack had become dissatisfied with 'small minds', though becoming increasingly commercially successful, was filling the bill as the battle hymn which he had envisioned against Ainsley. Few of his listeners associated it with the Island's situation with New Jericho. After overhearing a discussion Abe was having with his son about why Ainsley had left the Mainland, Zack wanted something more powerful. He unsuccessfully tried to badger Abe into writing some new lyrics, but Abe refused. Zack had essentially written 'New Jericho' himself.

Zack plays the song without any accompaniment.

NEW JERICHO - SAME OLD HATE 86BPM TEMPO - KEY OF G IN 4 / 4 TIME

Temple of New Jericho
part of the same tired old show
of unwarranted hatred
claiming to be sacred

Ainsley,
tell us more about indecent exposure

Ainsley,
tells us who paid for non-disclosure
self-proclaimed prophet
historically dishonest
right reverend of fallacy
guiding people into moral bankruptcy

Ainsley,
you are a blight upon Wannasea

Ainsley,
depart our island and leave us be

Ainsley, you pitiful disgrace
your words are nothing more than human waste
packed chock full of self-righteous alarm
attacking those who have done you no harm

Ainsley,
tell us more about indecent exposure

Ainsley,
tells us who paid for non-disclosure

Ainsley look into the mirror
witness that condescending sneer

so full of malice and self-loathing
your very soul's afire and smoking

Ainsley,
you've become a blight upon our shore

Ainsley,
disappear, come round our island no more
self-proclaimed prophet
historically dishonest
right reverend of fallacy
guiding people into moral bankruptcy

Ainsley,
you are a blight upon Wannasea

Ainsley,
depart our island and leave us be

Beth has stood at the coffeemaker open-mouth during Zack's performance. Neither Abe nor Zack had given Beth any indication that this song existed, much less was going to be performed at 'The Place'. She walks down to the kitchen end of the bar where Abe is sitting on a stool. Zack breaks into 'small minds'.

"When did you two come up with that?" Beth asks in a lowered voice.

"Zack finished it up this morning," Abe whispers back. "I didn't have much to do with it. You may also want to notice that Dave made it part of the livestream."

"You think this is going to cool things down with Ainsley?" Beth asks.

Abe shrugs his shoulders, before saying, "Should we really be concerned about Ainsley's feelings?"

Beth shrugs her shoulders before asking, "What does that line about indecent exposure refer to?"

"Hugh discovered that an indecent exposure incident is the most likely reason that Ainsley moved his church out to the island," Hugh begins. "Seems he was caught making unwanted advances to a few junior secondary school boys when he had the church in Somerset. Somehow, he got the local authorities to overlook the incident with the help of a some very powerful donors and Ainsley's commitment to move elsewhere."

'The non-disclosure references?"

"Seems they paid the kid's parents to sign NDAs," Abe says.

"How did Hugh come across this information?"

"Didn't ask," Abe says. "It's a non-specific reference in a song. Olivia told me there is no risk."

"Olivia knew what you guys were up to?"

"Not specifically," Abe replies, "I spoke to Olivia about it in the abstract."

Beth shakes her head before demanding, "No more damned battle hymns".

"No promises."

Beth returns to the coffeemaker, as Dave adds 'small minds' to the livestream. Once Zack and the Northenders have finished the song. Dave collects his equipment and heads out the back hallway to go up to the studio to put a copy on to YouTube. Dave then merges the audio recording of 'New Jericho' to the end of 'small minds', so that when people purchase 'small minds', they will now receive both songs.

FIRST MEETING

Tuesday, 7:32PM. Beth sits with Marie and Abe in the corner table at 'The Place' where Abe likes to sit. Zack has been unable to join them due to his grandmother taking a turn for the worse earlier in the day. Beth estimates that there may be seventy people present for Olivia's meeting. Some she recognizes. Some she doesn't. Those she recognizes are mostly Island business owners. Beth was pleasantly surprised that Marie was not upset that she had given away their night out to attend this meeting. Marie was enthusiastic about attending.

"Welcome,' Olivia says through the microphone from the front of the stage. "Coffee and tea are available at the bar if you would like. I'd really prefer to have these meetings be as informal as possible. In that vein, I will offer to conduct these meetings unless there are other suggestions. By a show of hands let's see who agrees."

Almost the entire audience raises their hands.

"I suggest that our focus should be on defining concerns about this island's future and defining what we may be able to do to correct the situation. At present, the most pressing concern seems to be the New Jericho Temple and its protests and attacks on islanders and businesses. Is there general agreement?"

A collective "Yes" comes from the attendees.

"I have pulled together a list of New Jericho activities which I feel are detrimental to our island. Tonight, we won't focus on specific incidents, rather we will begin the process of trying to aggregate them. Your emailed invitation included a link to that list. Please, if anyone has knowledge of any other similar incident, please email me. As regards the New Jericho Temple, we know from their own website and flyers that Ainsley's stated goal is to use their extremist religious rhetoric and activities to force people from this island and take political control of it. When I first heard Ainsley's goal, I thought it was laughable. There aren't more than 500 people affiliated with the

New Jericho Temple. Unless I've missed something, no more than 100 of those 500 are willing to be Ainsley's activists. Unfortunately, Edgar Ainsley and that 100 are beginning to do a great deal of damage to our island."

"People are frustrated with all the flyers which they have posted everywhere," someone from the rear shouts out. "Is there anything which can be done about that?"

"I'm afraid our island's ordinance don't have much to say about postings in public places," Olivia says. "That said, our island's ordinances do not have anything to say about people pulling those flyers down if they don't like them."

"Then there are the attacks on individuals," another audience member calls out. "Beyond what has happened at 'Clyde's' I know of at least ten other instances of members of New Jericho attacking islanders."

"What needs to be done there, is to encourage any who are attacked to file charges against not only their attackers but against Edgar Ainsley for inciting such attacks," Olivia says. "Ainsley's words on his website are more than enough to prove 'incitement to violence'."

"Why don't you or someone else write an op-ed?" come from a person in the middle of the audience, who Beth recognizes to as the assistant editor at 'The Islander'.

"I'm willing to do that," Olivia states, "unless someone else offers."

There is no response.

"Can anything be done about Ainsley having people living in the basement of his church?" Ben, the bookseller from Island Books' rises and speaks. "It seems that there are at least fifty people living there right now."

"Is that something which you might be able to have looked into Betty?" Olivia asks of Betty Furness, who is the island councilwoman from the 5th ward which is comprised primarily of the far east end.

"I believe I should be able to have a review done," Betty Furness says. "None of those facilities in that strip mall are permitted to serve as dwellings. It is a commercial use only area. Does anyone other than Ben has knowledge of people living in Ainsley's church?"

A man and women from different sections of the audience rise.

"I have a shop in the same mall as New Jericho," the man says, "I can verify that there are people living at the old Hill's store."

"Same here," the woman adds.

"As a start," the councilwoman says, "I will have a building and permit inspection done at New Jericho."

"That seems like a good start," Olivia says, "but I think we need to try to come up with something to show that island is not moving toward becoming a haven for closed-minded bigots. Does anyone have any suggestions in that regard?"

Beth rises from her chair, "I think it might go a long way toward correcting the island's image if we overturned the current marriage statute as marriage being only allowed between a man and woman. We could move our marriage laws to be in line with those on the Mainland."

"Let's do a show of hands as to who agrees with that sentiment," Olivia requests.

About 2/3rds of the audience raises their hand.

"Betty," Olivia says, "as you are much more familiar with the process of changing the island's rules than I, would you mind describing how that would happen?"

"First the island council would need to approve having a referendum to change that particular legal code," Betty says. "Considering the current structure of the council, I am not certain that approval to have such a referendum is a given. It will require Ward 5 or 7 council members to approve. Currently the council seems averse to changing anything. The good news however is that there is an election coming up this September which could change that. I know for a fact that 2 of the 3 council members who have been tied to the Sylvester's operations on this island are not going to be running for re-election. I can see if my political party is willing to champion such an effort."

The island has 3 main political parties. The Fishermen's Party, which is the most conservative of the 3 and currently has 3 serving council members. The Farmworkers Progressive Union to which Betty Furness is affiliated and has 3 council members as well as the current Governor. The Mountain Centrist Party which has 1 council member. The Mountain Centrist Party, which supports environmentalism, nonviolence; social justice; currently represents Ward 6. Ward 6 is the ward in which 'The Place' resides.

"It will be great if you can do that," Olivia tells Betty, "but I would like to see this taken a step further. I suggest that we form an action committee to push this initiative. Could I have a show of hands as to how many agree with that suggestion?"

Most of the attendees raise their hands.

"I'd like to suggest that we appoint Beth Stolz as head of that committee," Angelique says from a table in the front.

"Show of hands," Olivia requests.

The response is the same as that for Olivia's original suggestion.

"Are there any other people interested in joining that committee?" Olivia asks.

Angelique, Marie and two others raised their hands.

"I think five is a good number for that committee," Olivia says. "Any objections?"

Silence.

"Beth will organize this committee over the next month," Olivia says. "Is this okay with you Beth?"

Beth nods her head as she writes down the names of those who are on the committee. Beth now knows why Abe refers to Olivia as 'The Shark'.

"Are there any other activities which anyone wants to suggest related to dealing with New Jericho?" Olivia asks.

Ben, the bookseller, offers to have his son set up a bulletin board style website with the capability of on-line meetings to which the group agrees. The group then approves having bi-weekly meetings at 'The Place'.

For the next thirty minutes, the meeting devolves into a general compliant session.

After Olivia tables the meeting closed and has it seconded, Abe rises from the table and says, "I'm going to go over to studio and see if Zack is back from the nursing home yet. He's not handling what is happening with Emma very well."

Beth and Marie nod goodbye to him as most of the rest of the attendees are to exit via the front entrance. In three minutes only Angelique and Olivia remain behind. The pair come over to the table where Beth and Marie and sitting.

"Got a few minutes?" Olivia asks.

"Sure," Beth says, not really understanding why Olivia and Angelique want to speak with either Beth or Marie.

"Thanks, for letting us use 'The Place'," Angelique says. "It is perfect for this kind of meeting."

"Also, thanks for taking on the action committee," Olivia adds as she and her sister take the two empty chairs at the table. "I'm not sure how to put this, other than to say I'm growing a little concerned about your grandfather."

"Why?" Beth says with concern rising in her voice.

"As part of these civil suites and legal proceedings against the Sylvester Bros.," Olivia relates, "Abe has made a rather odd request."

"What type of a request?" Beth asks.

"Abe is insisting that his wife's sailboat be returned to his possession," Olivia says. "Has he mentioned anything to you about it?"

Beth shakes her head negatively.

"Originally when Abe made this request, I thought, okay, maybe he wants to restore it," Olivia relates, "but that isn't the case. Abe wants the sailboat back exactly as it is right now. Once he has possession of it, he is planning on bringing it up here."

TABLES TURN

Friday, 12:27PM. Beth has traveled to the Mainland with Molly and Zack for a visit to the Halifax Office Supply Center. Beth had a sudden urgent desire for halibut. A restaurant two blocks down on the other side of the office supply store is known for it.

After purchasing both necessary and unnecessary office supplies, which have since been placed into Abe's station wagon, the trio is now walking the short distance to the restaurant.

"How are sales on your website going?" Beth asks.

"Terrific," Molly replies. "'not the same', 'this side of nowhere' and 'small minds' are selling really well. We are also starting to make a little money from the podcast and YouTube."

"Just so I have enough to pay for my trailer," Zack says, "that's all I care about."

"When are you expecting to get this trailer?" Beth asks.

"The agent says it should be six weeks until the transfer is complete," Zack says. "I'm thinking of having a little trailer warming party when it's finished."

From behind them, two men rush in front, then turn to face them.

"Aren't you that little monkey boy that's made up those stupid songs about us and Prophet Ainsley?" the man on the right shouts.

"I think it's time we showed this little half-breed what a godless piece of dung he is," the larger man on the left shouts as he approaches Zack with his right fist raised to strike.

Before either Beth or Molly are able to react, Zack has launched a karate roundhouse kick to the right side of the man's head. The man bounces off the nearby cement wall and appears to be unconscious.

The other man, now a little less confident, tries to bullrush Zack and tackle him. Zack performs a knee smash on the man's forehead and immediately begins raining blow after blow on the man's body.

"Zack!" Molly shouts, "You need to stop. You are going to kill him."

Zack places one more kick into the guy's side before regaining control of himself. He moves to where Molly and Beth are standing about five feet away from the incapacitated men.

"Should I call the cops?" Beth asks.

"What for?" Zack says. "They got mouthy and ended up getting what they deserved."

Zack begins walking toward the restaurant.

"Maybe we should go back to the island?" Beth says.

"Naw," Zack says as he continues toward the restaurant, "I'm hungry for halibut."

Slack-jawed Molly and Beth look at each other before following Zack into the restaurant.

"Where did you learn that stuff?" Molly asks Zack.

"In the army," Zack says as they are moved to a table in the rear of the restaurant.

"Haven't you been out of the army for almost three years now?" Beth asks.

"I still work out," Zack says. "When I was down at 'Dave's', I used to have a couple incidents like that a month."

"What if those guys call the police once they get themselves together?" Molly asks.

"I find that highly unlikely," Zack says as he looks over the menu, "You think they want to tell the police that they just got their asses kicked by a monkeyboy?"

They sit in silence for a few moments awaiting the return of their waiter before Zack adds, "That 'godless piece of dung' stuff is new, though. Haven't had anyone call me a godless piece of dung since Iraq."

EMMA'S PASSING

Sunday, 9:47AM. Abe walks through the sliding glass door into the studio. Zack is seated on the stool in front of the piano. Abe is somewhat surprised to see Zack. Usually unless there is something he is trying to produce, Zack doesn't come to the studio on Sundays.

"Grandma passed away last night," Zack says Abe.

"I'm really sorry to hear that," Abe says, "I know how much she meant to you."

Zack has his guitar cradled in his lap but is not playing.

"She died just about the same time I finished my last set yesterday," Zack says. "The nursing home says that she fell asleep at 9 and was gone at 10:30."

"Have funeral arrangements been made?" Abe asks as he sits down in the rolling chair at the table and moves it over near the front of the piano where Zack is.

"There will be a viewing at Flynn's on Monday evening," Zack says. "The funeral will be on Tuesday. Mom and dad are taking care of everything."

"Let me know if there is anything we can do to help," Abe offers.

"Dad doesn't think that it's going to be a very big funeral," Zack says. "There aren't many people around, who remember grandma anymore."

"Beth and I will be there," Abe says.

Zack fiddles around with neck of his guitar for a few moments before saying, "I know that in the condition grandma was in, dying is probably for the best. She couldn't remember anyone or much of anything. Everything frustrated her. These last few weeks, she had to be drugged up like a zombie to keep from hurting herself."

"Life isn't always easy," Abe says.

"I just don't understand why something like that happened to grandma," Zack says. "Grandma never harmed anyone. She never lost faith in my grandpa when everyone else did. She was a hard worker when she could work. It just doesn't seem right."

"It wasn't right," Abe says, "but this life isn't always about what is right or wrong. For better or worse, this life is about what was and what is. Our burden is to learn how to deal with it."

Zack sets his guitar down beside the stool.

"Abe," the young man says, "I don't know if I can handle having any more dead people in my head."

Abe looks at Zack curiously.

"What dead people are in your head Zack?"

"Grandpa, Chadwick and Williams," Zack says looking down at the tiled floor. "I'm not sure that I can deal with having Grandma in their too."

"You've talked to Dr. Schiller about this?"

"It's most of what the doc and I talk about."

"Who are Chadwick and Williams?"

Zack rubs his hands over the front of his jeans before answering, "They're my two mates from the army. They are the best friends that I've ever had. An IED blew them up while I was out scouting the other side of the stream. I still don't understand why I wasn't blown up with them."

"When you say that Chadwick and Williams are in your head, what exactly do you mean?"

"I hear them asking me to play something for them. I hear them asking me questions. I hear them talking like we used to talk in our CHU and APV."

"Do you ever see them?" Abe asks.

"No," Zack says with downcast eyes, "I only hear them inside of my head."

"When you hear them, do you think there is something wrong with you?"

"Sometimes," Zack says grimacing.

"I have been hearing voices inside my head for the past twenty-three years," Abe tells Zack. "I hear my wife telling me things. I hear my daughter's voice and her laugh."

Zack remains silent.

"I used to hear the voices so often that I started drinking alcohol to stop hearing them," Abe says.

"I play music," Zack says.

"Believe me that is a much better option than alcohol," Abe says. "I don't hear them very often, but you know something?"

Zack shakes his head.

"When I do hear their voices now, I am very thankful for it."

Abe waits for a full minute before asking Zack, "Have you had breakfast?"

"No, I wasn't feeling very hungry."

"The sun is out," Abe says, "Why don't we go out on the patio? There is some quiche left from last night, I'll reheat. Coffee or Tea?"

"Coffee."

"I'll be back in minute," Abe says rising from the chair and walking toward the hallway.

Beth and Marie are seated at the kitchen table. Six, who is lying beside Beth's chair, rises and greets Abe.

"Zack's grandma died last night," Abe says softly. "Zack's in the studio. He's not handling it very well. I'm going to get him a little breakfast out on the patio."

"You two go tend to Zack," Marie says. "I'll pull some food together."

Abe pours two mugs of coffee from a large coffeemaker on the counter. One with two sugars for Zack. One black for himself.

Beth enters the studio in front of Abe. Six follows them. Beth immediately goes up to Zack and gently pulls him off the stool before hugging him tightly.

"Emma's in a better place," Beth tells Zack.

The hug lasts for a good two minutes.

"Let's go out on the patio," Beth says. "It's nice out there."

She leads Zack out the sliding glass door from the studio. Abe trails behind carrying the coffee mugs. Six follows and sits in the space between the chairs with Abe and Zack now occupy.

They sit at the patio table closest to the kitchen's sliding glass door. Abe places Zack's coffee down in front of him.

"It's really going to be weird being down at grandma's house knowing grandma is never going to be coming back," Zack says.

"I'm going to go back in and help Marie," Beth says before going through the kitchen's sliding glass door.

"I'm not sure I can take having any more dead people in my head, Abe."

"From my experience," Abe says, "all you can do is wait until they go. What does Dr. Schiller tell you about it?"

"He says that I should try to take steps to separate myself from situations which bring on memories," Zack says. "That's one of the main reasons that I'm buying the trailer on the South End. I'm going to force myself to go down to the beach every morning. I'll swim. I'll workout. Whenever I'm doing things, the voices don't come as often."

"How soon before you can move into your trailer?" Abe asks.

"A little more than five weeks if there no issues come up," Zack says.

Abe sips on his coffee then rises from his chair and says, "I'll be back in just a minute."

Abe walks through the kitchen's sliding glass door. Beth and Marie are working on pulling together pancakes, eggs, and sausage.

"Beth," Abe begins, "would you mind if Zack stays in one of those bedrooms above my in-law suite until his trailer is ready?"

"Not at all," Beth says. "I think Josh might actually like having a little company."

Abe walks back out to the patio and sits down.

"You know Beth's just had the upstairs portion of my in-law suite refinished," Abe says. "Josh is moving in next week. There are three bedrooms and a bath. Would you want to stay there until your trailer is ready?"

"I need to help mom and dad with all the funeral stuff," Zack says, "but that might be a good idea after that's finished. Mom starts working day shift at the resort next Monday. I don't think it's going to be good for me to be in grandma's house with no one else around."

"It will give you time to get things ready to move into your trailer," Abe says. "Six and I will even go to the beach with you in the mornings until your trailer is ready. I can walk while you work out."

"I don't have much to get ready," Zack says. "All I have is duffle full of clothes and my guitars."

Beth and Marie arrive with the food. After placing it on the table, Marie walks up behind Zack and hugs him around the shoulders.

"I'm so sorry, Zack," Marie says.

"Thanks," Zack says.

"Did you see that op-ed which Olivia wrote?" Beth asks her grandfather.

"Haven't seen it."

"Take a look in 'The Islander' when you have a chance,' Beth says. 'Olivia really lit Ainsley up. She listed 14 assaults by his church members and basically put the island on notice that it shouldn't be tolerating Ainsley's bigoted thuggery any longer."

"'' Seems a good first step to me," Abe says. "Was one of those assaults Olivia listed the attack on Zack in Halifax?"

"No, she didn't list it," Beth says.

"Zack," Marie says, "has anything more come from those two guys you had a run in with last Friday down in Halifax?"

When Molly, Beth and Zack had come back out of the restaurant in Halifax, the two men had disappeared. The only sign of the struggle were a few drops of blood on the sidewalk.

"Not so far," Zack says. "I've been watching my back though."

For the next twenty minutes, talk around the table revolves around actions the villagers have taken against New Jericho. Posters are being torn down faster than they are put up. The ferry company has forced church members handing out flyers at the dock area to move to the other side of the traffic circle. Ainsley has now taken to roaming Main Street with his bullhorn ranting about the village's defiance of God's laws and threatening eternal damnation.

Once he's finished his pancakes, Zack rises from the table and says, "I'm going to go down to the funeral home now to see if there is anything I can help mom and dad with. I'll be back up tomorrow morning. Thanks for the breakfast."

"Don't forget to ask your mom & dad if there is anything that we can help them with," Beth says.

Zack walks to his blue Bug. Climbs in. Starts up the engine and disappears down the mountain.

"I'll get flowers sent over to the funeral home this afternoon," Beth says.

Abe, who is still finishing his breakfast, nods an okay.

Beth decides that it is time to talk with Abe about something which she has been putting off most of the week.

"Olivia tells me that you are planning to have grandma's sailboat brought up here," Beth says gently. "What exactly are you planning on doing with it?"

Abe looks up from his plate, wipes his mouth with his napkin, before saying, "I'm going to have a stand built on the far side of Becca's Garden. When the sailboat gets here, I'm going to put it on the stand."

"You are planning on fixing the sailboat up?" Beth asks.

"No, I'm not."

"Then what is the purpose of having the sailboat?"

Abe takes a long sip of his coffee before replying, "It's the only thing that I have left of your mother and grandmother. When I see it,

I will be reminded of them. When my time comes, I want my ashes placed on to that sailboat, have it taken past the south islands and sunk."

'It will remind me of the Sylvester Bros and Reginald," Beth says with a little more vitriol than she wanted. "Grandma and my mom are buried down at the cemetery beside Becca."

"Your mother and your grandmother were never in that cemetery when they were alive," Abe says firmly. "The last place they were, was in that sailboat. I want the sailboat left exactly as it is."

Beth raises her eyebrows and begins to say something before Abe adds, "You will be rid of the sailboat when I'm gone. Until then, after I get it back, it's going to be on the far side of Becca's Garden."

A NEW OPTION

Friday, 10:29AM. Beth is seated at the far patio table at the house. She is waiting for Angelique, who had called her last evening to arrange this morning's meeting. Angelique said it had something to do with an offer to join the bid on the old government center. Beth watches as a new Jaguar XF pulls up. Angelique comes out of the vehicle's passenger side. A well-groomed man in a dark business suit exits from the driver side. Beth walks out to meet them.

"Beth," Angelique says, "this is Jay Cuthbert from Island Resorts. Jay, my cousin Beth Stolz."

The pair shake hands.

"Do you want to sit out here?" Beth asks.

"I'd much prefer it," Cuthbert says.

Beth points them to the chairs before asking, "Coffee or tea?"

"No thanks," both say, so Beth sits down in the far chair.

"Beth," Cuthbert begins, "I am the Acquisitions Director for the company which owns Star of the South Resort. We have been paying attention to your bid for the old government center. Over the past few weeks, our primary owners have expressed an interest in joining your bid. Yesterday, after we completed working out the details of our proposal, I contacted Angelique to see if she might arrange a meeting with you."

"What do you mean by joining?"

"Our primary interest is in developing a casino/resort in the old quarry area," Cuthbert says. "Your business owns the only liquor and gaming license for that area. We'd like to discuss the possibility of working something out to make that happen. For starters we'd like to propose payment of $2.5million upfront with no strings attached other than raising the bid on the property to $4.5 million in total to cover the addition of permitting for the casino and resort. We would pay you $500,000 per year for the use of your liquor and gaming license in addition to a $1.25million per year lease on the properties. All the build out costs would be borne by Island Resorts."

"I'm somewhat confused," Beth says. "Why didn't you bid on the property on your own?"

"We would still have the gaming and liquor license issue," Cuthbert says. "Additionally, we are aware that Wannasea's Governor doesn't want outside interests owning that property because of the water and power generation stations. We came to feel that you're being the property owner would be much more beneficial for everyone concerned."

"Are you aware of our agreement with the Wannasea Historical Society?"

"We are."

"Are you aware of our plans for a restaurant and auditorium/meeting area in newer portion of the old government center?"
"To a lesser extent."

"If you don't mind," Beth says rising, "I'd like to bring my grandfather into the discussion as he is an active participant in our bid."

Beth walks into the studio. Abe and Zack are working on a sheet of lyrics at the table.

"Abe," Beth asks, "would you have time to come out and meet with a gentleman about our bid for the old government center?"

"Sure," Abe says rising.

"Zack," Abe requests, "why don't you continue putting down your thoughts for the lyrics?"

Beth leads Abe out to the front patio table. Introductions to Mr. Cuthbert are made as well as repeating what Island Resorts is offering. Abe sits down to the right of Beth.

"Why don't you explain to us exactly what your proposal is," Beth suggests.

"Our preference would be for you to take full ownership of the properties, then minus the historical society portion, lease the remainder of the facility plus your license to our organization."

"We could do that legally?" Beth asks Angelique.

"There is no reason why not," Angelique replies.

"This sounds rather like you want to do to us legally," Abe says, "what the Sylvester Bros tried to strong arm us into doing."

Cuthbert laughs before saying, "We aren't in the drug, gun running or money laundering business like the Sylvesters. Island Resorts is a legitimate business. We are one of the premier resort developers and operators on this island. Would you vouch for that Angelique?"

"I will."

"We would really prefer not to have a business operating up at the old center which is direct competition with our business here," Beth says.

"I don't see that as being an issue," Cuthbert says, "unless you are planning on opening a casino down here or bringing in acts focused upon acrobatics or magic."

"Our plan was more about moving our existing venue up there," Beth says. "We'd serve alcohol in the restaurant but there was no plan for gambling."

"Why were you thinking of moving your existing operation up there?" Cuthbert asks.

"Frankly," Beth says, "we've outgrown it. During the weekends and tourist season, we probably turn away more customers than we serve."

"Doesn't the property, which your current business sit on, abut the old government property?" Cuthbert asks.

"It does," Beth says, "I believe there are more than twenty acres of woodland before the parking lot of the old government center is reached."

"Why couldn't you expand your existing facilities on to that acreage once you have acquired the government center property?" Cuthbert asks. "Then minus the portion of the castle which the historical society will occupy, you can lease the remainder of the property to Island Resorts."

Beth looks toward Abe, who gives her a why-not look.

"We could," Beth replies. "There is another consideration, however. We have promised our longest-term employee the opportunity to operate the restaurant at the new facility."

"What type of restaurant?" Cuthbert asks.

"Seafood focused," Beth replies.

"I don't see why we couldn't accommodate that," Cuthbert says. "It will probably be easier if you handle doing the restaurant lease, however. I'd also suggest that having a restaurant, if it is of any quality at all, so close to our resort guarantees a money-maker. I also wouldn't think it will have much of an impact on our lease payments."

"How long are you proposing the duration of this lease to be?" Abe asks.

"Fifty years," Cuthbert says.

"What happens with all the facilities which have been built out after that fifty-year period?" Beth asks.

"Pending lease renewal or addendums, all those facilities would become your property."

"What if you decide after a few years to close the place?" Abe asks.

"Don't foresee any danger of that," Cuthbert says, "but the lease will have a clause that only after 10 years can the lease be broken. If it is, there would be a penalty of 25 million."

"What about taxes, insurance, etcetera on the facilities which you build?" Beth asks.

"We will be responsible," Cuthbert says. "Additionally, we will cover all of your existing bid production costs and pick up all new architectural costs in that area."

"Do you have any idea how many new jobs your resort would create if it's completed as planned?" Beth asks.

"If the resort is approved per our plan," Cuthbert says, "There will approximately 200 full-time staff positions created, another 100 part-time and 150 seasonal positions."

"You have this documented somewhere?" Beth asks.

"We do," Cuthbert says. "If you agree to sign a non-disclosure agreement, I will get you those documents as soon as possible.

"I will help you deal with getting those documents," Angelique injects.

"Is there anything else which I might be able to answer?" Cuthbert asks.

Abe and Beth go silent.

"Is what I am suggesting of any interest to you?" Cuthbert asks.

"Beth," Abe says, "it's your business now, I'm just along for the ride."

"I very much like the idea of the island having the number of new jobs which you mentioned," Beth says. "Nothing we were planning on doing at the old center would generate one-third of those jobs. That dynamic causes me to lean toward your offer. Would you be able to give us a few days to talk it over?"

"As long as you can make a verbal commitment to us before the end of next week," Cuthbert says, "we will be fine."

"We will try to get back to you by the first of next week," Beth says.

"I hope to hear from you then," Cuthbert says rising from the patio chair and extending his hand to Abe and Beth.

"Angelique," Beth says, "would you mind hanging around for a little while. There are a few things which we would like to discuss. I will drive you down to your office once we are finished."

"Sure," Angelique says, remaining in her patio chair.

Abe, Beth, and Cuthbert shake hands and say goodbye. Abe and Beth sit back down as Cuthbert climbs into his car.

"Is what Cuthbert was saying doable?" Beth asks.

"It is," Angelique replies firmly.

"Do you think that we would have any problems building out our existing business on the area of old government center property which abuts it?" Beth asks.

"I wouldn't think so," Angelique replies, "but I will find out for certain by the end of the day."

"Aren't you putting the cart before the horse?" Abe asks, "What if the island government doesn't except your bid?"

Angelique says, "I know for certain that they will. Particularly if the bid is increased to $4.5 million to cover the cost of having to deal with Island Resort's plan."

"Do you see any issues with what they are offering us as far as lease payments?" Abe asks.

"Only one," Angelique says, "I would suggest you tie the lease payment for the gambling license to the income from their casino operation. $500k to start is more than fair, but it's probably too low thereafter. I will figure out what sort of percentage those types of leases usually have and run it by Cuthbert to see if it is showstopper for them. Otherwise, I think it's a very generous offer."

"What do you think, Beth?" Abe asks.

"The island can really use all the jobs which that resort would create," Beth says. "I also think that I like the idea of expanding down here. I've been nervous for a while because I'm unsure that we have the skills or the drive to do what we were thinking about doing at the Quarry."

DECISIONS

Sunday, 3:41PM. Beth and Marie are seated in the upstairs office at 'The Place'. Over the past two days filled with discussions with Abe about the bid, Beth has decided to take Star Resorts up on their offer. Beth is now calling Angelique on her cell phone.

"Hey Beth," comes through the cell phone speaker as Beth switches it on and sits the device down on the office desk.

"Marie is here with me," Beth says in the direction of the phone. "I've decided that I would like to take Star Resorts up on their offer if everything can be worked out."

"What do you see as possible sticking points?" Angelique asks.

"The primary is the ability to expand 'The Place' using the lower portion of the castle property," Beth says. "Secondary considerations are working out the leasing arrangements on the restaurant and the payment for the use of our liquor and gaming license."

"Cuthbert has sent me documents which exclude the portion of the old government center building where the restaurant will be," Angelique relates. "He's agreed on a sliding scale based on casino income for increasing the license lease. Basing that scale on income versus profit is a big deal, so I'm kind of proud of that one."

"What about the building out the lower portion of the property?"

"I've looked through all the history of the land with the government center sits on," Angelique continues. "I suggest that your best approach is to have the section you want to use to expand broken out as a separate parcel. Spoke to the island Planning Commissioner about it yesterday and he said there shouldn't be any problem doing that. Also made a rather interesting discovery about your existing properties when I was going the history of the property."

'What's that?" Beth asks.

"Your great-great grandmother Alice Reginald actually owned the property, the building and licenses which were the Lakeside Bar and Grill from the time those parcels were split from the Reginald castle," Angelique says. "She had been renting the operation out from the time that it was built in 1924. She was renting it out to two of her cousins." "So Grandma Becca didn't purchase it?" Beth asks.

"No," Angelique. "She inherited it after Alice was killed. Your current properties have been in your family non-stop since 1913."

"Was the property originally purchased by Hugo and Alice when they were hiding out on the Mainland?" Beth asks.

"Hugo isn't on the old deeds. It was just Alice."

"Abe will be interested in that," Beth says.

"You are now ready to agree to join your bid on the castle with Island Resorts then?" Angelique asks.

Beth takes a deep breath before saying, "I am."

"I will get with Cuthbert and finalize all the documents," Angelique says, "I should have everything ready by Tuesday when I come out for the Concerned Citizens meeting."

"Speaking of that meeting," Beth says, "there are a few things which we would like to run by you.

"Okay."

"Marie and I started digging through the island rules on marriage," Beth begins, "and got distracted a little when we discovered that it's not just island marriage laws which are badly out of date."

"Welcome to my world," Angelique says with a laugh.

"Over the past week, we have spoken a few times with the other two guys on our committee. Like us, the guy from the flower shop is focused on changing the marriage laws, but the guy from the bed and breakfast started getting into things like zoning laws. This was what led us to research more on island rules. We also have become a little concerned that if we start campaigning to change just the marriage laws, we will be giving Ainsley a target which he can use to shift the discussion away from all the trouble which he is causing on the island. Perhaps the approach should be to have the island's legal code brought up to date including the rules on marriage? Along with marriage, we could pick out 4 or 5 other seriously flawed laws and call it the effort something like 'Updating our Island'?"

"That's a great idea," Angelique exclaims. "Our island's citizenship requirements are completely bonkers. Zoning, public lands and beach access. There is no end of citizen hot buttons which could be put into that effort. Do you know how citizenship on this island works?"

"No," both Beth and Marie say.

"Half of the people, who are permanent residents of the island, don't qualify for Wannasea citizenship as the laws are currently written. You either are born here or must be the child of someone who was born here. There are more Wannasea citizens living off the island than there are living on it. The only other avenue to citizenship is to have established permanent residence on the island for ten years. Then in addition to having to prove that residency, you must be approved by your ward council to file for citizenship. Few people who have moved to the island, bother with it."

"To be honest," Beth says, "after reading through them, most of our island's rules seem to read like they were thought up by someone out of the dark ages."

"They were," Angelique says. "Most were also thought up by our ancestors."

A POLITICAL TURN

Tuesday, 8:22PM. The meeting of Wannasea Concerned Citizens has just concluded. There were more than ninety attendees. Actions by and against Ainsley were reviewed. Primary among the review, the effort to take down Ainsley's posters and prevent flyers from being handed out. Councilwoman Furness had also announced that the building which Helmsley is using as a church will be inspected for code violations tomorrow. Beth had given a review from her committee, explaining the move away from focusing strictly on Wannasea marriage laws. By and large the attendees are now in agreement that the New Jericho Temple is now on the defensive.

Angelique has asked Beth and Marie to remain at the table in the rear corner where they have been sitting with Abe and Zack during the meeting. Angelique and Olivia approach their table with a gentlemen Beth knows to be Vic Newton. Vic is approximately Abe's age. He is dressed in tweed and looks the picture of an aging male islander from fifty years ago. Vic is also the head of the Mountain political party.

"Beth and Marie," Angelique says, "this is Vic Newton, the chair of the Mountain Centrist Party."

Vic holds out his hand, "Beth I believe we last spoke at the ceremony for the new government center? You gave quite the performance."

Beth nods her head though not remembering having spoken to Mr. Newton.

They exchange greetings and pull up chairs.

"The Mountain Centrist Party is an artifact left from Alice Bailey Reginald," Newton begins. "Alice was our Party's founder. Up until the early 1970s, the Mountain Centrist Party had been the island's premier political power. Over the past 50 years, the party has devolved into becoming an anachronism for old people complaining about essentially meaningless grievances."

He pauses for a moment.

"We like your thoughts on updating the island, " Vic Newton says. "It's long past time this island had some fresh blood working toward updating it."

"Thanks," Beth says, "but my primary focus is making the island's marriage laws work for everyone."

"I understand," Newton says. "Olivia has been talking to me about what's been going on with your meetings. Based on our discussions, I asked if she could arrange for us to meet."

"Why?" Beth says without malice.

"The Mountain Centrist Party is dying," Newton explains. "Ward 6 is the last bastion of support which we have and I'm afraid what Sheffield did with Sylvester Brothers puts our party at even greater risk of dying. The Mountain Centrist Party is actually on the verge of being absorbed by the Farmer's Party and ending its almost century long run."

"We much prefer that doesn't happen," Olivia says.

"Okay," Beth says apprehensively, "but I don't see what that has to do with me."

"Your great-great grandmother was our party's founder," Newton states. "She remains the very essence of what the Mountain Centrist Party actually stands for."

"All due respect, Mr. Newton, Alice Bailey has been dead for over 62 years," Beth says looking directly at Newton.

"The three of us," Angelique says pointing to Olivia and Newton, "really don't want to see her party die."

"That's all very nice," Beth says, "but what is it exactly you are hoping I may be able to do about it."

"We want you to run for the council seat in this district under the banner of the Mountain Centrist Party," Newton says looking directly into Beth's eyes.

"Do you know that I am gay?" Beth says somewhat belligerently.

"I do," Newton replies. "You are also Alice Bailey's great-great granddaughter. Her party still carries a lot of weight in this ward. Some of us have come to believe that there is a lot of Alice in you. We believe that you can easily win the September election in this ward. We also feel that you might help us save the Mountain Centrist Party."

"There is also a good possibility that I am now pregnant," Beth announces.

The table goes silent for a long moment before Newton says, "I don't see that your being pregnant should stand in the way of being elected. In fact, it may be boost."

"I'm not sure that I'm going to have the time to run for public office," Beth inserts. "In addition to possibly being pregnant, I am in the process of being involved in the purchase of the old government center and I have a business to run."

"I promise you," Newton says, "if you agree to run for council, our party will do all the heavy lifting. You likely will not have to do anything but give a few speeches. Possibly a debate. We will do as much as possible to assist you."

"I think you should consider it," Marie says. "We won't really be that involved in the new government center build out now. Sallie and I can take care of running things at 'The Place'. We only have two more trips to the clinic in Hanover. Even with the pregnancy, you should have the time available to run."

"Beth," Angelique says, "we really think you are on to something with 'Update our Island'. We know you have a passion for this island. It's time to take that passion in a somewhat different direction."

"Both Angelique and I will help you out, however we can if you run," Olivia says.

Beth has not seen this coming. She isn't sure what to think.

"May I have some time to think this over?" Beth requests. "Running for office is not something which I have thought about even in my wildest dreams. I was brought up by a great-grandmother, who believed that running for public office is a one-way ticket to personal extinction."

"We understand," Angelique says, "but think of the future which you can help make possible, not only for your own child, but for the rest of the children on this island."

"We will make your running for council as least burdensome as possible," Newton promises.

"How soon will you need my answer?" Beth asks.

"By the end of this month should be fine," Newton says.

The end of the month is a little more than 2 weeks distant.

"I'll do my best to have an answer by then," Beth says.

"Good," Newton replies, "we will be looking forward to hearing from you."

After a round of handshakes for Newton and hugs for Angelique and Olivia, everyone departs but Beth and Marie. They remain seated at the table in the corner.

"You knew they were going to ask me," Beth says, "didn't you?"

"Angelique told me about it this morning."

THEO AND A WALL FALL

Sunday, 10:12AM. Abe is seated at the table in the studio looking through a journal in an aged brown leather cover.

"Grandmother was an assassin," Abe says to Beth as she races past him on the way to the bathroom in the rear.

This past Monday, the fertility clinic in Hanover had told Beth that she is now 5-6 weeks pregnant. Until yesterday, Beth wasn't so certain that she believed them. Now, two days into morning sickness, she has become a firm believer.

Beth closes the door to the studio bathroom as Abe returns to the journal. A week ago, Josh brought down to Abe a chest which belonged to Becca from the upstairs area of the in-law suite which was being refurbished. Abe was familiar with chest. The chest was where his mother had stored her 'family' things. In it were a couple bibles with inscription for the births of Bailey and Reginald children, books which had long gone out of fashion and children's clothing. Most of which had been Beth's. All items with which Abe was more than familiar.

Starting Monday, Abe had decided that he would have the written and photographic items from the chest scanned so there will be copies for Beth, Hugh, or anyone else who wants them. At Molly's urging, he'd taken those items to the island's photography/office supply to have copies made.

Last Friday, Abe thought he had Becca's chest completely emptied. Then he noticed something strange. The bottom on the inside was a little warped in the middle. Worried, Abe lifted one end of the chest to see how it looked on the outside. Not only wasn't there any warp on the outside, but through looking closely at the bottom of the chest, Abe was able to tell that there was at least five inches between where the inside bottom started, and the outside stopped.

Abe had knocked on the inside bottom. It did not sound solid, though it didn't sound hollow either. Abe spent the better part of an hour trying to see if there was some mechanism in the trunk which would release the warped bottom layer. He finally gave up and went to Becca's shed by the garden and pulled out the tool kit. He used a long handled plain screwdriver to, as carefully as possible, pry the bottom up. It lifted without too much difficulty to reveal 3 leather bound journals. The journals were dusty and faded but were otherwise intact.

When he opened the first one on his left, his grandmother Alice's handwriting jumped out at him. Abe immediately enlisted Molly to help scan the pages in the journal. When the task had been completed on the first journal, aside from going with Zack, Josh and Six to the beach on Saturday morning, Abe had done nothing but read through the journals. Not all his grandmother's writing was in a language which Abe understood. Molly showed him how to use Google Translate to figure out what language the writings were in.

To Abe's astonishment, one of the languages is Romanian. Abe began feeding chunks of words into the translator. First Abe had learned that his grandmother had been carrying goods from the Mainland to the factions opposed to the Reginald's rule. Twenty minutes ago, he'd become fixated upon an eight-page section toward the end of the first journal. Alice wrote that her two male cousins were extremely upset that Theo was forcing himself on their sister. Alice helped devise a plan to undermine the wall at the East Lake which Theo habitually walked past at least 3 days a week right after sunset. After Alice discussed the plan with her contact on the Mainland, they sent Aldridge, a tunnel explosive expert, to the island to enhance her plan.

Alice's and her cousins' original plan had been to try to undermine the last section of the lake retaining wall so that pulling out a couple large boulders at select points would cause it to crash. The Mainland convinced Alice that the use of explosives would not only be more efficient but will leave her and her cousins at much less risk of being apprehended for the incident.

"Which grandmother was an assassin?" Beth says returning from the bathroom and sitting down in Molly's chair at the desk. Her face is now somewhat pale.

"Alice," Abe says with a wide smile and his eyes shining bright, pointing to the journal. "I have the story right here written in her own words."

"I can't make anything out but Wannasea and a few names," Beth says. "What language is it in?"

"Romanian," Abe says handing her his tablet. "Here's a translation of Alice's entries."

Beth looks at the screen:

Tuesday - Cousins Will and Simon work on tunnels with Aldridge from sundown until first light. All is ready. Theo will pass the wall after the sun has fallen. Explosives are in place and primed in the tunnels. Everything is set to bring down Reginald and the east lake wall.

Wednesday - Raining, we wait until tomorrow night.

Friday - The deed is done. Catherine whistled as Theo came our way. The explosives went off in the tunnels just as Aldridge said. The wall and the top third of the lake fell. Theo is gone. Long live freedom. Long live Wannasea.

"I'm not sure I understand," Beth says.

"Theo was Hugo's half-brother," Abe says. "He was going to be made king of this island by Nine. Alice, her cousins and a munitions expert from the Mainland had the large wall at the far end of East Lake collapse and kill him"

"So those lines in your song are true?" Beth says.

"More or less," Abe says. "This is proof that Grandmother Alice was involved in Theo's death. That was something which was always rumored but this journal is the first direct evidence that there is truth to that rumor."

"Bottom line, your grandmother helped to kill her husband's half-brother," Beth says.

"And helped to save an island from the tyranny of the Reginalds," Abe adds.

"We are part Reginald, you know."

Abe gives Beth a curious look before saying, "Why are you sticking up for the Reginalds?"

"I think pregnancy is making me a little weird," Beth says as she returns the tablet to Abe. "Or maybe it is because I have one of those little Reginalds growing in me and I'm hoping no one decides to drop a wall on them."

"From all reports, Theo was a very bad sort."

"From all reports," Beth says with a smile.

Beth thinks for a moment, "Does anyone else know that you have these journals?"

"Molly," Abe replies, "but she has no idea that I've just discovered that Alice was actually the force behind the killing of Theo."

"Would there be any problem not telling Molly or anyone else that Grandma Alice is a confirmed assassin at least until October?"

"Why?"

"Her Mountain Political Party is disappearing," Beth says. "Knowing she was an assassin might be enough for it to be killed off and buried."

"You really think so?"

"Yes."

"Okay," Abe says, "I will concentrate on translating the journals and leave Molly out of it. I am really hoping that I can present what is in these journals when the new Historical Society Museum opens at the castle though." "Based on current plans that's unlikely to happen before the end of this year at the earliest."

"I'll keep this and any other controversial discoveries to myself until then," Abe promises. "How are you coming on making a decision to run for island council?"

"This morning sickness isn't making be feel any better about it," Beth says, "and I can't really see myself as a politician."

"This island probably doesn't need any more politicians," Abe says. "It could however use people like you, who have a serious interest in this island's future. Don't you want to make the island better for this child that you are carrying?"

"I guess so," Beth answers, "but I think there may be people around more qualified than I am to do that?"

"Where?"

"Olivia or Angelique?" Beth says.

"Olivia and Angelique don't live in Ward 6," Abe says. "Outside of a bunch of old farts, and I'm including myself in that category, I don't know anyone else in this ward, who is as qualified as you."

"I'm only 25," Beth says, "and I'm pregnant."

"Grandma Alice was 17," Abe says, "and she was risking her life."

"I thought you always said that Grandma Alice was a real piece of work, who made your father's life miserable?"

"She was," Abe says, "but that doesn't mean that she wasn't brave and did a lot of good things for this island."

"What do you think they'll say about me, sixty years from now?"

"You have the rest of your life to determine that," Abe says.

Beth's stomach revolts. She rises from the chair quickly and goes back into the bathroom.

As she moves past Abe, he says, "Your grandmother used to eat ginger when she had morning sickness."

"Not approved by the Hanover Clinic," Beth shouts from behind the closed bathroom door.

Zack comes into the room through the sliding glass door. He had been down to the southeast beach with Josh and Six.

"What have you gotten out of the journals?" Zack asks.

"That my grandmother knew Romanian," Abe replies.

"I'm thinking about asking Beth if she'd let me play a few Sunday night sessions of only sea and folk songs," Zack says to Abe "Since we put music to your 'How Tomas Wanna's Sea became Wannasea', we now have at least a dozen of our own sea type songs. I'd also like to do some songs with my dad and uncle just for the fun of it."

"But 'The Place' isn't open on Sunday,"

"We'd only be open from like 6 until 9PM. We could just serve coffee, tea, and bottled drinks," Zack says, "Molly and I can take care of clean up and whatever else needs to be done.

"I'm pretty sure Beth doesn't want to put anything more on her plate right now," Abe says.

"Who doesn't want to put what on whose plate," Beth says as she walks from the bathroom.

Zack explains his request.

"Talk to Marie and Sallie," Beth says, "If they are okay with doing it, I am too."

WINDFALLS

Friday, 1:42PM. Abe and Zack are in the studio working on song selections for the sea song/folk performance which Zack plans to give at 'The Place' on Sunday evening. Sallie had been the primary driver in convincing Marie to allow the performance. She was going to use it to also unveil the updated menu of 'Sam and Sallie' items. Sam, her boyfriend, would be available to assist in the kitchen as he is off work at his normal job from 2PM on Sundays. They will open for food at 4PM and end the food service at 7. Only drinks would be served thereafter. Zack, his father, uncle, and the percussionist from Northenders would be on from 7:30 until 9PM.

Molly, who is sitting at the desk, is reviewing ticket sales on the website. After getting approval for the performance, Molly had arranged ads in the Thursday and Friday additions of both 'The Islander' and 'Halifax Times'. Currently 98 of the 120 available tickets for the performance are sold at $15 each. Molly has also been instrumental in arranging a livestream of the performance. It had taken until Wednesday noon to convince Zack to make it a paid stream event. They are charging $4.99 per view.

"Zack," Molly calls over toward the piano, "how many people did you say you thought might sign up for the livestream if we charge for it?"

"My guess still is there will be more people here in person," Zack says not looking up from the list which he is proposing for the opening set.

"I should have bet you," Molly says. "Come over here."

"I don't bet, remember?" Zack says, handing the music list to Abe, rising from the stool, and walking to the desk.

"Look at this," Molly says pointing to a livestream pre-sales figure which has just gone to 4,378. "At $3.65 profit per view, that's around $16K before we pay Dave and your band."

Abe rolls his chair over beside Molly.

"That's pretty impressive," Abe says, "and you still have two days' worth of sales to go."

"Can you tell where the sales are coming from?" Zack asks.

"Seems to be mostly around Halifax, Swansea and Hanover," Molly says.

"Better throw 'Orange All Around' on your list," Abe advises Zack.

"Didn't I tell you," Molly says beaming.

Zack does a two handed, palms down wave of exultation toward Molly.

"All hail the great and powerful Molly," Zack says with a wide grin.

"One of these days you are going to appreciate me," Molly says shaking her head.

"I already appreciate you, Molly," Abe says from her side.

Molly gives Abe a that-isn't-who-I'm-looking-for-appreciation-from look.

'It is really great, Molly," Zack says patting her gently on the back.

For the past month, Abe and Molly have been trying to persuade Zack to split the music he performs into two categories: folk and sea songs, blues, and soft rock. The pair are hopeful this concert will drive Zack in that direction.

"Now will you give me approval to split your music catalogue on our website into two categories and charge separately for each?" Molly asks Zack.

Currently Zack has one catalogue with 15 songs in it which is being sold for $9.99. Zack and Abe currently have a total of over 12 songs for each category.

"Let's wait until Sunday," Zack says.

"If we wait until Sunday," Molly says. "Odds are good that you will be costing us money."

"I'm with Molly on this one," Abe says.

"Are you guys trying to tell me that just like my psyche," Zack says, "my musical production is also bi-polar?"

"We are telling you," Abe says, "that you are what you are, and we are here to help you make the best of it."

"I do like what you are Zack," Molly adds.

"I do too," Abe says.

"Okay," Zack says, "make two catalogues but let's only charge $8.99 for each."

They agree, Abe and Zack go back to working on the Sunday song list. Molly dives into modifying the website for two catalogues and populating it.

Five minutes pass before Beth enters the room. She is now doing much better at managing morning sickness. The clinic in Hanover has provided her with a dietary plan which includes plenty of fluids, snacking and smaller meals in addition to taking B-6 supplements. At least for the moment, Beth seems to have the nausea under control.

In addition to morning sickness, Beth has been advised to spend less time on her feet. After discussions with Marie, Beth has turned the day-to-day management of 'The Place' over to Marie and Sallie. Her function now is basically that of running payroll and accounting.

"Vic Newton will be here in a minute," Beth tells Abe. "Do you still want to be with me to meet him?"

"Sure," Abe says. "I'm ready to go when you are."

"It's sprinkling a little," Beth says, "Is it okay if we meet him at your place?"

"Good by me," Abe says. "I'll go over and put on the kettle."

Abe rises from his chair and heads toward the sliding glass door. Just as he reaches it, Vic Newton knocks on the glass.

"Long time, no see." Newton says.

"Was kind of out of commission for a while with the right ankle fracture," Abe says. "I'm just starting to get back into circulation now."

Beth comes up behind Abe and guides him out the back door.

"If Abe is now working on getting back into circulation," Beth says, "he might just get there by the time he turns 90."

The two older men laugh, as Beth leads them over to the Abe's portion of the in-law suite.

"Have you talked Olivia into running in Ward 2?" Beth asks.

"She says she's going to run if you will," Newton replies as the entire the sliding glass door.

"Make yourself at home," Abe says, "I'll get the kettle going."

Newton sits in the far chair. Beth takes the chair beside him.

"Any more trouble with New Jericho out here?" Newton asks.

"We had some protesters out Wednesday night," Beth says, "but they must be so far away from 'The Place', they have become mostly a curiosity for our customers."

"What's your verdict on running for Ward 6?" Newton asks.

"I will do it under one condition," Beth says.

"What's that?"

"If I have any issues with my pregnancy," Beth states, "I can drop out immediately with no questions asked."

"We will agree to that," Newton says. "I wasn't joking when I told you that we are planning on making running for the seat as easy as possible for you. Currently no one has filed to run in your ward. I think that Cathy Sheffield is hoping that we will eventually come to her and beg her to run again. My plan is to have your filing ready to submit, then on the final day before the party caucus, we submit it. That will keep Sheffield and more than likely everyone else out of the picture."

"What do I need to do at this point?" Beth asks.

Newton opens his attaché and pulls out a binder which contains one two-page form and one six-page form.

"The two-page form is to join the Mountain Centrist Party," Newton says. "Please take a look at it and sign it if you don't have any questions."

Beth takes the two pages, glances through them and takes the pen which Vic Newton offers her. She signs the form and returns it to him.

"This is your candidate filing form," Newton says. "I'd suggest taking a good look at it. When you finish, give me a call and I'll come to pick it up. Hopefully you'll have it finished by this time next week."

Newton hands the six-page form over to Beth.

Abe returns with a tray containing three mugs, spoons, tea bags, instant coffee, milk, sugar, and a tin of Danish shortbread.

"That protégé of yours certainly has the New Jericho people stirred up over that song of his," Newton says.

"Which song?" Abe asks as he distributes the mugs.

"The one which goes, "Ainsley, you are a blight upon Wannasea. Ainsley, depart our island and leave us be."" Newton says trying to sing that stanza. "Half the shops around the ferry terminal now play it for the enjoyment of Ainsley's people handing out flyers. I'm told the same thing is going on down at the strip mall where Ainsley has his church."

"Good," Abe says. "We are always hoping to reach our target audience."

Abe sits down at the empty chair closest to the sliding door and begins fixing himself a cup of tea.

Beth continues to go through the candidacy form. She uses the pen to strike out a line referring to commitment to travel. She pushes it toward Vic Newton, who glances at it, then initials above it.

Abe reaches into his top shirt pocket and pulls out a check. The check is for $25,000 and is made out to the Mountain Centrist Party. He places it on the table and slides it over to Newton. Newton's eyes go up when he sees the amount.

"That's more money than the Mountain Centrist Party has taken in the past four years," Newton says.

"Zack has told me that he is going to donate his proceeds from website sales of 'small minds' and 'New Jericho' to the Mountain Centrist Party at the end of this quarter," Abe says. "At the moment that stands at around $17K."

"I don't know how to thank you," Vic Newton says.

"Just make sure that you do your best to see that Beth and Olivia are elected," Abe says. "I'm fairly certain if that happens those two can take it from there."

A SEA SONG EVENT

Sunday, 4:22PM. Beth, Marie and Abe are seated at Abe's usual table by the rear of the stage area. They are in the process of finishing up the sandwiches and soup from the Sam & Sallie menu. The pair have kept things simple. Fried grouper, grilled halibut, grilled steak, tuna salad, clam chowder, seafood gumbo and vegetable soup are the limit of the food being served. Sallie has brought Josh, Randy and two of Josh's friends in to help in the kitchen and bussing tables. The dining room area has Ana, Emily and four teenage girls, who had worked at the place this past summer.

"This clear broth clam chowder is wonderful," Abe says as he finishes his soup. "The halibut sandwich was darned good too."

"Sam and Sallie may be on to something," Marie says.

After reconsideration, Sallie has asked Beth earlier in the week to forego expanding 'The Place's' menu during their normal business days. She and Sam have decided they will try out their menu when Zack has such events as well as offering a catering service on their days off to test their menu plans for the restaurant.

There are approximately thirty other customers scattered throughout tables on the dining area floor. Molly has set up a stand at the front to handle those how have come for Zack's performance. She turns website tickets into glow-in-the-dark stamps on the back of hands. Zack, his dad, and the rest of the band have been up at the studio since 1:30 practicing playing together and formalizing their playlist.

"What did Olivia have to say this morning when she called?" Beth asks Abe.

"The criminal trial for Reggie and the Sylvester Brothers starts next Wednesday," Abe says. "They are separate proceedings. She does not think that I will have to testify in Reggie's trial. The deposition that I've made probably will be enough. Which is fine with me because I'm not sure that I can control myself if I actually lay eyes on Reggie."

"What about the Sylvester Brothers?" Beth asks.

"That's more uncertain," Abe says. "The murder charges have the biggest penalty, so there is a good chance that I will have to go in to testify both against them and as an injured party during the penalty phase."

"Where are the trials being held?" Marie asks.

"Swansea district court," Abe says. "If I have to be over there for I while, I'll stay with Hugh."

"How did Reggie and the Sylvesters plead?" Beth asks.

"Reggie has some kind of plea deal that he's trying to work out," Abe relates, "but Olivia says he is wasting his time because everything the prosecutors need came from Cecil and three other Sylvester gang members, who have turned state's evidence. The Sylvester Brothers pled not guilty, but Olivia says they may be on the verge of working out a plea to avoid the death penalty. In addition to your mother and grandmother, there are four other murder charges being tried against the Sylvesters related to their drug business in Halifax."

"We better scoot if we want to make the movie," Marie says about her and Beth's plan to catch a first run movie in Halifax.

"We'll probably be back late so don't worry about us," Beth says as she rises from her chair, kisses Abe on the check, then heads with Marie toward the front entrance.

Abe sits in silence contemplating whether to go back up to the studio for a few moments until Sallie comes out of the kitchen and sits down in the front chair at his table.

"What do you think?" Sallie asks Abe.

"Excellent," Abe says, "and I'm not just saying that to make you feel good."

"Sam knows what he is doing," Sallie says.

Prior to sitting down to eat, Abe, Beth, and Marie had noticed Sam's skills when they had gone into the kitchen to say hello. In a few minutes, it was obvious to them that Sam operated his kitchen much differently than Sallie. Sallie, who learned running the kitchen from Becca, was all about everyone being able to do every task in the kitchen. Sam was about people doing specific tasks and doing them as well as possible. What struck Abe about Sam was that he also appeared to be an extremely patient and proficient teacher to those he assigned tasks.

"Seems he does,' Abe says, "How are you guys feeling about Beth backing out of building the venue at the old government center."

"I'm kind of bummed that we won't be working directly with Beth so much once the restaurant is up and going,' Sallie says, "but Sam and I have been doing some talking with people about Island Resorts. They certainly appear to be a first-class operation. If Sam and I can produce good food at not too unreasonable a price, we shouldn't have much trouble keeping the customer base that Island Resort is going to hand us. We do have hopes of building up a local following though before the restaurant gets going."

"Seems that it will be this time next year before it's ready." Abe comments.

"At the earliest," Sallie replies. "Looks like we have a few more people coming in, I'd better get back to work."

Sallie rises from the chair and heads to the counter to check on the tea and coffee production.

Abe pulls his wallet from his pocket and puts down a ten-dollar bill on the table before rising and heading to the cash register.

"What are the damages?" Abe asks Ana, who is currently tending the register.

"Sallie said it was on the house," Ana says.

"She's not going to make any money that way," Abe says.

"You want to go argue with her?" Ana asks.

"No," Abe decides, 'Tell both Sam and Sallie that we said thanks."

"Will do."

Abe heads out the front entrance and walks up to his in-law suite and goes in the front door. Taking off his jacket and placing it on the sofa, Abe walks to the desk and sits down. The second of Alice's journals is open on the fourth page. Abe sets the alarm on the clock atop the desk to 7PM before sitting down. Abe goes back to working on translating Alice's entries about covert work which she was doing with her cousins, who at the time were operating the Lakeside Bar and Grill.

The next two and half hours pass in blur of Romanian, French and English words before the alarm goes off. Abe rises, picks up his tablet, places it in the inside pocket of his jacket. He returns to 'The Place'.

Prisha and Saanvi are now seated at his table. Abe exchanges greetings with them and sits down, noticing that the band is not on the stage yet.

"Would you like me to get you something to drink?" Saanvi asks.

"Thanks very much but I'm good at the moment," Abe says. "What do you two think about this trailer Zack has bought on the south side?"

"I like it," Saanvi says. "I think it will be good for Ralph over there if he sticks to going to the beach like he has been.'

"I'm not sure that I like Ralph being alone," Prisha says with a little concern creeping into her voice. "Ralph doesn't always do well when he is alone."

Sam and Dave, the audio-visual guys come in and begin setting up for the livestream. They nod to Abe as they head for to the stage.

"I'm sure he'll spend plenty of time here," Saanvi tells her mother.

"Also," Abe says, "Josh has kind of attached himself to Zack. Any place Zack goes, Josh tries to tag along."

"That's good," Prisha says. "Do you know what he and the band are doing now?"

"I haven't seen them since 2PM," Abe says, "but I would guess they are going over a few last-minute changes."

"Hank is very excited about playing tonight," Prisha says. 'He practiced his fiddle every night this past week in preparation."

Zack and the crew come through the front entrance carrying their instruments. After Zack sets his acoustic guitar down against the stage's back wall, he and his father walk to Abe's table. They both hug Prisha and Saanvi, who have risen to greet them.

"Are you ready to play?" Prisha asks her husband.

'I hope so," Hank says with a laugh. "I've never performed in front of a camera before."

"Don't worry Dad," Zack says, 'After a few minutes playing you won't even notice that Sam and Dave are there.'"

"We better get set up," Hank says as he and Zack return to the stage.

Abe surveys the crowd. Molly had said that 112 tickets were pre-purchased. Abe sees only two open tables and there are a few people standing at the bar. Abe checks the clock over the bar. 7:22. He pulls his tablet out of his jacket pocket, switches it on and creates a new file called "SundayEvent". After Abe enters "Sea Songs", he notices that Zack is pointing at him to start the introductions. Abe rises, walks to the stool which Sam has set out, picks up the wireless microphone and switches it on.

"Welcome to 'The Place'," Abe says. "Tonight, as you all know, will be a special performance of folk and sea songs by the Zack Tillerman Group. Attending the performance requires the payment of a $15 cover charge per person. If you have not already done so, you can see Molly at the stand at the entrance to make your payment. Please note that this event is being livestreamed. We encourage you to join in on the stanza if you know the words to the song. There will be three sets. The first is a selection of sea songs. The second, folk music followed by a session of the type of Wannasea Island tunes which many of you have heard played here over the years."

Abe sees that Dave is indicating that the live stream has begun.

"We will begin this evening with a selection of sea songs," Abe says, "so with no further ado, here is the Zack Tillerman Group."

Abe clicks off the microphone and returns to his table.

"Welcome folks," Zack says into his microphone. "My father began teaching me how to play music with sea songs. I'm going to start this evening playing the first song my father taught me to play, 'Blow the Man Down'.

Molly and Abe had spent the past week convincing Zack that he should announce each of his songs and offer a little personal tidbit when he did so. At least for this first song, it appears that Zack will take their suggestion.

The band breaks into the song. Most of the crowd joins in the stanzas with Zack's uncle urging them on.

"This next song still remains one of my favorite sea songs," Zacks says as the band breaks into "Roll the Old Chariot Along".

The crowd volume picks up a little.

"Now we are going to perform some of our own sea songs," Zack says. "This first song, 'Shan't Deceive Her' was written by Abe and I about two months back.

Abe is surprised that the crowd volume does not diminish all that much.

Zack follows up with 'Comes the Tillerman' and 'Barrett's Privateers'.

"Now just in case our new friends down at the New Jericho Temple think that we have forgotten about them," Zack says, "here is 'New Jericho same old hate'.

There is scattered clapping and whistling as the band breaks into the song. They repeat the last line, "depart our island and leave us be", four times.

Hank and Zack's uncle put down their instruments.

"Now we are going to have a little change of pace," Zack says, "I'm going to do two new songs for you. This first one Abe and I wrote yesterday."

125

REALLY WISH TEMPO - 82BPM KEY A MAJOR 3 /3 TIME

really wish that I had not

said what popped into my mind

did not expect the pain it brought

the words, much too unkind

really wish that I had not

raised my voice and anger up

when the argument became so hot

it led to our breakup

really wish that I had not

walked away and washed my hands

I spoke before I thought

Making unreasonable demands

really wish that I had not

said what popped into my mind

did not expect the pain it brought

my words, much too unkind

really wish that I had not

raised my voice and anger up

when the argument became so hot

it led to our breakup

really wish that I had not

walked away and washed my hands

I spoke before I thought

making unreasonable demands

really wish that I had not

said what popped into my mind

really wish I could undo the pain

instead of only being able to begin again

I spoke before I thought

making unreasonable demands

really wish I could undo the pain

instead of only being able to begin again

"This next song," Zack says, 'was created last Monday earlier in the week by Abe and I. The song begins the folk portion of tonight's proceedings."

EXPECTATIONS – TEMPO OF 66BPM, KEY OF C MAJOR IN

always gave

more than I received

but what I gave

left you aggrieved

all I ever expected

was for you to be you

all the while you hoped

to mold me into something new

expectations and a nervous breakdown

expectations leading to a showdown

expectations to which I could not ascend

expectations brought our end

was it ever as simple

as just wanting to be with you

will it always be as uncertain

as not being able to

expectations and a nervous breakdown

expectations leading to a showdown

expectations to which I could not ascend

expectations brought our end

failure to meet your expectations

destroyed our reputations

left us both in sorrow

with little hope for tomorrow

always gave

more than I received

but what I gave

left you aggrieved

expectations and a nervous breakdown

expectations leading to a showdown

expectations to which I could not ascend

expectations brought our end

expectations and a nervous breakdown

expectations leading to a showdown

expectations to which I could not ascend

expectations brought our end

Zack's father and his uncle return to their instruments.

"This next song is one of the first songs which I played at 'The Place'," Zack says. "Here is Jim Croce's 'Operator'.

Zack follows this up with 'Stuck in my Mind', 'Don't Blame it on the Alcohol', 'Carried Away' and 'Not the Same'.

Abe notes that 'Don't Blame it on the Alcohol' gets the loudest audience response.

After 'Not the Same', Zack introduces the band members.

"Now for all of our fans in Hanover," Zack says, "here's a round of 'Orange All Around'."

There seem to be at least three tables who are fans of the Orange.

"We are now going to take a short break before we do a few Wannasea songs," Zack says putting his guitar down.

The original plan had been for Dave and Sam to stop livestreaming at this point but Abe notices that they continue to record. Dave is scanning his camera slowly over 'The Place'. When he returns to pointing the camera to the stage, Zack is seated on a stool only his father and uncle are now behind him.

There had been a long on-going discussion between Abe and Zack about doing Reggie's songs. Abe didn't want to have them performed but Zack had insisted.

"Those songs belong to you, Abe," Zack kept insisting. "It's time for you to reclaim them."

Abe had finally relented.

"We are going to start the Wannasea portion of the evening with musical adaptation of one of Abe's poems," Zack says "This song will tell the story of how Wannasea came to be called Wannasea. This is the first time this poem has been set to music."

THE ISLAND OF WANNASEA - 122BPM TEMPO - DMAJOR KEY - 2/2 TIME

from volcanic eruption
and lava filled destruction
an island arose
where only a sailor goes

Wannasea
where I ever long to be

Wannasea
always home for me
in the sea birds flew
across Clarence of swirling blue
building nests in cliffs
among an island's lasting gifts

Wannasea
where I ever long to be

Wannasea
so blue its sea
green, more green
greenery, all that's to be seen
where black lava had been
green became the island's scene

Wannasea
where I ever long to be

Wannasea
so blue its sea
midst the foaming waves

131

NG RIPPEL

lie dark tidal caves
where lonely pirates hid
the evidence of what they did

Wannasea
where I ever long to be

Wannasea
so blue its sea
many came and many went
as an island made an ascent

from remote farming nation

to preferred tourist destination

Wannasea
where I ever long to be

Wannasea
always home for me "

Wannasea
where I ever long to be

Wannasea
always home for me

Wannasea

where I ever long to be

The band follows that with 'The Kingdom of Wannasea', 'Hugo Flies', 'Alice's Rule and 'Dark Ringlets'

"We are going to end the evening with a song which has not been performed in public before," Zack says. "The name of this song is 'Beyond Time'".

Zack and the band break into the song with Abe and Zack had created for Marie and Beth's wedding ceremony. Zack had been telling Abe that he really liked the song, but it didn't really fit into his style. Yesterday morning, after they had come back from the beach, Zack had gotten Abe to modify the song toward the meaning Zack wanted. That meaning was beginning to make Abe wonder if there wasn't much more going on in Zack's life than anyone at 'The Place' knew.

BEYOND TIME (2ND VERSION) - 99BPM
KEY OF C 3 / 4 TIME

through hurried days
and worried nights
love moves beyond time
time which flows in many ways
up the valley and to the heights
hand in hand, we should climb

trying hard to avoid pitfalls
our love often sputters and stalls
like the hands of a failing clock
we could not move past other's talk

eternity flows
around you, around me
weaving our souls into time
you, the one I chose
but it's not always me you see
wondering if you'll ever truly be mine

trying hard to avoid pitfalls
our love often sputters and stalls
like the hands upon a failing clock
we can't move past other people's talk

past the minutes
around the hours
beyond all time we go
the future becoming witness
to a love which might be ours
and not something from long ago

trying hard to avoid pitfalls
our love often sputters and stalls
like the hands upon a failing clock
we can't move past other people's talk

through hurried days
and worried nights
love moves beyond time
time which flows in many ways
up the valley and to the heights
hand in hand, we should climb

past the minutes
around the hours
beyond all time we go
the future becoming witness
to a love which might be ours
and not something from long ago

Abe has typed into his tablet that 'Expectations' seems like something of mystery to the audience, 'Really wish' a better reception, 'Beyond Time' received the best live audience response.

'Thanks for coming folks," Zack says before setting his guitar beside the stool.

The audience gives a long round of applause. Dave and Sam stop their livestreaming. The minute Zack puts his guitar down, Molly is upon him.

"Why did you have that last segment livestreamed?" Molly says to Zack angrily.

"I thought it wouldn't hurt to give our internet audience a little extra," Zack says.

"That little extra just cost us about $2,000."

A DECISION

Monday, 1:22PM. Molly is still angry with Zack. By extending his Sunday livestream performance by 30 minutes, the cost for the production had gone up $2,346.00. Zack's suggestion that adding the last segment was good advertising was going nowhere with Molly. By 11, Zack had decided that today was the day to go do a walk-through of the trailer out on the southside which he is purchasing. Abe is using the time to translate his journals.

"Zack is beginning to get out of control," Molly says out loud.

Abe is unsure whether the comment is directed at him or simply something Molly is doing to let off pent up frustration with Zack.

"I'm becoming more convinced by the day that Zack has no interest in the business side of his music," Molly said. "I think that he'd be just as happy right now if he were playing down at the ferry dock and collecting money in his guitar case."

"That's very likely valid," Abe tells Molly. "Zack keeps saying that the music is the most important thing to him."

"Music isn't going to pay his bills," Molly says.

"I don't think Zack has any bills at the moment," Abe says. "His car is paid off. He has the money to buy his trailer in cash. Most of the time, he eats here or at his moms for free."

"Don't you start siding with him," Molly warns.

Abe weighs for a moment telling Molly that it was just an observation but thinks better of the idea.

"How long is it before your graduation?" Abe asks.

Molly is due to graduate from the Wannasea extension with a degree in accounting this May.

"A little more than 11 weeks, now."

"What are you planning on doing after you graduate?'

"I honestly have not given it much thought," Molly says. 'I've been so busy here with Zack's music business that I haven't really had time to think about it."

"You aren't attending any of the recruitment sessions?"

"No," Molly says, "I haven't even taken the time to put together my resume."

'That is definitely something very un-Molly,' Abe thinks to himself before saying aloud, "You are planning on sticking with what you are currently doing for a while?" Abe asks.

"At least until the end of the summer," Molly says. "You realize that Zack's music business has made us a good deal of money. We've already earned over $350,000 in profit since we started. I don't see how I can earn anything anywhere close to that amount doing accounting for one of the resorts. To get a really good entry level position, I'd almost certainly have to move over to the Mainland and I'm not sure I want to do that."

"Music is a fickle business," Abe tells Molly. "You can be riding high for a while, then BOOM, the bottom drops out."

"So why have you been in the music business for fifty years?" Molly asks.

"I really haven't," Abe says. 'Writing lyrics is my side job. I've been lucky enough that it's produced enough money that I can work on historical journals and other writing without needing to worry about how much income those efforts produce."

"What would you have done if you had no income from songwriting?" Molly asks.

"Fairly certain that I would be over at Swansea University teaching," Abe says.

"You would have left the island?"

"If that's what it took to make a living, I would have," Abe says knowing that he is saying the words without real conviction that they are factual.

Beth comes into the studio through the hallway entrance.

"Well, we got it," Beth announces.

"Got what?" Abe asks.

"The old government center," Beth says with a broad grin. "Angelique just called to inform me that the island made their decision this morning. Seems the bidders from Qatar dropped out and there aren't really any other qualified bids. The island government has decided to proceed on finalizing our offer."

"That's great," Molly says, "I know you've been hoping that your bid was going to be the one chosen."

"Did Angelique say why the people from Qatar dropped their bid?" Abe asks.

"Rumor is that they didn't like what is going on between the island and Ainsley's church," Beth says. "Maybe I should send Ainsley a thank you card?"

"So how soon will you take ownership?" Abe asks.

"Probably 3-4 weeks," Beth says. "That's fast but Island Resorts wants to start construction as soon as they can. They have hopes of opening their resort the first part of next year."

"What about the restaurant and performance area?" Abe asks.

"Same time," Beth says.

"And the Wannasea Historical Society and the renovations of their portion of the castle?" Abe asks.

"The Society will have to wait until the auditorium work is done at the turret area," Beth says, "but they can start working on the rear and west sections as soon as Angelique is able to have their lease formalized."

"Are you still looking into creating another land parcel from the purchase so you can expand down here?" Abe says.

"That will be my primary work for the next few months," Beth says. "While we are on the subject of the old government center, there is something that I've been meaning to speak with you about."

"What's that?" Abe asks.

"The way this joint bid with Island Resorts is structured," Beth says, "I really don't need you to be involved in ownership of that property if you don't want to be involved. I have enough money to do the entire purchase myself. I'll also have plenty left to create the retreat/resort which I am hoping to create."

Abe thinks for a long moment.

"Guess there really isn't any need for me to be involved," Abe says, "unless you need someone to help take care of the ownership aspects when the baby comes."

"I will always want your advice," Beth says. "But it's time for me to deal with those responsibilities on my own."

A TRAILER WARMING

Sunday, 1:05PM. Abe has just turned his Volvo off of West Road on to South Mountain Way. He is headed toward Zack's trailer warming affair, though he is running a little late.

Abe has spent the last three days in Swansea attending the penalty phase of the Sylvester Brothers trial. Both brothers had agreed to serve three consecutive 20 year sentences in exchange for dropping five of six gun running charges. Abe had spent most of Thursday and Friday at the Swansea courthouse watching the proceedings. He had not been called to testify on the items which he retrieved from Janie's sailboat or during the penalty phase. His depositions were all that had been required.

Abe is glad that he had gone to the proceedings even though very little of the trial was focused upon the murder of Janie and Julia. Abe could not at this point say whether he is satisfied with the trial's outcome or not. Abe remains angry, but most of that anger is directed toward Reggie, who had not been present at the trial. Reggie's trial is scheduled for next month. Two days of seeing the Sylvester brothers in person had left Abe feeling numb. Numb that two such malevolent individuals had been able to take away the lives of his wife and daughter. Numb that the trial treated murder so clinically.

In talking with the lead prosecutor for the district, who helped Abe create a victim impact statement, Abe admitted that beyond seeking some measure of revenge from Reggie and the Sylvesters, his secondary consideration was wanting to know if the Sylvester brothers had killed his wife and daughter in part because they were from Hugo and Alice Reginald's family. As the proceedings wrapped up on Friday with the acceptance of the plea deal, the prosecutor told Abe that he had been able to pose the question to both brothers during the negotiations. Neither of the brothers had any idea that the women which they had killed were from the Reginald family. Both were insistent that their initial intention had been to scare the women away from going to the police or the Press. The pair had insisted that Julia and Janie's response had triggered their killing. The revelation has left Abe feeling more than ever that Reggie was the person most responsible for what had happened to his wife and daughter.

Abe has stuck with his insistence that Janie's sailboat is to be turned over to his possession without anything being done to it other than hauling it to the Constabulary wharf in Wannasea village. Abe is disheartened that he will not receive the return of the plastic box containing Janie and Julia 's wallets. Those items must be retained in the evidence bin in the event of future appeals.

Zack's trailer warming had started at noon. Abe stayed at Hugh's over the past three days and had taken Hugh and Helen out to brunch this morning in return for their hospitality. He gotten talking to Hugh about some of the things which had been discovered in Alice's journals, being careful not to tell Hugh of the existence of those journals. The discussions had been primarily about what Hugh might know of Alice's Bailey's family. Hugh had told him of some his research revealed that most of the Baileys were involved in covert activities tied to the Mainland, both prior to the fall of the Reginalds on Wannasea as well as during the second world war. Unfortunately, Hugh had not yet been able to find specific names and dates, leaving Abe with one more avenue of his grandmother's life to research. It had also left Abe thirty minutes late leaving for his return to Wannasea.

Abe turns the Volvo on to South Shore Drive. About a third of the mile down that road, he swings the car into the parking lot for the beach. He seen Beth's VW parked there and figured this was about as close as he was going to be able to get to Zack's new home.

Abe is relieved to be able to walk the approximately two and a half blocks upward toward the trailer park.

There are a good number of people attending Zack's party. Beth and Marie are seated with Saavi on the side steps. Zack's parents and his uncle are seated at a picnic table on the deck along with 3 other people, who Abe doesn't know. Josh and Randy are standing along the deck railing along with several waitresses from 'The Place'. Abe makes his way around saying hello when Zack pops out of the trailer and says, "Let me give you the tour."

"I really like this deck," Zack says. "There's a roll out awning if it gets too sunny."

Today is rather overcast so the awning remains in place.

"Does not appear that there are many people living in this park right now," Abe says.

"Less than 1 in 4 of the trailers are occupied now," Zack says. "In the summer though, the park will be full.'

Zack leads Abe inside. There are people, mainly from 'The Place', seated on the couches, side chairs and at the 3 stools which serve as a dining area. Sallie is behind the counter of the galley style kitchen. At Molly's urging, Zack has arranged for Sam and Sallie to cater for him.

Zack leads him back the hallway to the two bedrooms and a large bath behind the kitchen.

"There are 920 square feet," Zack says. "I think that's the perfect size for me."

Abe is surprised at how well kept and clean the trailer is. It has a sea-mist green motif throughout. 'All in all, it's a nice little place,' Abe thinks as he finishes Zack's brief tour.

"There is still some clam chowder left," Sallie tells Abe as he walks past the kitchen.

Abe isn't all that hungry but can't pass up the offer. He takes a small bowl from Sallie as Zack leads him back outside and around the corner.

"There are drinks in the coolers," Zack says pointing to two large coolers along the side of the beige colored trailer with dark green trim.

Zack takes Abe to a small patio table where Molly sits with Dave, the A/V guy.

"Take my chair," Dave says, "I've got to get going now anyway."

Abe sets his soup down on the table and takes the chair which Dave has vacated.

As he does so, Molly hands the color section of the weekend's Hanover Herald to him.

"Look inside at pages 4 and 5," Molly instructs Abe.

Abe opens the section to the corresponding pages and sees an article called 'An Island Phenomenon". There is a picture of Zack playing at 'The Place'. Abe notes that it must be recent as the 'Northenders' are backing Zack up. There is another picture of Zack on the beach, in his orange swimsuit and black T-Shirt top. Zack is never without that top on the beach, even when he goes swimming. The t-shirt prevents Zack having to answer questions about the nasty scars on his back. There is also a picture of Zack dressed in a tuxedo sitting in front of a cello beside three young women in formal attire with other musical instruments.

"I thought you didn't want to do interviews?" Abe asks Zack.

"I don't," Zack says taking a seat on the deck chair on the other side of Molly.

'So how did this story come to happen?" Abe asks.

"For the past couple weeks, I've been running into this guy named 'Ray Simmons' down at the beach when I work out," Zack explains, "He's a decent sort, so I started doing my workouts with him."

"He's also a freelance reporter," Molly notes.

Abe looks at the small picture of the author at the bottom of the article. He remembers having seen the fellow talking with Zack on a couple of his forays to the beach before he had dives head first into Alice's journals.

"He's from the island?" Abe asks.

"No, he lives in Hanover," Zack says.

"Enterprising sort," Abe says.

"He's actually a nice guy," Zack says. "I'm going to have lunch with him tomorrow after I meet with Doc Schiller over in Hanover."

"The reporter also talked to Saanvi at the bank," Molly relates, "and went to the resort to talk with Prisha."

Abe takes a couple spoons of Sallie's soup. It's as good as the last time.

Abe begins reading through the article. He discovers Zack was something of a cello prodigy when he was in secondary school. Zack had been a member of a locally acclaimed string quartet which is shown in the photograph.

"You play cello?" Abe asks.

"Along with the violin," Zack says. "The fiddle was the first thing which my dad taught me to play."

The article indicates that Zack dropped out of the string quartet and gave up an opportunity to attend a music conservatory north of Hanover. Zack had enlisted in the army instead.

"Why'd you stop playing with this group?" Abe asks pointing to the picture.

"I had a falling out with one of them," Zack says avoiding Abe's eyes.

Abe goes back to reading the article and discovers that Zack had not really taken up playing the guitar until he was in the army. The article mentions Zack being injured but says nothing about the circumstances of the event leading to that injury's impact on his life. The rest of the article is a review of the music which Zack has released. It ends proclaiming that Zack is well on his way to becoming the most popular musical artist on the Mainland, who has not released recordings through music stores or the formal music industry.

"It's a nice article," Abe says.

"I think so, too," Molly adds.

Abe finishes his soup.

"I've been doing a little thinking about this organization which we've formed," Abe says facing toward Zack. "I'm beginning to think it may be holding back your career."

"Honestly, Abe," Zack says, "my career is exactly where I want it to be."

"I think if you had professional musical guidance," Abe says, "it could take you a lot further. All you need to do is say the word and I will see if my agent can take you on or get you with someone, who can help you grow."

"I think we are doing just fine," Zack says.

"We have made quite a bit of money, you know," Molly interjects. "The after-performance sales from last Sunday have now brought in more than the event sales."

"I'm planning on doing another livestreamed performance next Sunday," Zack says. "We are going to call it 'Blues and more'."

"I released ticket sales on Thursday," Molly says, "and 'The Place' is already sold out."

"Zack," Abe replies, "aside from helping you to write songs, I haven't been much help at all in expanding your musical skills or getting you into the sorts of venues which you ought to be playing. I've come to think you'd be much better off at this point with professional management."

"I don't want to play in any other musical venues," Zack says firmly. "I could not have written the songs which we now have by myself. If I'm still playing at 'The Place' ten years from now, that will suit me just fine. I mean it when I say that I am not going to play music off this island."

A STRING IS PULLED

Thursday, 9:05AM. Zack is knocking on the sliding door to Abe's kitchen. Abe is sitting down at his dining table finishing a cup of tea. He is absorbed in Alice's third journal.

Abe rises, unlocks the door, and allows Zack to enter. Zack has his acoustic guitar on his back.

"What brings you out so early?" Abe asks.

"I've had an idea for a song that I like to do for the blues livestream on Sunday," Zack says. "I'm hoping that you will help me come up with it."

"Do you want to go over to the studio?" Abe asks.

"Could we do it right here?" Zack asks. "If not, we can go up to my trailer."

"Do you mind if I ask why you don't want to go over to the studio?" Abe asks.

"The song I'm thinking of is rather personal," Zack says. "I'd rather not work on creating it in front of Molly."

"If you can't do it in front of Molly," Abe says, "how are you planning on performing it in front of an audience."

"It's not the same thing," Zack says. "If I start putting the song together over there Molly is going to start asking me questions. Questions which I'm not going to want to answer."

"What's the deal with you and Molly?"

"In case you haven't noticed," Zack says, "Molly likes me in a much different way than I like Molly."

"Meaning Molly sees what we are doing as something other than a business arrangement?"

"I don't want to put it that way," Zack says. "I do really like Molly but it's pretty much the same way that I like my sister."

"Okay," Abe says. "I'm game to work on the song here. Want some coffee or tea?"

"Tea would be good," Zack says.

Abe picks up his tablet, the journal, and his mug. He stops at the kitchen counter to switch on the half-full electric tea kettle.

"Let's go to the front room," Abe says.

While Zack is setting up, Abe phones Molly. Abe asks Molly if she would mind going down to the village to pick up the copies of the non-journal items from Becca's trunk. The photography company had called yesterday notifying Molly that they are ready.

"Once you have them," Abe asks, "would you mind going into Halifax and have 3 copies made of each one of the photographs?"

"No problem," Molly says, "Do you think Zack might want to go with me?"

"Zack has something he's working on at the moment," Abe explains, "so he can't go."

"Would you mind if I also go to the music store and purchase some new music stands?" Molly asks. "The ones that you have are not only ancient but falling apart."

"Knock yourself out," Abe says as Molly disconnects the call.

"I'm not sure Molly isn't wise to us," Abe says, "but I think we are good until later this afternoon. Sure, you don't want to go over to the studio?"

"Let's stay here until we have a handle on the lyrics," Zack requests.

The tea kettle is whistling.

"I'll fix my tea," Zack says putting his guitar down on the couch and going toward the kitchen area. "You can get ready to do word magic."

"It's not magic," Abe says, "and there really isn't all that much to doing it."

"I'm really hoping to make this song special," Zack tells Abe. "You remember that picture of the string quartet which Ray Simmons put in the Hanover Herald article about me?"

"I do," Abe says putting the journal into the center desk drawer then locking the drawer.

"There's some history to it," Zack says as he places a jasmine tea bag into the mug which has been taken off the rack behind the kettle. "I joined that string quartet when I was thirteen and had just finished my primaries. The three girls in that photo are from well-to-do families on the Mainland. None of them went to the same primary school that I did. None of them lived anywhere near the neighborhood where I lived. I was in that string quartet because I could play cello. Not that any of those girls weren't proficient musicians, but they were there because of who their families are."

"That's not going to make much of a blues song," Abe says.

Zack finishes pouring water into the mug and returns to the couch.

"Going into my third year in the string quartet, things got rather hot and heavy between me and the first violin," Zack says looking at the coffee table rather than Abe. "Abby is from one of the oldest families in Halifax. Her old man runs the biggest shipping company over there."

"Uh-huh," Abe says looking down at his tablet keyboard but not typing anything.

"Abby's parents liked me fine as a cello player," Zack continues. "They didn't like me so much as Abby's boyfriend."

"Why is that?" Abe asks.

"I had two strikes against me," Zack says. "My family is lower middle class and I'm mixed race. In Abby's world, it's one strike and you are out."

"Did the girl's family confront you?" Abe asks.

"Not directly until the end," Zack says. "Abby kept telling me that as long as we stayed away from being a pair publicly, it would eventually work out. We used to come out here to the island when we wanted to be together. We'd either go to grandma's or out to her family's resort house when no one else was there. This went fine for almost a year until Abby became pregnant in the third month of our last year in sixth form. She kept telling me that she was working out a way that she could pull together enough money so that we could run off, get married, have the baby then return in a few years. That fantasy lasted about a month until her parents discovered that she was pregnant. In an instant Abby was shipped off to Switzerland and her parents went out of their way to erase all evidence that I had any part in her life."

"Where did that leave you?" Abe asks.

"Out of the quartet. Out of any chance of attending the conservatory. I quickly learned that I'd wasted all my last sixth form years."

"When did you decided to go in the army?"

'I had to get away," Zack explains. "When it finally dawned on me that Abby wasn't coming back and her parents were working on black balling me, I figured the Army was one way out."

"How did they black ball you?"

"They made sure any chance that had at further education was taken away," Zack says. "They went so far as to see that my dad was fired from his job as an electrician for a contractor down at the docks. It was tough for him to find anything but piece work for a long time."

"You haven't seen this girl since?"

"About four months before I left 'Dave's' over in Halifax," Zack says, "Abby came into the bar for about twenty minutes with one of the other girls from the quartet. Before I had a chance to speak with her, she left. Last Friday, she was out at 'The Place'. She stayed until ten minutes before the last song."

"Were you intending to speak with her before she left?"

"I was," Zack says, "but seeing her left me kind of paralyzed."

Abe rises from his desk chair, goes into the kitchen, refills the kettle and turns it on.

"You want some more tea?" Abe asks.

"No, I'm good."

Abe stands by the kitchen counter and waits for the kettle to boil before carrying it back over to his desk along with a new tea bag and a spoon. He puts the tea bag into his mug, fills it and carries the kettle back to the kitchen.

"Do you blame this girl and her family for your going into the Army?" Abe asks.

"Not really," Zack says. "I had other choices. My mom has a cousin in Atlanta where I could have gone to get myself back together. I picked going into the Army. Neither Abby nor her parents put me in the Army."

Abe returns to his desk and sits down. He pulls a wire bound notebook from the left corner of the desk, opens it to the first blank page. Abe picks a pen out of the black plastic container and draws a line in the center of the page. On the top portion Abe writes "During". Below the line he writes "After". He wheels the chair across the oak plank floor over to the front of the coffee table and hands the notebook and pen to Zack.

"Write at least 3 words in each of those sections which best describe your feelings about what happened between Abby and you. The top is for how you felt while you were together. The bottom is how you have felt since.

Abe wheels back over to the desk and opens his tablet. He creates a new file which he names "Abby". He then completes making his cup of tea and sits back and drinks it while Zack thinks and writes.

After ten minutes, Zack rises from the couch and carries the notebook and pen back to Abe at the desk.

"Who do you want this song to be for?" Abe asks.

"Abby," Zack says without hesitation.

"I take it that song we wrote called 'Expectations' and what you did in re-writing 'Beyond Time' were about Abby and you?"

"In a manner of speaking," Zack says as he returns to the couch and picks up his guitar. "Those two songs were meant to be more about explaining to the audience how I feel."

"Do you want this girl back?" Abe asks.

"I don't think so," Zack says. "I'm not going to say that it couldn't have worked out if Abby and I stayed together but where things are now, seems too far gone. The problem is that does not stop me from thinking about her."

"Why don't you play around with melodies which you think may fit what you want to go into this song," Abe suggests. "I'll see what I can do with lyrics."

Abe looks at what Zack has written down on the tablet.

During

Wonder

Sweetness

Connected

Protective

Love

<u>After</u>

Erased

Uncertain

Directionless

Alone

Abe and Zack spent the rest of the day crafting a song which will be called 'Six Year Blues'. Most of the words end up coming from Zack.

THE CANDIDATE

Saturday, 4:13PM. Beth, Marie and Abe sit at the far patio table working on finalizing campaign slogans. Tonight at 5PM, Beth will be making a presentation to the Mountain Centrist Party's Ward 6 caucus. At 6PM, the caucus will determine who the party's candidate will be. The trio have managed to create 12 possible slogans.

"Abe," Marie says, "why don't you pick the four which you think might work best."

"Tell you what," Abe says, "I like 'Fix Ward 6 - Beth for Council'. Why don't you pick one Marie and then Beth will pick the final two."

"' What Alice began is Beth's plan'," Marie states, "is what I like best."

Abe types their choices into a file on his tablet.

Beth takes a few moments to study the list which they have put together. Beth pats Six's head, who sits beside her chair, before choosing 'Update our Island' and 'Fairness builds our Future'.

"We better head up to Southside Primary School," Beth says. "Roberta asks us to be there no later than a quarter till five."

Southside Primary School is where the Mountain Centrist Party Caucus for Ward 6 is to be held. Roberta Johnson is the party functionary, who Vic Newton had assigned to work with Beth on her candidacy. Roberta had been two years ahead of Beth at the Wannasea School. She is Director of the local foodbank.

Abe pastes the list into an email which he sends to Newton, Roberta Johnson, and Beth.

Beth leads Six back into the studio and shuts the sliding glass door behind him. She then walks to Abe's car. Marie is sitting in the driver's seat with Abe seated behind her. Beth climbs into the front passenger seat. In silence they make the short ten-minute drive to the school on the other

side of the mountain.

As the Volvo approaches the parking lot, about a dozen of Ainsley's followers can be seen protesting at the main entrance to the parking lot. They are making it as difficult as possible for cars to enter.

"I'll go around the back way," Marie says as she maneuvers the Volvo past the east end of the building then follows the narrow road which leads to the athletic fields, then around in a half circle to the front parking lot.

Marie parks the car in the second row. They climb out and go through the school's front entrance to calls of 'Satan's Spawn", "Abominations", "God will hold you to account", "Wannasea is God's preserve" and "All those not following God's rules must be removed".

Roberta Johnson is waiting for them just inside the door.

"How do you like your reception committee?" Roberta says pointing out toward Ainsley's protesters.

"They are out there for me?" Beth asks.

"Apparently so," Roberta says.

Abe looks out the glass of the entrance door, then says, "I don't see Ainsley out there with them."

"He's down at Ward 2," Roberta says. "Seems Olivia has now surpassed Beth as a threat in New Jericho minds."

"How many people are in there?" Beth asks, pointing toward the auditorium.

"Forty-four, I think." Roberta responds. "That's about normal for a Ward 6 caucus. Let's sit down for a few minutes. They don't expect us in there until five."

They sit in the row of chairs lined up against the front wall of the primary school's auditorium.

'I'd advise keeping your speech as brief as possible," Roberta says. "At this point, most of those inside are only interested in the fact that you are Alice Bailey's great-great granddaughter. We can work in what we hope to accomplish with your candidacy later."

"How many people usually vote in the Ward 6 general election?" Abe asks.

'Anywhere between four and five thousand depending on what the hot button issues happen to be," Roberta says.

"How many are eligible to vote in Ward 6?" Abe asks.

"About 10,000,' Roberta says, "but at least a third of those people live off the island. Island citizenship requirements are archaic. Hopefully that is something we can work toward correcting."

Roberta, Beth, and Marie engage in small talk about their experiences in this same primary school.

Roberta checks her watch, "Time to go in."

They enter the rear of the auditorium and walk down the right hallway toward the front of the auditorium's stage. Most of the people in the audience appear to be fifty or older. Abe and Marie take two empty seats behind the last row in which the participants are seated. Roberta walks with Beth up to the stage which is occupied by two male senior members of the Ward 6 Mountain Centrist Party.

"You're on your own now," Roberta says to Beth, who begins walking up the side steps.

"Ladies and gentlemen," the man at the lectern says, "Beth Stolz, who is seeking to become our candidate for Island Council from Ward 6, will now say a few words."

Beth walks to the lectern, adjusts the microphone, "Good afternoon. It is indeed an honor and privilege to be considered as the Mountain Centrist Party candidate for Ward 6. As many of you know, I am Alice Bailey's great-great granddaughter. I have been taught almost from the time when I could first talk that Alice stood for bravery in the face of adversity, fairness for all and progress. I promise you that if you choose me to be your candidate for Ward 6, I will do my best to follow that tradition. Thanks so much for considering me as your candidate."

Beth turns and walks directly off the stage to where Roberta, Abe and Marie sit.

"The caucus vote won't occur until 6PM," Roberta whispers. "There really isn't any reason for you all to hang around here. I'll give you a call as soon as I know the result."

Marie, Abe, and Beth make their way back to the Volvo. Ainsley's followers renew their shouts as Marie steers the Volvo behind the school.

"Persistent lot," Abe comments, 'aren't they?"

"What is it exactly they are trying to accomplish?" Beth asks. "I haven't seen anyone else out here but us and the members of the Mountain Centrist Party inside. Do they think shouting insults is going to change anyone's mind?"

"I think what they are trying to accomplish," Abe says, "is to make Ainsley happy."

"Ainsley has a weird sense of happiness," Marie says as she steers the Volvo on to the West Road cutoff.

They ride in silence until Marie pulls the Volvo into the parking lot of 'The Place'.

"I've got to get back to work," Marie says as she turns the engine off and passes the keys back to Abe.

"Do you have time to eat a bite with us?" Beth asks.

"I do if it's quick," Marie replies.

"Abe?"

"Sounds good to me," Abe says as he follows Marie and Beth to the front entrance.

'The Place' is packed. Not one table is free.

"What do you guys want?" Marie says, "I'll go in the kitchen and make our order."

Abe opts for soup and salad. Beth a fruit salad

"Let's eat on the back patio," Beth says.as she leads Abe through the dining area, down the back hallway and out on to the patio, which is 2/3rds full of dinners.

"Won't even be tourist season for another two months,' Abe comments.

"The sooner we get going with expanding this place, the better," Beth comments.

"Have you worked anything out with the architect?" Abe asks.

"We are currently considering building an outdoor performance center capable of accommodating 3-400 on the other side of where the storage shed used to stand," Beth says. "I am hoping on being able to afford having the Stage and 2/3 of the seats be covered. Am also thinking of expanding the patio by 50% more, but I'm not all that sure how our food business is going to fare once Sallie is gone."

"Any plans on who might replace her?" Abe asks as they sit down at a picnic table at the rear corner of the patio toward the house.

Beth shakes her head, "I was thinking just last night that over the past 62 years, 'The Place' has only had two people in charge of the kitchen. Becca and Sallie. How do you replace that?"

"Not easily," Abe says.

Beth and Abe pull out their cell phones and check their messages until Marie returns with a tray full of food and iced tea.

They are halfway through their meal when Beth's cell phone rings.

"It's Roberta," Beth explains rising toward the table and walking toward the woods at the rear of the patio.

"Hey Roberta," Beth says after she connects the call.

"Welcome to Island politics," Roberta says. "You are now the Mountain Centrist Party's Ward 6 candidate."

"How well did I do?" Beth asks.

"You got 39 out 46 votes," Roberta says. "Cathy Sheffield only had 32 out of 44 during the last election."

BLUES AND MORE

Sunday, 7:16PM. 'The Place' is packed in anticipation of Zack's second Sunday evening performance. Abe, Beth, and Saanvi are seated at Abe's normal table near the side wall section of the stage. The dining room area has been mainly full since opening at 4PM. Much of the patio area is also filled with diners.

Zack had brought the 'Northenders' into the house's studio at 2:30 to enable them to better learn 'Six Year Blues' as well as the other songs which Zack has lined up to perform. Sam and Dave, the A/V guys, had been brought to the studio at 5 to record 'Six Year Blues' for placement on the website.

Molly is once again at the front entrance, exchanging tickets for a hand stamp. Molly had been on the warpath with Zack, Sam, and Dave to make certain that tonight's livestream performance will not exceed 90 minutes. Over 8,000 livestream pre-purchases have been made. The livestream service has told Molly that only 10,000 streams are available at one time. If this performance reaches that number, she will need to cut off advertising for the livestream on the ZackTillerman.com website.

Sam and Dave come in through the back hallway and begin setting up their audio and video equipment.

Abe looks out into the audience wondering if Zack's Abby is sitting at any of the tables.

Five minutes pass before first the 'Northenders' come in and begin setting up, then Zack comes in carrying his electric and acoustic guitars. He sets the acoustic guitar to the rear of the stage and straps on the electric guitar.

Zack looks toward Abe and nods. Abe walks in front of the stage and clicks on the wireless microphone.

"Welcome to 'The Place'," Abe begins. "Tonight, will be a special performance by 'Zack Tillerman and the Northenders', they are calling 'Blues and More'. The first 90 minutes of the performance is going to be livestreamed on the ZackTillerman.com website. Please do not walk between Dave, the cameraman, and the stage."

Dave makes a polite wave to the crowd and begins recording as Abe nods to him.

"Here without any further ado are Zack Tillerman and 'the Northenders',' Abe says to complete the introductions.

"The first song was written by Abe over twenty years ago," Zack says looking out into the audience. "It's called 'This side of nowhere'. Abe and my grandfather once knew how to get there."

Zack and the band break into the song. This is the first time this song has been performed at 'The Place' but it seems as if the crowd knows it well. The performance is tight and hard driving. The band plays,

"'cause this side of nowhere is where I reside

rented lot in a double-wide

this side of nowhere my new place in the sun

snarling dogs and nowhere else left to run"

three times before the audience will let them end the song.

"Now," Zack says, 'in the same general vein, here is 'Don't Blame it on the alcohol'."

This is the best Abe has heard Zack play the song. The crowd is into it. They do the song twice before the crowd is satisfied.

Zack follows up with 'Stuck in my mind' and 'Expectations'. The songs don't receive quite as good a response as the first two.

"Now we are going to do a blues tribute song," Zack says nodding toward the 'Northenders'. "Here is Muddy Water's "Baby Please Don't Go".

This is the first time Abe or Beth have heard Zack perform this song. It's good. Damned good.

Zack takes a few minutes to introduce the members of 'The Northenders', before announcing they will play 'Stuck in my mind'.

They follow this up with 'Hard Case'.

Abe is beginning to realize that despite the lack of professional support, Zack is getting better at performing. In no small measure, 'the Northenders' are helping make that happen.

"Here is another blues tribute," Zack announces. "Robert Johnson's 'Crossroad Blues'."

Zack lets 'the Northenders' take the lead on the song. The results are pretty good.

Zack and the band then do 'not the same', 'really wish' and 'carried away' without taking a break between songs.

Abe looks at the clock behind the bar, 8:50.

"Here is our last livestream song of the evening," Zack says. 'It's a song which Abe I wrote earlier in the week. It's called 'Six Year Blues'.

<u>SIX YEAR BLUES</u> TEMPO OF 83BPM KEY OF D MAJOR IN 3/4 TIME

six years ago
I came to know
what I thought heaven sent me

became fool of all fools
skirting society's rules
and learning, we weren't meant to be

no turning back
the non-stop attack
as your friends turned against me

notes I play
unable to sway
what eyes chose not to see

what once was sweet
left incomplete
as resentments against me grew

I am sure
we'll both endure
what next six years brought me
six years ago

I came to know
what I thought heaven sent us
music so sweet

we took our seat
and played as long as they let us
was no turning back
the non-stop attack
as your family turned against me

walking away angrily
averted the calamity of becoming
their greatest enemy

six years ago

I came to know
what I thought heaven sent m

I am sure
that I shall endure
what past six years have sent me
the edicts they placed
left me erased
with nothing left to discuss
six years ago

I came to know
what I thought heaven sent us

I am sure
was no easier for you to endure
what those six years have brought us
the edicts they placed
left me erased
with nothing left to discuss

Six years ago
came to know
how to be the fool of all fools
skirting society's rules
and learning, we aren't meant to be
became fool of all fools
by skirting society's rules
and learning, we weren't meant to be

Zack signals Dave to cut off the livestream but does the last stanza three more times for the live crowd.

"We are going to take a short break now," Zack says, "We will be back to play four more songs before we close out the evening. I'm open to requests for those songs, so if you have something special, you'd like us to try to play, write it down on a slip of paper and hand it to a waitress."

Abe looks around the dining area. All the tables are still full.

Zack unstraps his guitar and sets it against the stool before heading out the back hallway.

After Sam and Dave remove their equipment and head with Molly out the back entrance and up to the studio to work on prepping their recording of the performance for follow up sales, Zack and the band return to the stage.

They play 'Small Minds', 'Expectations', 'This side of nowhere' and close out the night with 'don't' blame it on the alcohol'. Zack and the band exit the stage to ringing applause.

As 'The Place' clears out, Zack comes over to Abe's table. He gives his sister a hug before sitting down.

"No Abby?" Abe asks.

Zack shakes his head and says, "No Abby."

AN INTERVIEW

Three weeks later, Monday, April 8, 1:56PM. Beth is seated at the table nearest to the front entrance of 'The Place'. She has placed a tray with cups, tea, coffee, and cookies in the middle of the table. She is waiting for a reporter from the 'Islander', who has asked to do an interview with Beth about her candidacy in Ward 6.

Beth has her notebook open and is reviewing plans for the building of an outdoor event performance area where the patio area of the place resides. A large scallop shell like structure with proper acoustics to be built out within the southwestern corner of the newly redefined business property. The Shell-like structure planned to hold up to 500 and will extend to the back entrance to 'The Place'. The unseen outer portion of the shell will contain solar panels which it is hoped will eventually not only cover the cost of operating this new area but provide ½ of the power for the existing facility. The southwestern section has been chosen because there is a natural depression on that side of the property which will make building the stage and seating much easier. A new restroom facility is to be built in the southeastern corner of the property. Blue composite beams and a surrounding set of gates will enclose the facility. The patio eating area will be moved outside of the gated area to the west side. Another large food service area will be added facing west to serve the patio dining area. The existing food service window will be used for the performance venue. The mobile kitchen will be moved outside the main business and the kitchen will once again be rebuilt.

Beth likes this latest plan, with one notable exception: the price tag. The total cost is projected to be $4.2 million. If Beth chooses to go this route, she is going to have delay doing anything as regards building the resort/retreat behind the patio area which she still wanted.

A knock comes on the closed front door. Beth gets up from the table, walks to the door and opens it. A young lady, who appears to be in her mid-twenties dressed in jeans and a red sweater enters carrying electronic equipment.

"Valerie Smythe," the young woman says holding out her free hand to Beth.

Beth guides the reporter to the table and helps her set down her laptop, two small microphones attached to an audio recording device which plugs into her laptop's USB port.

"As I mentioned on the phone," the reporter says, "I plan on recording our conversation. I'll write a short article about your candidacy and will put the full interview up on 'The Islander's website."

"I'm fine with that as long as you provide me with a copy of the recording," Beth says. "The Mountain Centrist Party wants to put it up on their website as well. There are coffee and tea if you are interested."

"It's really quite nice up here," Smythe says as she pours herself a cup of tea, "I haven't been up here for ages."

"You should try out the walking path which goes around the mountain," Beth suggests.

The reporter pins one of the small microphones to the collar of her sweater before handing the other microphone to Beth. Beth places it on the collar of her flower print shirt.

"Are you ready to start?" Smythe asks.

Beth nods her head affirmatively.

Valerie Smythe: This is Valerie Smythe, political reporter for 'The Islander' newspaper conducting an interview with Bethany Stolz, the Mountain Centrist Party's candidate for the Ward 6 council seat. We are currently sitting down at 'The Place' located at 111 Mountain Way. Beth is the owner/operator of this establishment. Beth, would you mind telling us how long you have been here?

Beth Stolz: I am currently 25 years old. I have lived here my entire life. I began working in the kitchen when I was 15. When I was 19, I took over the running of the dining room area from my grandfather. For the past 3 years, I have run the entire operation other than the scheduling of the music acts. I now do that jointly with my grandfather.

Valerie Smythe: How long has your family operated 'The Place'?

Beth Stolz: My great-grandmother, Rebecca Stolz, acquired the business 63 years ago after her mother and husband were assassinated by a car bombing down in the village. Since that time, my great-grandmother, my grandfather and grandmother and I have operated 'The Place'.

Valerie Smythe: I will note for our listeners that it was recently discovered that Ms. Stolz's grandmother and mother were murdered by a mob operating out of Halifax. How has this discovery impacted your life?

Beth Stolz: I was eighteen months old when my grandmother and mother were taken from me. Although I have almost no memory of either of them, there remains a hole in my heart over losing them. What the recent discovery of those murders has brought to our family is a small bit of closure. Prior to the discovery, none of us could be certain what had happened to my mother and grandmother. For my grandfather in particular, knowledge of their fate has brought us some at least some relief.

Valerie Smythe: What has caused you to become involved in politics?

Beth Stolz: The reality is that I've been involved in politics from the moment that I was born. You could not be the great-great-granddaughter of Alice Bailey Reginald and not be aware of the history of Wannasea independence and her movement to make this island a better place for all. The use of politics to better conditions for everyone on this island has been instilled in me from a young age.

Valerie Smythe: What makes you feel that you are qualified to be an Island Council member?

Beth Stolz: In addition to being successful in the operation of this business, I have continued my great-grandmother's practice of making this facility a haven for young people in need. We offer assistance, jobs, a place to live when needed to island youth, who have been left with few other options. I have expanded that practice to offer those who come here to work the opportunity to start or continue their education if they so desire. This effort has taught me much, not only about the needs of the island's young people, but the emotional and financial stresses on their families.

Valerie Smythe: Isn't this rather odd in that you have not yourself completed a university degree?

Beth Stolz: My degree is in real world experience. This facility currently directly employs 16 people with another half-dozen or more relying upon its continued operation. When I took the operation over from my grandfather at 17, it was not profitable. Currently we not only provide jobs and assistance for many of those who work here, we turn a profit in the process. As far as continuing education is concerned, I am a firm believer in it. I have taken over 150 equivalent semester hours either in courses down at the Wannasea Extension or on-line which have assisted in the growth of this operation as well as my personal base of knowledge. I'm currently taking two online courses. One in Property Development, the other in Political Processes. I will continue to take such courses as needs arise. I firmly believe that every individual's education is a continuing process which does not necessarily require the acquisition of a degree in higher learning.

Valerie Smythe: Your corporation recently made a successful bid for the old Wannasea Government Center. Would you tell us a little bit about you plans for that facility.

Beth Stolz: One of the primary drivers for having become involved in the bid to purchase the old government center was the desire to see our old Castle become a heritage site operated by the Wannasea Historical Society. The second driver has become to acquire the space to expand our facility here. We hope to build an outside performance venue for up to 400 in addition to expanding our outside eating space. The remainder of the property at the old center will be developed into a resort/casino and inside theater operated by Island Resorts. When that facility is completed, it will offer approximately 200 new full-time jobs in addition to the normal part-time and seasonal work which comes with such facilities.

Valerie Smythe: What will your primary agenda be as councilwoman?

Beth Stolz: First to update the laws of this island to reflect present day realities. This will start through changing the current citizenship, voting, marriage, and ship registration regulations. Secondly, I hope to push to increase the number of full-time jobs available on our island. Currently too many people are pushed into moving away from the island because they cannot make enough money over the course of the full year to support themselves here. The resort up at the Quarry will be a first step in that direction. If ship registration rules are changed, we hope to make the island a year-round day stop for cruise ships. As mentioned previously, I will also focus on expanding the Island's educational and healthcare facilities and opportunities to better meet our island's needs.

Valerie Smythe: Do you have any political ambitions beyond becoming a Ward 6 member of Island council.

Beth Stolz: No.

Valerie Smythe: As I drove in this morning, I could not help but notice there are a handful of New Jericho Temple supporters at the boundary of your property carrying rather uncomplimentary signs and shouting insults about you and those who choose to be your customers. What do you have to say about those protests?

Beth Stolz: The New Jericho people are entitled to present their opinions as long it does not interfere with the operation of our business. It seems that their main issue with me is that I am gay and currently pregnant. I will make no apologies for either condition. I met my life partner when we were in the second grade, we have been friends for 17 years. We have been a couple for five years. We have decided that we want to raise a family on our island. I'm sorry that upsets the New Jericho people so much.

Valerie Smythe: Many say that you are the person, who discovered our island's hottest new musical talent, Zack Tillerman. Would you care to comment on your discovery?

Beth Stolz: (laughs out loud). I did not discover anything as it relates to Zack. Zack has always been a musical talent. His sister, Saanvi, who has long been my friend, asked me last summer if I might be able to find a way to bring Zack to 'The Place' as a worker and performer. Having been Saanvi's friend, I had met Zack more than a few times. After Saavi's request, I worked out interviewing Zack with my grandfather. The discovery part comes to anyone who takes the time to listen to Zack playing music. When Zack feels the music, it really is something special. What my grandfather and I heard then, is now obvious to almost anyone who listens to Zack play.

Valerie Smythe: I have heard you play on some of Zack Tillerman's recordings. One stands out, 'We didn't start the fire'. Are there any plans for you to continue such recordings?

Beth Stolz: I'm hoping that other than singing and playing for my children, my music career is now behind me.

Valerie Smythe: Thank you very much for your time, Ms. Stolz.

Beth Stolz: My pleasure.

The reporter turns off the microphones and closes out the recording session.

"That certainly is not what I expected," Smythe says.

"How so?"

"When I came out here, I was certain that you were just running for office on the back of Alice Reginald's name in a half-hearted attempt to keep the Mountain Centrist Party alive," the reporter says. "Off the record, if I could vote on this island, you would have just earned my vote."

OPEN SESSION

Monday, May 6, 3:40PM. Beth is again sitting at the table closest to the front entrance of 'The Place'. She has six-12oz. plastic bottles of water, two large thermal carafes sitting in front of her. One holds coffee. The other holds Wannasea Tea. There is an assortment of sweeteners as well as cookies on a tray in the center of the table. Beth has her own bottle of water in front of her from which she has been taking sips every so often in accordance with instructions from her midwife and the Hanover Clinic.

Roberta Johnson had suggested that Beth hold what she referred to as 'an open door' meeting for Ward 6 voters to discuss with them their concerns. Beth has set aside 3;30-6:30 PM on every other Monday for these meetings. Today is the first meeting. As yet, no voters have arrived. Roberta had asked Beth to allow her to come to these sessions, but Beth had chosen to do them alone.

Yesterday had been a rather eventful day at 'The Place'. Sallie had come in at a little before 10 to drop off some supplies which were to be used for another Sunday performance by Zack and the Northenders. When she arrived, Sallie discovered that not only had the parking lot been seeded with nails and broken glass, but the entire white stucco front of Abe's had also been splashed with a wild assortment of paint. Beth had called the Island Constabulary. Abe had called Defense One.

After an hour and a half, Defense One had been able to establish that both the sharp objects on the parking lot pavement and the paint had been delivered by two individuals in a battered white van. The paint had come from two paintball guns. The battered white van turned out to be the same one which usually sits on the other side of the road leading to the entrance to 'The Place' where the New Jericho Temple protesters have taken to hanging out. Interestingly, today there are no protesters at their normal posts.

Marie had managed to persuade Jack Druce, after he had taken the appropriate pictures and received recordings from Defense One, to allow them to clean up the mess prior to the 4PM opening. It took three hours and the help of everyone at the house to clear out the tacks, nails, and broken glass from the parking lot. Josh took a crack at using the pressure washer to clean off the paint splotches. His efforts did very little to remove the stains other than to send multi-color streaks downward. Despite the vandalism, Zack's fourth Sunday event billed "Sunday Night Jam" went off with a full house at 'The Place' as well as a sold-out livestream. Livestreams are becoming increasingly profitable for ZackTillerman LLC.

This morning Beth had filed another claim with her property insurance company, though she isn't certain why she has bothered to do so. At this date, almost 6 months after the Sylvester Brothers attempted destruction of 'The Place', Beth and Abe have as yet been unable to recover one cent from their policy. Abe has taken to proclaiming that business continuation policies seem to only apply to the continuation of the insurance company's business. The only response from their insurance carrier thus far has been to raise their rates because they have been moved into a higher risk category.

As it is a rather pleasant day outside, Beth has propped the front doors open. Through them walks a grey-haired lady in Bermuda shorts, floral print shirt and sandals.

"Come on in and sit down," Beth says as lady adjusts her eyes to the relative darkness inside. "There are tea, coffee and cookies if you'd like."

The woman strolls to the table and takes the chair across from Beth.

"I'm Ada Jenkins," the woman says as she pours herself a cup of tea. "I live over on South Mountain."

"Nice to meet you," Beth says rising to shake the lady's hand. "What concerns you?"

"I'm very worried about the increase in car traffic which is going to occur due to your expansion here and what is being built up at the old quarry," the lady says before taking a sip of her tea.

"Did you express these concerns to the Island Government during their impact session review last month?" Beth asks.

"No, I didn't," the lady says. "I guess I should have."

"Let's not worry about that," Beth says. "What is it exactly which concerns you most about a possible increase in traffic?"

"I'm worried that it will make it harder for me to get over to the North Side to the ferry and to purchase provisions," the lady says as she sips on the tea. "I'm also worried that it will become a danger for the kids going to school."

"I'd suggest keeping in mind that when the old government center was open," Beth says, "there were normally about 150 people working there each weekday. Most of whom drove their own cars to work. Additionally, there was a great deal of traffic to the center from people going there to conduct various business."

"I'd kind of forgotten about that," the lady says, "but isn't this new casino thing going to generate a lot more car traffic.'

"It is not projected to do so," Beth says, "Island Resorts is going to operate a trolley service to and from the facility and ferry. They will also have a shuttle van service down near the ferry."

"Does the trolley service just go between Wannasea village and the new casino?" the lady asks.

"It is projected to have stops all over the island," Beth says.

"Will non-guests of the casino be able to use it?"

"I'm told that they will. There will be a charge of $.75 per trip however," Beth responds.

"What about the increased traffic once your new facility is complete?"

"We are going to be a stop on the trolley service," Beth says. "Additionally, it is less than ¾ of a mile from the ferry dock to this business. Many people now choose to walk up here for events and such. Our parking lot is planned to be a little smaller than it currently is, so we are going to be encouraging people to walk or use the bus or trolley for our events."

"You don't think there will be any more traffic than there was when the old government center was in operation?" Ada asks.

"I don't expect there to be during the day," Beth says. "In the evenings, there may be. It's not possible to know for certain at this point."

"I see," the lady says pouring herself a little more tea.

"Ms. Jenkins," Beth asks, "you wouldn't happen to be related to Jerome Jenkins, the drummer in the Northenders?"

"I'm his grandmother."

"Would you mind if I ask you how many of your grown children or grandchildren are able to have enough work on this island so that they can afford to live here?" Beth asks.

"I have seven children," Ada Jenkins answers. "Five boys and two girls. Only my youngest daughter can still afford to live on the island. She was lucky enough to get an office position at 'Star of the South Resort'. Two of my thirteen grandchildren are now off the island. The other grandkids are either in school or too young to be out on their own."

"The Quarry project is going to create at least 200 full-time jobs and who knows how many part-time and related jobs. Only through having facilities such as the one being built at the old government center, is the employment picture on this island going to change."

"I'm worried that the island is going to change with it," the old lady says.

"My job will be to try to see that change occurs in the best way possible," Beth says.

"Thanks for listening to me," Ada Jenkins says rising from the chair. "If you are elected, will you be doing more sessions like these?"

"I will," Beth says, "but I'm planning on one session per month. It will be on the first Monday of the month during the same time with a 'open session meeting' from 5:30 to 6:15PM. I'm also always available by voicemail, email, or text message as well as through the Mountain Centrist Party website."

"Thanks for your time," the old lady says as she goes back out the front entrance.

After taking a sip from her bottle of water, Beth picks up her tea mug and takes it behind the bar where she washes it out in the sink. Beth is glad that she is no longer making weekly trips to the Hanover Fertility Clinic. She now has been assigned a PA midwife at the maternity section of the Wannasea Island Health Facility. Next Tuesday, Beth will have an ultrasound performed at the facility. If there are no further complications, her baby is planned to be delivered there.

After placing the mug on the draining board, Beth walks around the backside of the bar. At approximately 20 months, her pregnancy is really beginning to show. Beth is also beginning to experience serious back aches. She walks around the dining room area for a few minutes before going back to the table and sitting down.

Last week, Beth had approved the plans to turn the patio area into an event venue. Although, she was a little disappointed that she is going to have to put plans for the build out of the resort/retreat on indefinite hold, Beth isn't that certain that she can deal with much else at this point.

Beth sees a man and woman dressed in casual clothes, who appear to be in their forties walking toward the front entrance. As the pair enter and their eyes adjust to the change in light, Beth can see that both are people she remembers seeing among Ainsley's protestors during their first protest at 'The Place'. They also appear to be rather angry.

Beth quickly rises from her chair and calls back to them as she moves toward the kitchen entrance, "Welcome. Please pour yourself some coffee or tea. I must run into the kitchen for a moment to turn off a kettle of water which I just put on."

Beth fast walks to the kitchen and goes through the swinging doors. As she moves to the backside of the mobile kitchen toward the garage style doors, she pulls her cell phone from her front pocket. She opens it. With her hand cupped over the microphone makes a call to Abe.

As soon as Abe answers, Beth loud whispers into her cell phone, "Please get down to the dining room as fast as you can. I think there are a couple of Ainsley's people here who are looking to cause trouble."

"Don't disconnect this call," Abe says through the earpiece, "Zack and I will be right down."

Beth moves toward the coat rack at the rear door and pulls down a light jacket she often uses if she is carrying the trash out at night. She goes to the kitchen utensils and pulls out a 10" long kitchen knife which she slides into the inside pocket. She hears Abe telling Zack something in her cell phone, then the phone goes silent. Beth places the phone in her front pocket with the microphone side out.

She composes herself and walks back out of the kitchen toward the table. The two visitors are standing, they have not seated themselves. She walks to the chair she had been sitting in but does not sit down.

"Sorry about that," Beth says as politely as she is able. "Now what is it that you would like to talk to me about?"

"YOU SATANIC ABOMINATION!!!" the man shouts at her. "HOW DARE YOU HAVE THE AUDACITY TO TRY TO ESTABLISH DOMINION UPON GOD'S ISLAND."

"YOU SOULESS BITCH OF SATAN," the woman adds. "YOU NEED TO TAKE YOUR DISGUSTING PERVERTED WAYS OFF OF OUR ISLAND."

"When was it exactly that either of you were elected to rule this island?" Beth asks angrily, "I've lived on this island my entire life and have not been informed that you are now in charge of me or anyone else. Additionally, I and every member of my family have lived on this island as far back as anyone remembers. Where is it exactly you are expecting me to go?'

"Almighty God has given us that dominion," the man shouts back at Beth.

"You will be going straight to hell when God has finished with you," the woman says.

'Which may turn out to be much sooner than you think," the man adds.

"Are you residents of Ward 6?" Beth asks. "These meetings are only open to residents of Ward 6. If you aren't residents of Ward 6 then you will have to leave."

"WE ARE THE CARETAKERS AND PROTECTORS OF GOD'S ISLAND," the man shouts. "GOD HAS INSTRUCTED US THAT SATANIC SPAWN SUCH AS YOU HAVE NO RIGHT TO BE UPON OUR ISLAND."

"GOD HAS SEEN YOUR UNNATURAL ACTIVITIES," the woman shouts. "HIS VENGENCE IS NIGH!"

Beth hears Zack's Bug pulling up to the front entrance.

"Are you members of the New Jericho Temple?" Beth asks. "If you are, I will remind you that you are legally prohibited from being on these premises."

"WE ARE THE RIGHT HAND OF GOD," the man shouts menacingly. "COME TO PASS JUDGEMENT AND TAKE BACK HIS ISLAND FROM SINFUL ABOMINATIONS SUCH AS YOURSELF!."

"The lady asked you whether or not you are residents of Ward 6," Zack calls to them as he enters the front entrance. "If you are not, you need to leave."

"WE GO WHERE GOD COMMANDS US TO GO!!!" the man turns toward Zack and begins moving in his direction.

Zack puts his hand on Abe's arm to keep him from moving forward. The man steps closer. The woman with him seems uncertain what action she is to take next.

"The last time we checked," Zack says, "God is not registered to vote in our ward. Now it is time for you to leave."

The man rushes toward Zack, who hits him in the side of the head with a karate slap then in a flash, knees him in the groin. The man slumps to the floor as the woman with him runs around Abe and out the front entrance.

"Call the Constabulary," Zack tells Beth.

Beth pulls her cell phone out of her pocket and dials the Constabulary as Zack hovers over the man, who writhes in pain. The man makes a move to rise but Zack puts a hold on the man's neck which prevents him from moving without cutting off his breathing. When her call is answered by the desk sergeant, Beth explains what has transpired and is informed that an officer will soon be there.

"Thanks guys," Beth says after she hangs up the phone. "Do you mind if I go call Roberta?"

"Go ahead," Abe says, "Seems Zack has this under control."

Beth pockets her cell phone and heads back toward the kitchen wondering why she let her I've-got-this attitude prevent her from not taking Roberta up on her offer to be present at these sessions.

'I have to make better decisions when there is anything going on which might involve New Jericho,' Beth tells herself.

After entering the kitchen, she puts the knife and jacket back before calling Roberta Johnson.

"Hey Beth, what's up?"

Beth explains the situation to Roberta.

"These New Jericho types are becoming more and more confrontational," Roberta tells Beth. "I'm going to talk with Vic. You need to have me and someone else around when you are doing any political activity open to the public."

"I should have listened to you," Beth says sheepishly.

"I also have a couple cans of mace which I'd like you to carry in your purse," Roberta says.

"I don't usually carry a purse," Beth says.

"Start."

DUPLICATES

Tuesday, May 14, 10:18AM. Beth is lying on the examining table of the maternity section of the Island's clinic. Marie is by her side. She has just had the nurse run the ultra-sound scanning device over her protruding abdomen. The Nurse is now finalizing the output from the scan.

"We have a couple things which may be surprises to you," the nurse says to Beth and Marie. "The first surprise, you need to know about. The second is your choice."

"I'm not a fan of surprises," Beth says, "I always prefer to know as much about what I am dealing with as possible.

"Me, too," Marie says.

"All right then," the nurse says printing out the ultrasound image on the thermal printer at the bottom of the ultrasound station.

The nurse pulls off the black and white image and takes it to the examining table. She allows Beth and Marie to look at the image for a few moments before saying, "You will notice that there are two babies in there."

Beth and Marie had been told by the Hanover Fertility Clinic that multiple births were not uncommon with their procedures. This is the first time that Beth and Marie had any inclination that information might apply to them.

"If you take a close look at the baby in front," the nurse says, "you will see that it's a male. I'm afraid that it is impossible to tell the sex of the baby in the back."

"We are having twins," Marie says excitedly.

"And at least one boy," Beth adds.

"You can keep the photo," the nurse says. "Your midwife will be here in a few moments to discuss the next steps."

Beth and Marie look at each other as the nurse exits the room.

"Wow," Beth says pointing to the negative image from the ultrasound. "Twins. Can you believe it?"

"We'll have to believe it," Marie says. "We are also going to have to start buying almost two of everything for the babies' room."

"It's been a long time since there was a boy at the house," Beth says. "Do you know how to buy boy's things?"

"Sure," Marie says. "Having helped to raise Randy and Josh gave me plenty of training."

Physician's Assistant Colleen Hendricks, their fifty-three-year-old midwife, comes into the room holding Beth's chart.

"How are you reacting to the news of twins?" the PA asks with a big smile.

"Still processing it," Beth says.

"The Hanover clinic suspected that it would be multiple conceptions," the midwife says. "They asked that nothing be mentioned to you until we had confirmation. As you can see, we now have confirmation."

The midwife then explains to them the seriousness of following through with Beth's current regimen of vitamins, staying hydrated, limited exercise. She provides Beth and Marie with a pamphlet on multiple births.

"Everything has been going fine with your pregnancy so far," the PA says. "Now that it is warming up, I cannot emphasis enough how important it to stay hydrated. Always carry a bottle of water with you. Make it a regular habit of taking sips of water throughout the day.

You'll need to drink at least 64 ounces of water a day, so the sooner you are in the habit of consuming that much water, the better."

"I'm going to want to see you every week for the time being," the midwife says. "Are Tuesday mornings at the same time good for you?"

"Tuesday morning is fine," Beth answers, "that will allow Marie to come along without missing work.

"If anything out of the ordinary comes up," the PA says, "please notify me immediately. Do you have any additional questions?"

"Will I be able to have the babies here," Beth asks, "or am I going to have to go over to the Halifax hospital?"

"It depends on how your pregnancy progresses," the midwife says. "If everything is normal, then you should be able to have your babies here. I delivered a set of twins at this facility in November for a family from the east end."

"Are there any restrictions which I should put on myself as far as work or my campaign for Island council?" Beth asks.

"Pace yourself,' the midwife suggests. "If you begin feeling tired, adjust your schedule to do less. Be prepared to have to take time off."

"Is the schedule for birth still projected to be the second week in September?" Marie asks.

"It is," the PA says. "You are entering the phase of pregnancy when your body is going to begin changing rapidly. These changes are even more pronounced for someone having twins. You want to become aware of what your body is telling you and adjust yourself accordingly."

"Thanks," Beth says to the midwife.

"Congratulations,' PA Hendricks says. "You can now at least start thinking about a name for the boy."

GRADUATION

Sunday, May 26, 6:36PM. Beth is seated with Saanvi and Prisha at Abe's usual table at 'The Place'. Only Sallie and her boyfriend Sam remain in the building after the conclusion of a graduation party for Molly which had started at 4. Everyone else at the party, including Marie and Abe, have left to go down to the Wannasea Extension to attend a concert which Zack and the Northenders are giving tonight beginning at 7:30 for graduating students. Marie had arranged for Sallie and Sam to cater for the event. A total of 52 people had shown up. 24 of whom are currently working at 'The Place'.

Over the past four weeks, in addition to 12 seasonal workers, 'The Place' has added a pair of sisters Jennifer, 14, and Judith,16, whose drug addicted single mother had deserted them, plus a 15-year-old transgender male named Alfie, who is an escapee from New Jericho Temple's gay conversion program. Beth had to put the sisters into Marie's old room temporarily. She is beginning to hope that Molly will soon move on to another living arrangement other than up at the house as this is the usual progression for those working at 'The Place', who have graduated.

"Are you going to tell me about Ray Simmons?" Beth asks Saanvi after taking a sip from the bottle of water sitting in front of her.

Zack had disclosed last week that his sister was now dating Ray Simmons, the Hanover Herald reporter. Seems they had hit it off when Simmons was interviewing Saanvi for the article on Zack. The reporter had asked Zack's sister out for coffee. They had now been going out steadily over the past two months.

Saanvi blushes a little before responding, "Ray and I just like doing things together."

This is unusual for Saanvi. Beth knows from her long history with Saanvi that she does not go out with just anyone. When Saanvi had worked at 'The Place', she had spent most of her four summers working pushing away suitors.

"What sorts of things?" Beth asks.

'We like to go to movies," Saanvi answers. "We go on hikes and walk on the beach. We've been going to museums and historical sites over on the Mainland. Ray knows a lot about the history of the Swansea and Hanover districts."

"I think she is serious about this one," Prisha says with a big smile.

"Do you like him?" Beth ask's Saanvi's mom.

"I think he may be a keeper," Prisha says chuckling.

Saanvi gives her mother a look of displeasure.

"Tell us how it's going with those twins," Saanvi says hoping to move the discussion away from her love life.

"I'm now drinking enough water to float a boat," Beth says. "But the midwife says things are going as well as possible."

"When is your due date?" Prisha asks.

"Sometime around Sep.10," Beth responds.

"When is this election?" Saanvi asks.

"Sep. 3ʳᵈ," Beth replies.

"If you win," Saanvi asks, "when will you have to begin attending island council meetings?"

"October 14ᵗʰ," Beth responds. She does not choose to tell them that on Thursday afternoon, she had a long discussion with Vic Newton and Roberta Johnson about continuing her run for the Ward 6 council seat. Beth had begun to think that having twins and running for council were mutually exclusive. Vic and Roberta have promised to do everything possible to make the candidacy easier on Beth. What had been two debates between Beth and the two other candidates for the position was now being trimmed to one debate in early August at the new government center. Roberta would now handle the bi-weekly Monday afternoon voter sessions with Beth only doing one 30-minute session at 6PM. Roberta has asked Beth to give her candidacy another month to see how she feels about it.

"Don't you think running for council and having two babies may be a little much?" Prisha asks.

"It may be,' Beth says, "but I'm going to give it try. If there is any adverse impact on my pregnancy, I'll stop immediately."

"Let us know If there is anything we can do to help?" Saanvi says.

"You wouldn't happen to know where I might be able to find a good nanny capable of handling twin babies?" Beth asks with a laugh.

"Actually, I might,'" Prisha says. "One of the ladies working the desk in the afternoon at the resort just had a baby about six months ago. She is good with kids and is a hard worker. The afternoon shift and the baby are really stressing out her marriage. She wouldn't be able to live in, but I think she could do a terrific job for you during the day. Do you want me to ask her if she might be interested in becoming your babies' nanny?"

"Sure," Beth says, "If she is, just ask her to give me a call."

Beth takes a long sip from her bottle of water. Over the past few weeks, Beth has begun to worry a little about how living arrangements are going to work out up at 'The House' when the babies come. She already has too many people living there. The room she hoped to use as a nursery is now occupied. She has also begun to worry that having Zack, Abe, and Molly in the studio most of the day is not going to work out when the babies are sleeping.

"I'm also beginning to look around for a kitchen manager to replace, Sallie," Beth says. "She is going to be leaving after the first of the year to start up the restaurant up the mountain."

"Are you planning on keeping the same menu?" Prisha asks.

"I'd like to," Beth says, "but it may not be easy. Sallie's something of a savant at making her soups. Probably is going to be hard to find someone to keep up the quality."

"When would the new person start?" Prisha asks.

'The plan is September," Beth says, "but I'd be willing to take on someone now to give them more of a chance to learn."

"That's the time when the resorts lay off their summer help," Prisha says. "You may find there are some good people available then. I'll ask around at my resort."

"What is Molly planning on doing now that she has graduated?" Prisha asks.

"I don't think that she has plans to do anything any differently than she has been doing since Zack, Abe and she started up their LLC," Beth says. "They seem to be making quite a bit of money."

Beth's cell phone rings. She pulls it from her purse which hangs on the back of the chair. The phone shows that the caller is Olivia.

"Sorry," Beth says to Saanvi and Prisha, "I need to take this call."

"Hey Olivia," Beth says. "What's up?"

"I'm hoping that Angelique and I can come up and talk with you," Olivia says. "Are you tied up right now?"

"I'm with Saanvi and Prisha at 'The Place'," Beth says into the cell phone.

"We are going to have to be going," Saanvi announces to Beth. "Ray is picking me up at 7:30 to go to the movies down in the village."

"I ought to be free in fifteen minutes or so," Beth says into the cell phone.

"I'll be there then," Olivia says then disconnects the call.

"Have you heard anything about Ralph starting up some kind of business with the audio-visual guys from the Extension?" Saanvi asks.

Beth has noticed that Zack has been spending more time than usual with Dave and Sam the past few weeks. She also knows that Dave has just graduated from the Extension.

"Haven't heard anything about it," Beth says. "What have you heard?"

"Not much," Saanvi says, "other than they are planning on setting up some sort of audio business in SouthTown."

SouthTown is one of the oldest small villages on the island. Its residents are primarily black and retired.

"Seems kind of an odd place to start an audio business," Beth says.

"That's what we thought," Prisha says shaking her head.

"I will talk with Abe about it,' Beth promises. "Abe always seems to be in the know about what Zack is up to."

"Thanks," Prisha says.

"Do you mind if we arrange a baby shower for you in early August?" Saanvi asks.

"Of course not," Beth says. "Just let Marie know what you are planning because she was starting to consider doing something but wasn't sure that is an appropriate thing for a marriage partner to do. We are kind of operating this whole pregnancy thing without a playbook."

"Tell her that I'll give her a call tomorrow," Saanvi says rising from the table a gathering her purse.

"If there is any at all that you think we can help you with," Prisha says also rising, "please let me know. I've discovered that since Emma has been gone, I've got a lot more free time than I am used to having."

Beth rises and walks to the pair to the front entrance and bids them a good evening. She then walks past the full length of the bar and into the kitchen area. Sallie is cleaning the new prep area on the other side of the mobile kitchen. Beth can hear Sam inside the structure.

"We're almost finished," Sallie tells Beth. "I think the party came off pretty well."

"It did," Beth says. "Molly seemed to really be touched that we arranged it and so many people showed up."

"When is the mobile kitchen unit going to be pulled out of here?" Sallie asks.

"Tuesday as far as I know," Beth says.

The mobile kitchen is going to be pulled from inside the kitchen area, through the garage doors and parked beside the west wall which is behind the bar area. The plan is to continue to use the mobile unit as much as needed until the installation of the new kitchen is completed. Then the unit will be returned. Currently that is projected to be in late July.

"We stopped by the old government center," Sallie says. "They are really making big progress up there as well as at the Quarry."

"Cuthbert says your restaurant should be ready no later than the end of February," Beth says. "The auditorium is going to be done in April. Supposedly the first phase of the casino/resort is also going to be ready then."

"Lots of things going on," Sallie says. "Are you sure it isn't getting to be too much for you?"

"I'm okay for the time being," Beth replies. "The minute, I'm not, I'll let everyone know."

"Not going to take any chances with these two guys," she adds pointing toward her protruding stomach.

"We are counting on you not to," Sallie replies.

"How are the newcomers working out?" Beth asks.

"The sisters are great," Sallie says. "Aside from being very shy, they are willing to do anything we ask them to do." "Alfie?" Beth asks.

"Alfie is very entertaining," Sallie replies, "but work doesn't seem to be very high on his list of priorities."

"Anybody home?" Beth hears Olivia calling from the dining room area.

"Be right out," Beth says.

"We should be finished up in about ten minutes," Sallie tells Beth. "There is a container of leftover clam chowder in the left fridge if you want to take it up to Abe."

"Thanks," Beth says pulling her checkbook from the maternity blouse pocket. She writes Sallie a check for the agreed upon amount then returns to the dining room area.

"I'm over in the corner," Beth says pointing toward Abe's table by the stage. "Do you guys want anything to drink?"

Beth grabs three bottles of water from the cooler.

Her cousins shake their heads negatively, go to the table where Beth's purse still hangs from the back of chair and sit down. Beth places the three bottles of water on the table, then joins them.

Aside from speaking with Angelique by phone about developments regarding the buildout of the old government center property, Beth hasn't spoken much with her cousins over the past few weeks.

"First of all, congratulations on the twins," Angelique says.

"Thanks," Beth says with a chagrined smile, "I think."

"We need more members of the Stolz family on this island," Olivia says. "Who's going to stir up trouble if there aren't more members of our family doing it?"

Beth laughs.

. "We have a few legal things," Angelique says, "one of which includes a possible solution to your space crunch, as well as a campaign thing, we'd like to talk over with you."

"Let's talk possible solutions to my space crunch first," Beth says.

"That will involve going over a legal issue," Angelique responds. "I had a long conversation with the Island Planning Board yesterday afternoon. What they would like to see done is for all the land belonging to the old government center and castle to be split off and merged into your existing business parcel."

"That would include the Quarry?" Beth asks.

"No,' Angelique says, "Remember the Quarry is a separate parcel completely. They would like for you to merge the Quarry property along with the 5 acres which will be left from the old government Center and Castle into another new parcel."

"Do you know why they want this done?" Beth asks.

"We think so,' Olivia replies. "The Planning Board wants you to commit your liquor and gaming license to only apply to the Quarry and old Government Center parcel."

"I don't really see a problem with that," Beth says.

"Keep in mind," Olivia says, "by taking that step, you may potentially be giving up a large chunk of future income because the way things are currently structured, you could use that license on all your parcels."

"I don't see us selling liquor or running a casino here," Beth says.

"You might be talking about cutting yourself off from 10-15million if you ever want to sell this property," Olivia advises.

"Selling won't be on my radar," Beth says. "Abe has discovered that this property has been in my family's possession from the time it has been legal property. Come what may, this is where I plan on staying."

"I suggest that if you are willing to make those parcels adjustments," Angelique says, "that you ask the island for something in return."

"Such as?" Beth asks.

"Permission to begin building out your resort/retreat area as soon as the re-parceling is finished," Angelique says. "The property here will be designated as commercial residential space."

"Don't know what good that's going to do me," Beth says. "I'm kind of out of money to build out the remaining space unless I want to start putting my family at future financial risk. With these two on the way, I'm not going to do that."

"That's where we have another idea," Angelique says. "There is a guy named Steve Harmony, who has been trying to build modular tiny houses on a parcel west of SouthTown. He can't get the island to permit it. The island will not allow any residential dwelling which is less than 500 square feet."

"The tiny houses which he wants to build are really cool," Olivia says. "He's got a model at his workshop which we looked at this morning. Once you get the base infrastructure in place, if you use small buildings like Steve wants to produce, you would be able to have them built rapidly as you need or can afford."

"I'd really rather not go into business with anyone else," Beth says. "Particularly on this property."

"You wouldn't have to," Angelique says. "Harmony is only interested in getting his product in place at this point. He is convinced that once he does, people will see their value and force the island to let him build more of them on unpopulated parcels on the back side of the island."

"We think those type of dwellings would fit a big need when it comes to seasonal workers," Olivia says. "At the moment, many of those workers are crammed into apartments meant to hold one or two people at most."

"You actually think the island would permit building them out here?" Beth asks.

"The Island planning commission's primary focus is the land close to the water," Angelique says, "Property in the center of the island has been an afterthought for a long time. I'm convinced that Island will agree to allow those buildings on your property, if you agree to the changes in your business parcels."

"Any idea what these little houses would cost," Beth asks.

"We were told,' Olivia responds, "anywhere from $22K-55K each."

"How soon do you think it could happen?" Beth asks.

"I think the permitting can be finished in two weeks," Angelique says.

"How long does it take to put one of these tiny houses up?" Beth asks.

"From what Steve was telling us this morning," Angelique responds, "depending on their size and complexity, it usually takes 3-7 days to build out once the pad and utilities are in place. You really ought to go over and talk with him. I think you'll like the way he thinks."

"He can also probably help you get some votes out his way," Olivia says. "Now let's talk about something else which may impact your planning, the settlement of the lawsuit against the Sylvester Brothers."

"I thought that was going to take years to finish," Beth says.

"We did too at the start," Olivia responds. "The clamps have been put down so hard by the Mainland government on those two that they've basically decided their only recourse is to settle all their pending litigation and try to make themselves as comfortable as possible while spending the rest of their days in prison."

"What's that going to do for us?" Beth asks.

"Bottom line," Olivia replies, "Abe and you will be coming into large settlement sometime around the end of August."

"What is large?" Beth queries.

"85 million," Olivia says. "That's after fees and everything but taxes."

"Really?"

"Really."

"Does Abe know this?" Beth asks.

"He won't until tomorrow," Olivia says. "Dad wants to tell him, so please don't say anything."

"I won't," Beth promises.

"He's also going to get your grandmother's sailboat back," Olivia says. "That is unless you'd like me to play some legal games to keep it retained as evidence."

Beth thinks for a moment, before saying, "No, Abe should be able to have the sailboat back and do with it whatever he chooses. I've made peace with having it sit on the backside of Becca's toolshed while Abe is around."

"Our dad has really been scratching and clawing to get everything out of the Sylvester Brothers that can be gotten," Angelique says. "I've never seen him operate like he has in this lawsuit."

"Maybe I should ask your dad to go after our insurance company next?" Beth says.

"What's the problem with your insurance company?" Olivia asks.

"They still haven't paid anything against the calamity and destruction the Sylvester Brothers caused here," Beth says. "I'm out of pocket over $200,000 on that."

Olivia gives Beth a puzzled look, "I explained to Abe way back when that if he and Dad didn't want the insurance company involved in the civil lawsuit against the Sylvester Bros., the only viable alternative was to not give them grounds to litigate. Maybe Abe didn't understand that meant the insurance company couldn't cover anything related to the Sylvester Brothers actions out here?"

"Apparently not," Beth says taking a sip from her water bottle.

"That pretty much wraps it up on the legal front," Olivia says. "Do you feel up to getting into the personal and politics stuff now?"

"Sure," Beth replies.

"First," Angelique says, "we want you to know that if there is anything at all that we can help you with either here or with your campaign all you have to do is ask. I'm not talking about legal work; I mean things you want your family to help you with."

"We aren't joking about wanting to have two more little Stolzes on this island," Olivia says, "We want to make sure those twins are your first priority and if your campaign has to suffer, let it suffer."

"That's kind of been how I'm approaching it," Beth says. "I'm going to try to avoid anything which puts my babies at risk."

"We are a little worried about Ainsley," Olivia says. "We've been doing some digging into what caused him to move out to the island and we think that he's caught wind of it."

"Beyond what Abe and Zack put into the New Jericho song?" Beth asks.

"Seems there is more to it than what's in Zack's song," Olivia says. "Ainsley's story is that what occurred over on the Mainland is just one big misunderstanding. Young boys did not appreciate how much he cared about their wellbeing. Over reactions by their parents."

"If that were they case," Beth inserts, "why did Ainsley pack up his whole church and move out here?"

"His story is," Olivia replies, "that Satan has taken over the Mainland and coming back to his home island is the only alternative to allow the formation of God's Army for the coming war against Satan. He's brought almost 200 people over to the island now to join this so-called army."

"We have discovered," Angelique answers, "that there is quite a bit more than just some misunderstandings over in Halifax. There also may be an expansion of some of the reported activities which occurred on the Mainland, now happening on the island."

"Is the Constabulary looking into it?" Beth asks.

"Not at this point," Olivia says. "But that may not be too far away. In any case, we want you to understand that Ainsley has become like a cornered animal lashing out in every direction. One of those directions will likely be toward Abe, Zack, and you. We want to make certain that everything that can be done to protect you is done."

LITTLE HOUSES

Friday, May 31, 3:03PM. Beth is seated at the patio table closest to the house's parking lot. She is looking over a set of brochures which Steve Harmony gave her twenty minutes ago. On Tuesday afternoon, Abe, Marie, and Beth had gone out to Harmony's business not far from SouthTown. Harmony had recently purchased the Island Holiday Trailer business which had been operating on the island for twenty-five years. In addition to holiday trailer sales and service. Harmony is very much focused on building modular small houses which fit into the island both ecologically and aesthetically. Beth and Marie had been impressed with the flexibility of what Harmony had shown could be built into his modular structures. Harmony badly wants to show off the effectiveness of some of his smaller single dwellings which the Island government currently will not allow.

As Beth studies the brochures, Abe and Marie have gone out to the lower portion of the old government center property with Harmony and his site prep engineer to determine what might work best for the location.

Although Beth likes the way Harmony's small units look and their adaptability, the big driver for the choice of small houses is that it will give her the flexibility to add units as she needs and can afford them.

Marie and Beth have decided that if they go the small house route, their units will not have stoves, toilets, or showers. There will be a central bath, restroom, and washer & dryer area for the property. Each individual unit will have a small sink area with running water, a microwave and a 9000 BTU mini-split heating and cooling unit to do with a multiple purpose kitchen nook in the front and a couch area in the rear below the loft area which will contain a bed. Their current thinking is to build out single and double occupancy units. Angelique has been going back and forth with the Island Planning Commission to determine minimum space for each unit. She has brought down their defenses by noting that there are currently no restrictions on the size of resort rooms or condos. Angelique has told Beth that they may be amenable to changing the ordinance to include lot size with 300 square foot dwelling on 500 square foot lot as the minimum.

Zack comes out of the studio, comes to the table, and pulls out a chair.

"Do you know if Sallie has anything scheduled down at 'The Place' this coming Sunday?" Zack asks about possible use of the facility for a livestream event.

"I believe she has a wedding and reception," Beth says. "Want me to give her a call?"

"No," Zack says, "I'll go down and talk to her in a little bit. Would you have any problem if I used 'The Place' for a livestream on Monday or Tuesday evening? The Northenders and I have worked on a couple mixes for new songs we would like to try out along with our normal blues stuff?"

"Marie is the lady to talk to about that," Beth says. "I know that she'll want you to do it Monday, because the cleaning people are now in all day Tuesday.

"Monday will work," Zack says. "I'd like to make this a livestream only event. Having it on Monday will be a good excuse for not having a live audience."

"It's okay with me either way, " Beth says, " but Sallie and Marie need to approve it."

Zack nods his head and picks up one of Harmony's brochures.

"These are nice little units," Zack says.

"They are," Beth says. "You ought to go down to Island Holiday Trailers and take a look at what Harmony has."

Zack looks through the brochure for a minute or so, then queries Beth, "Do you have any idea what Mollie just asked me a few minutes ago?"

Beth shakes her head.

"She asked me if I will rent her my spare bedroom," Zack says.

Beth looks at Zack before responding, "I'm taking it that you don't think that is a good idea."

"It's not," Zack says. "I've done everything that I can think to try to make Molly understand that I'm not interested in starting anything up with her."

"What have you told her?" Beth asks. "That I like her just fine as a business partner and friend," Zack says, "but I have no interest in starting a romance with anyone at this point in my life. I have too many things to sort out."

"I'd guess she's taking that to mean that you really aren't ruling her out as a love interest?"

"I have ruled her out," Zack say, "but I really like Molly, I don't want to hurt her feelings."

"Sometimes feelings have to be hurt."

Zack goes back to looking at the brochure.

"What are you and Dave up to down at SouthTown?" Beth asks.

"We are looking to lease a space in the old drug store building," Zack says. "We are hoping to turn it into a recording studio. Dave and Sam are also going to run their audio and video business out of it."

"I thought Sam still had another year of school to finish?'

"He does, but he thinks he'll have enough spare time to help Dave out."

"Are you going to be selling anything out of this building?" Beth asks.

"Audio and video equipment add-ons," Zack says, "but I'm not going to be involved in the retail operation. My only role will be in the recording studio."

"Are you planning on doing most of your recording there once this new studio is up and running?" Beth asks.

"That's the current plan," Zack says. "I'll also be trying to recruit the musicians, who keep asking to play with me, to do recording sessions there. We will do our best to try to make it a first-class recording studio."

"Sounds interesting," Beth says. "May I give you a piece of advice?"

"Sure."

"Don't have Molly do the accounting for this new business of yours," Beth says. "Have Sam or Dave come up with someone else."

"That's probably a good idea," Zack says. "I don't need to get in any deeper with Molly than I already am."

Beth takes a long sip from her now always present bottle of water.

"Guess I better go down and talk with Sallie,' Zack says rising from the patio chair and heading around the north corner of the house.

Beth continues to browse the brochures for five minutes until Marie, Abe, Steve Harmony, and his engineer return from their review of the portion of the new property which is proposed to be merged with the existing business parcel.

They four pull up chairs at the patio table where Beth sits. "What's the verdict?" Beth asks.

"Seems creating small house, modular village on that property is very doable," Marie says.

"There are some exceptions from what we were originally discussing," Steve Harmony says. "Really makes no sense to put concrete pads in place for each housing unit. It would be best to use cement pillars. You wouldn't be able to move houses around if you wanted to, but other than that seems like a win. It means fewer trees need to come down. Should also make any under the house maintenance you will need to do, easier in the future."

"It also helps address possible issues with some of the steeper portions of the property," Harmony's engineer offers.

"What do you think, Abe?" Beth asks.

"I like what's being proposed," Abe says. "This plan will be much better than having a central hotel/resort setup. If we do things right, it will look as if what we build has always been here."

"I've made a free-hand sketch on my tablet for what you seem to want," the site engineer says putting his tablet down in the center of the patio. "We should be able to use it as a starting point for formalizing the site plan."

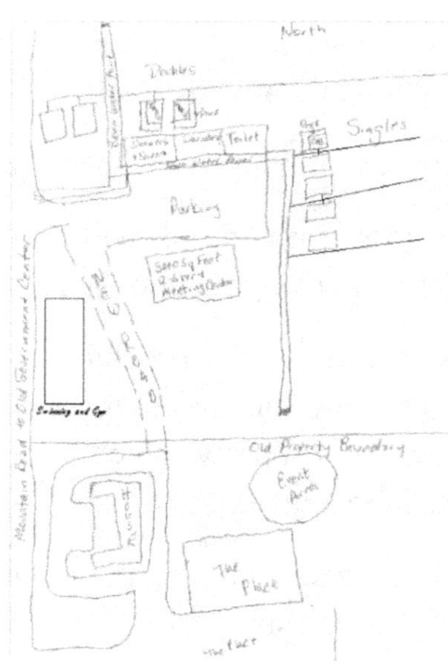

"Steve," Beth asks," What did you say the price will be for the single and double units?"

"Without changes to the current proposed configuration, $20,700 for each single unit, $28,422 for the double units."

"How many would you need us to commit to putting in place to start?" Beth asks.

"At least 5 singles and 3 doubles," Steve says.

"How soon will have a projection for the site prep, parking lot, restrooms and everything else but the meeting center?" Beth asks.

"A good guestimate," the site engineer says, "is that you are likely looking at between $250-$300K for that setup. The power, water and drain connections for each cabin probably will run around and additional $7-800 per unit. I should be able to work out final numbers by the end of next week."

"What about projections for the meeting center and the gymnasium?" Abe asks.

"Since you are looking to have that worked on last," Steve Harmony says, "why don't you give us three weeks or so. During that time though, feel free to contact us with any changes you might want."

"How soon would you be able to start?" Beth asks.

"After Island approval," Steve Harmony says, "we would get to work the following day. Site prep and the common facilities likely will take 8-10 weeks to finish. After that we can do a single unit every 3 days and a double every five."

"What are your thoughts, Marie?" Beth asks.

"I like the fact that we will be trying to integrate all of these buildings into the property," Marie says. "Not changing the property to fit the buildings. We keep most of the trees. Going with stone and mulch pathways appeals to me."

"Anything else you would like to discuss?" Steve Harmony asks. After receiving no queries, he continues, "If anything comes up contact me. Email probably works best for specific technical questions. For general questions, call me. Bill and I will now go to work finalizing the estimates and making sure that we aren't missing anything."

The two men from Island Holiday Trailers rise from their patio chairs and walk out to their pickup truck in the house parking lot.

"I was kind of skeptical about a modular individual unit approach," Abe says, "but the more I'm seeing, the better I like it. Where do we stand with the Island?"

"Angelique says that they want to draw a hard line on the lot size which the tiny houses sit on," Beth says. "That seems okay to me. The only real sticking point now is how many units we can have. Steve Harmony says that the property could handle 120 single units plus 100 double units easily. The island wants to limit that to 80 single units and 50 doubles."

"How many units do you think will need in the next five to ten years," Abe asks.

"*80 singles and 50 doubles are about twice what I was thinking of having when we were looking at one building,' Beth says, "but I suggest that we let Angelique bargain with them. So far everything she has negotiated with the island has turned out to be to our advantage.'

"We have at least a week until the property transfer is complete," Marie says. "Why don't we see how things look after that."

"I'm good with that," Abe says. "Are you still thinking of starting with 5 single and 4 double units?"

"That will meet our immediate needs," Beth says nodding her head affirmatively. "It will also use up all the funds that I will have available for the time being."

"I think it's good that we don't really have to build out anything until we actually need it," Marie says.

"I wouldn't fixate so much on what money you have available right now," Abe says, "Once this settlement from the lawsuit is complete, I'm going to make $2 million of it available to you. I'm hoping to help make your facility something the Wannasea Historical Society will want to use to house visitors attending their conventions and events. I'd also like your permission to pay for the build out the Meeting House as well as the Aquatic Center. There is a stipulation, however. I want to name those facilities the Rebecca Stolz Meeting House and the Jane and Julia Stolz Aquatic Center."

"I like that," Beth says.

"I would also pay for all of the solar panels and associated power equipment which is proposed to be placed on the common use buildings," Abe adds.

"That's really nice, Gramps," Beth responds. "When are you thinking of having this Meeting House and Gymnasium started?"

"As soon as you get this first phase of your little houses finished," Abe says.

"Right now, that looks as if it is going to be in September," Beth says. "Which is the same month as the election and when the babies are due. I'm good with the power equipment but maybe we ought to postpone dealing with a Meeting Center and Gymnasium until the first part of next year?"

BREAKING BAD

Thursday, June 13, 10:13PM. Beth and Marie are seated at the desk of the upstairs office at 'The Place' working on reviewing payments. The pair have gotten somewhat behind in their accounting duties due to the construction now occurring at 'The Place'. The event area at the rear of the property is now projected to be finished in October. They have just received approval to begin the construction of little houses on the expanded business plot.

"The Island has hit us with the new tax assessment," Marie says handing Beth the quarterly bill.

Beth takes a look at the bill which is a 15% increase over what had been paid the previous quarter. She notes that the property value assessment has increased significantly.

"I think they've already factored in the merger of this property with the lower portion of the old government center property," Beth says. "I'm going to see if I can get Molly to give us a couple days of her time to do a review of these tax assessments, so we don't get ourselves in trouble."

"Sounds like a good idea," Marie says.

Beth's cell phone, which is laying atop the desk rings.

"Beth Stolz," Beth says into the phone's microphone.

'Mrs. Stolz," Beth hears Judith, one of the new girls who is working with Sallie, say through the speaker, "someone is shooting up your house!"

"Are you guys, okay?" Beth asks as her pulse begins to race.

"Emily, my sister and I have gone into the upstairs bathroom and locked the door," the excited voice of Judith says. "We brought Six in with us."

"You guys stay in there," Beth says, "I want you to stay on the phone with me. Don't hang up no matter what happens."

"Okay," comes from Beth's cell speaker.

"Marie," Beth says rising from the desk chair. "Call the Constabulary and tell them that someone is shooting at our house."

Marie pulls out her cellphone. She calls the Constabulary, then follows Beth out of the office and down the stairs. Zack and the Northenders are still playing in the dining room area which remains full. Beth walks around the corner of table and motions to Abe, who is seated at his usual table with Saanvi and Ray Simmons. She explains the phone call to Abe, who goes on to the stage and motions for Zack to stop playing. While Abe is doing this Beth goes to the front security panel and locks down all the doors.

Using Zack's microphone, Abe says, "We are currently having some type of criminal incident occurring at the property above us. We ask everyone to remain seated and stay within the building until the Constabulary has given us an all-clear."

There is an audible murmur from the crowd.

"Until then,' Abe says turning to Zack, "would you mind playing the folks some music?"

Zack nods his head. He and the band restart the 'small minds' song which they had been playing.

Marie goes into the kitchen and checks to see that everyone there is safe and knows the situation. Both Beth and Abe come into the kitchen while Marie is explaining the situation to Sallie, Alfie, and Josh.

"The Constabulary should be at the house any minute," Beth says to Judith through her cell phone. "How are you guys doing?"

"A little frightened," Judith says, "but we are doing better now."

"When did the shooting start?" Beth asks.

"We thought we heard somebody breaking something in the parking lot about ten minutes ago," Judith says. "We were laying on our beds watching a video. When we looked outside, we couldn't see anything because the parking lot lights were out. Then we started hearing what sounded like shots and glass breaking downstairs, we went into the bathroom. I called you after we got the bathroom door locked."

"Does it sound like anyone is in the house?" Beth asks.

"I can't be sure," Judith replies. "I still hear pops and glass breaking but we don't hear anything which sounds like it is coming from upstairs."

"Stay away from the bathroom door," Beth says. "It might be a good idea if you go into the bathtub and the shower for the time being."

Beth hears Judith instructing her sister and Emily to move into the shower.

"Six thinks we are going to give him a bath," Judith says with a nervous laugh.

"Was there anybody else in the house but you three?" Beth asks.

"I don't think so," Judith replies. "The house was empty when we came in a little after 9. We didn't hear what sounded like anyone coming in after we came upstairs."

"I'm going to talk to Abe and Marie for a couple minutes," Beth instructs Judith. "Keep this call open and shout out to me if anything changes."

"Do you think I should go up there?" Abe asks.

"Absolutely not," Beth says. "Let's work on keeping everyone calm in here."

Sallie, Marie, and Beth go into the dining room. Abe pulls his cell phone from his jacket pocket and calls Defense One.

"Let's give everyone a free tea or coffee," Beth says moving to the tea making area. "Marie, you round up the waitresses to help us distribute. Sallie and I will pour."

Beth has poured her second cup before she hears Judith say through the cell speaker, "The shooting has stopped."

"Good," Beth says, "but you guys stay right where you are until we have an all clear."

"Okay," Judith says.

Beth pours four cups of tea before she hears Judith say, "I think the police are here. We hear sirens outside."

"Stay put," Beth says. "If anyone tries to open the door or bangs on it make them identify themselves."

"Okay," Judith replies.

Beth goes back to pouring tea for a few moments until she sees that she has an incoming call from Jack Druce.

"Judith," Beth says into the mic, "I have to take another call, so I'm going to put you on hold to answer it."

Not waiting to hear Judith's answer, Beth places the call on hold and answers the call from Jack Druce.

"Never felt happier to get a call from you," Beth says into the speaker.

"There are three of us up at your house," Jack Druce says, "can you tell me a little bit about what occurred?"

Beth describes what Judith has told her and tells him they've also kept the customers and all the staff inside of 'The Place'.

"You've had a lot of windows and car damage up here," Jack Druce says, "Whoever did it has taken off. I'll go tell the girls in the upstairs bathroom."

"They are pretty shaken up," Beth says. "I'll let them know that you are coming. Would you call me when you think it's safe to turn people loose down here?

"Will do," Druce replies.

Beth disconnects the call from the policeman and restores Judith's call.

"Judith," Beth says into the phone, "the police are there now. A gentleman named Jack Druce is going to be knocking on the bathroom door in a few minutes. It will be okay to open the door for him."

"That's wonderful," Judith says. "Six is getting a little whiney in here now."

Beth uses her shoulder to keep the cell phone to her ear as she continues to pour tea. After a few minutes, she hears an exchange between Judith and Jack Druce.

"Mr. Druce says you can let the people leave down there now, "Judith says. "I think we are okay here."

"I'll be up to see you in a few minutes," Beth says. "Call me back if you need anything else."

"Thanks Mrs. Stolz," Judith says.

Beth takes the cell phone from her shoulder and puts it into her back pocket.

"I'll go up to the house and see the girls," Marie says. "Why don't you hang out here until we know exactly what has transpired."

Abe, who has just come back out from the kitchen, adds, "I'm going up with you."

Marie goes to the security system and disarms it before she and Abe go out the front door. Beth waits until Zack and the band have completed their current song before walking to the stage.

"We have been given the all-clear from the Constabulary," Beth says through Zack's microphone. "You are now free to leave whenever you'd like."

"If you want to stick around, however," Zack says leaning over Beth's shoulder. "We will play you a few more songs."

Beth walks to Abe's table and sits down beside Saanvi.

"What's going on?" Saanvi whispers, as Zack starts playing 'Six Year Blues'.

Beth whispers what she knows to Saanvi and Ray Simmons.

AFTERMATH

Friday, June 14, 10:22PM. The back patio area and parking lot of the house are a mess. Abe's Volvo, Beth's and Zack's VW Beetles and a variety of Vespa scooters have been shot up with hard, round, green, plastic-coated projectiles which the Constabulary believes to be lethal breaker balls for a paintball gun. The .68 caliber projectiles are strewn around the parking lot, patio and inside the studio and kitchen.

The sequence of events based upon the video which Defense One has from the two cameras mounted on the light poles is that at slightly before 10PM last evening, four individuals carrying paintball guns and dressed in dark clothing walked across Mountain Way to the back of the house. Their first action was to shoot out the lights on poles. Two of the individuals then began shooting up the cars and scooters. The other two went on to the patio and began shooting projectiles at the sliding glass doors to the kitchen and the studio. Once the glass to the studio was shattered, all four individuals spent a good five minutes shooting projectiles into everything within the studio. The overhead lights, piano, amplifiers, the desk, chairs, and table. Nothing had been left untouched.

Defense One was able to record most of the shooters' movements through their night vision technology. They were also able to identify phone numbers associated with two cell phones which the shooters were carrying.

Marie and Abe are now working with two detectives from the Constabulary to document the damage. They are currently inside the studio. Beth sits with Judith, Jennifer, and Emily at the table closest to the kitchen. The girls are waiting to be interviewed by the detectives.

Olivia's BMW pulls into the parking area. She parks her car at the far south corner of the upper driveway then walks briskly over to where Beth sits with the girls.

"Be careful," Beth calls to Olivia, "there is glass and little round balls everywhere."

Olivia carefully negotiates her way to their table and brushes debris off the chair before sitting down.

"If this can be tied back to New Jericho," Olivia says, "we are going to sue Ainsley until he begs for mercy."

"The police have a couple cell phone numbers," Beth says, "hopefully they can tie those phones to actual people."

"Do you think it's the same individuals, who shot paint balls at the front of 'The Place'?" Olivia asks.

"Probably," Beth replies, "but they haven't been able to tie that first incident to anyone as yet."

Olivia stoops and picks up one of the round projectiles and holds it up toward Beth.

"Do these have metal inside?" the lawyer asks. "The constabulary says there is a small titanium ball in the middle," Beth replies. "They are banned from use on the Island for all the good that does us."

"Looks like they made one hell of a mess," Olivia says.

"Wait until you see the studio," Beth says, "but that really isn't the worst thing. Three of our girls were inside when the shooting was going on. If any of them had happened to be in the studio or the kitchen at the time, they likely would have been killed."

"New Jericho is completely out of control," Olivia says disgustedly. "Did Defense One get good recordings?"

"They did," Beth says. "Four people came onto the property from the other side of Mountain Way. There is no indication that they had a vehicle anywhere nearby. They covered themselves up fairly well. Hugh is saying that the best evidence from the Defense One may come from the audio. Seems all four of the people, who did this, were very chatty with each other."

"Who is running the case for the Constabulary?" Olivia asks.

"Jack Druce," Beth replies.

"Good," Olivia says.

"Do you happen to know Ray Simmons?" Beth asks.

"The name doesn't ring any bells," Olivia says. "Who is he?"

"He's a free-lance reporter," Beth replies. "He wrote that article about Zack in the Hanover Herald a while back." "I remember the article," Olivia says. "It was quite good."

"Seems Ray's usual reporting is the investigative type," Beth says. "He happened to be down at 'The Place' last evening when the shooting was going on. Seems about 16 months ago, he was working on an expose about Edgar Ainsley. When Ainsley moved over here, the Herald lost interest and told him to drop his research. Last night Ray told me that he wants to pick it back up. He spoke with Hugh for a while this morning. Would you like to talk with him about Ainsley?"

"Sure," Olivia says, "I also have a few other people. knowledgeable about Ainsley, who might like to speak with him."

"I'll text you his cell number," Beth says reaching for her phone.

Abe, Marie and the two detectives come out to the patio from the studio.

"Are you girls ready to be interviewed?" the lead detective asks.

The girls nod their heads affirmatively.

"Why don't we go into my place while the detectives are talking to the girls," Abe suggests to Beth, Marie, and Olivia.

Abe's sliding glass door has not been damaged. Seems the primary focus of the attack was on the studio and secondarily the kitchen. Abe leads the three women inside.

"Tea?" Abe asks after they take seats at his kitchen table.

Marie and Olivia nod their heads.

"I'll settle for water, Gramps," Beth says.

Abe fills the electric kettle and turns it on, before pulling two bottles of water from his refrigerator. He puts the water along with fixings for the tea and a packet of cookies on a large tray and carries it to the table.

"The detectives think that Zack was the primary target of last night's attack," Marie says. "They made it a point to pretty much destroying his car and the studio."

"Why Zack?" Olivia asks. "Are you sure that their target wasn't Beth?"

"Beth is probably part of it," Abe says as he remains standing waiting for the water to boil, "but they certainly made it a point to go after whatever they associated with Zack."

"Why?" Olivia asks.

"Zack stopped two of the church people from attacking Beth and kept one of them around to be arrested, a few weeks ago, " Abe says. "Zack is the person, who knocked out two Ainsley goons out over in Halifax. Zack is the person, who sings the 'New Jericho' song."

"Knocked them out?" Olivia says incredulously. "Beth, you told me that was just some kind of run in with two people, who said something about being from New Jericho. You didn't tell me that Zack laid them out?"

Beth manages a sheepish grin as she takes one of the bottles of water and opens it.

"After it happened," Beth says, "Zack told Molly and I that he didn't think it was all that big of a deal since he was used to dealing with those sorts of things at the bar where he had previously worked in Halifax."

"What actually happened with the two guys down in Halifax and the guy over at 'The Place'?" Olivia asks.

Beth gives a general description of Zack beating down the two attackers in Halifax.

"That's not what I'd call a run in," Olivia says. "That's what usually passes for attempted assault." You guys really should have called the Halifax police. If you had, we would know who those individuals were. What happened with Zack down at 'The Place' the other day?"

Abe describes how Zack knocked the guy, who had been harassing Beth to his knees then kept him incapacitated until the police came.

"Zack Tillerman never ceases to amaze," Olivia says shaking her head slowly.

BROKEN WINDOWS

Wednesday, July 3, 6:42PM. Beth sits at Abe's normal table near the stage at 'The Place' with Saavi and Prisha, who have come up to hear Zack perform folk and sea songs with his father. Pregnancy has finally slowed Beth down. She thinks her body is growing larger by the minute. Her back has begun to feel as if she is carrying the weight of the island. Construction, her campaign, and all other concerns have become subservient to her pregnancy.

"Have they finally caught the people, who shot up your house?" Saanvi asks.

"Supposedly they have arrested two of them," Beth says.

"Are they part of the New Jericho Temple?" Saanvi asks.

"The Constabulary won't say at this point," Beth replies.

"Have you been able to put the house back together," Prisha asks.

"Actually, Beth says, "Abe has dealt with most of that. He's done a great job of working with contractors to have things put together. He's really upset that they shot up my grandmother's piano so badly. He's had four people out to look at it and all of them have told him that it is beyond repair."

"That's a shame," Prisha says. "It's hard to have things destroyed when they have sentimental value."

"I think that if the island had not brought him my grandmother's sailboat last week," Beth replies, "we would have to have him restrained from going down to New Jericho and trying to take matters into his own hands. The only good part about any of it, is dealing with the attack has taken Abe's mind away from Reggie Reginald's trial."

"You have gotten rid of your VW?" Saanvi asks.

"It was shot up pretty badly," Beth says, "I decided that with these two guys, I needed something bigger, so I've bought a Volkswagen Caddy."

"You liked your Beetle, so much," Saanvi laments.

"The price of parenthood," Beth replies with a sigh.

"Do you know what Ralph is planning on doing with his car?" Prisha asks Beth.

"He said this afternoon that he is going to find someone to get it to the point that he can drive it," Beth responds. "The insurance company totaled it and gave him a check yesterday. Seems he wants to keep all the dents and holes and drive it around the island that way."

"Why?" Prisha says shaking her head.

"You'll have to ask him," Beth says with a shrug. "If there is one thing that I have learned over the past year, it is that your son does things in his own mysterious way."

"That's certainly one way of putting it," Saanvi says with a laugh.

"How is all the other construction coming?" Prisha asks.

"The company working on the event stage and area says," Beth replies, "that they will be done by the end of next month. Steve Harmony and his crew have just gotten started on the common area for the little houses."

"The kitchen here?" Prisha asks.

"Almost completely refinished," Beth says. "I can show you if you'd like?"

Prisha puts her hand on Beth's arm, "Maybe later. You know I've been doing some thinking about helping you to find someone to replace Sallie."

"You've found someone?" Beth says with sudden interest. Finding someone to replace Sallie has been put on the back burner and Beth knows time is running out.

Prisha takes a sip from her mug of Wannasea tea before answering, "I've been thinking that maybe I'd like to do it if you'll have me."

"You are serious?" Beth replies with sudden enthusiasm.

"My resort treats me well," Prisha says, "but there is no future in it other than what I am doing now. I'd much rather be preparing good food than tending the front counter and serving the reheated drivel that island resorts call a continental breakfast."

"If you are serious," Beth says, "we will take you on as soon as you want to start."

"I'd like to wait until the summer tourist season ends," Prisha says. "I feel that I owe resort that much. I'd also need to make at least $20 per hour.'

"We can do better than that moneywise," Beth says. "You don't know how big a relief it will be to have you running the kitchen. You would be able to start sometime around the first week of September?"

"Second week actually," Prisha says.

Abe walks in through the front entrance carrying his tablet in his right hand. He comes to the table and takes the empty chair at its front.

"Prisha may be coming to replace Sallie," Beth says to Abe with a wide grin.

"That would be wonderful," Abe says. "How many years has it been since you worked here."

Prisha does a mental calculation, "Twenty-four. Beth was still in diapers when we moved over to the Mainland."

"Any luck with grandma's piano?" Beth asks.

"Zack knows this guy, who is supposedly a wood-working wizard, out on the west end of the island," Abe says. "He just reviewed the state of your grandmother's piano and said that he would like to take a shot at repairing all the wooden portions. He's going to have someone come pick it up tomorrow."

"Will he be able fix the soundboard and the rest of the musical mechanism?" Beth asks.

"After he gets the wood finished," Abe says, "he'll bring it back to the studio. Hugh has put me in contact with a company over in Swansea which will come out and hopefully take care of that end. I sent them some pictures of the inside of the piano and they are confident that it can be repaired."

Sam and Dave, the audio/visual guys, come in through the front entrance and start setting up on the rear corner of the stage.

Abe turns his chair around and moves it next to Beth as close to the stage as possible.

Hank, Zack's father, comes in carrying his fiddle. He is followed by two members of the Rummies, a group Hank had played with on the Mainland twenty years back. The pair have agreed to play with Zack and his father this evening. A grey-haired, slim woman carries a bass fiddle, she is trailed by an older gentleman carrying a case filled with variety of percussion equipment.

As soon as Dave has come off the stage and has his video camera on his shoulder, Zack motions to Abe to start the introduction.

Abe takes the wireless microphone which is lying on Zack's stool at the front of the stage, switches it on, then after Dave gives him a thumbs up, says, "Welcome to 'The Place'. Tonight, you will hear a variety of folk and sea songs. We have also created a special song for this performance which you will hear just a little later. So here without any further ado is Zack Tillerman."

Zack and the band break into 'The Place' which is quickly followed by 'New Jericho'. Zack is playing the song with a cold fury which Abe has never seen before. They play the song through twice before going to 'Tomas Wanna's Sea'. When the song ends Zack sits down on the stool and pulls the microphone a little closer.

"This next song," Zack says, "is the new one which Abe mentioned. Abe found part of the lyrics in some writings from over 100 years ago. After a couple weeks of research, he was unable to find any trace of the rest of the song. We decided to try to recreate it. The result is what we are calling 'Wannasea Pirates'. Hope you like it."

Abe had found the main stanza of the lyrics in Alice's 3rd journal. He had spent the better part of June trying to find if those lyrics came from any known song. He had reached a dead end. When he showed the lyrics to Zack, his first reaction was to push Abe into creating an entire song around it. They finished the task on Sunday afternoon.

WANNASEA PIRATES TEMPO OF 121 BPM KEY OF D IN 4 / 4 TIME

It's Wannasea pirates we be
The bane of your shores
The scourge of your seas
It's Wannasea pirates we be

we'll waylay your boats
we'll steal all of your goats
if we find you've no gold
we'll take what can be sold
leave all what remains
in the most miserable of pains

For it's Wannasea pirates we be
The bane of your shores
The scourge of your seas
It's Wannasea pirates we be

If you ain't got no gilders
We may take your children
And put them to work
'til the bosun they irk
Then we'll set them afloat
Without a lifeboat

For it's Wannasea pirates we be
The bane of your shores
The scourge of your seas
It's Wannasea pirates we be

NG RIPPEL

What we can't steal
don't hold no appeal
to the scurvy likes a me
for 'tis a Wannasea pirate I be
we ain't got no fear
when the Navy is near
we're much faster and quicker
than those limey nose pickers

For it's Wannasea pirates we be
The bane of your shores
The scourge of your seas
It's Wannasea pirates we be

If you don't stop your trip
We'll broadside your ship
If we comes aboard
Ye'll meet the tip of me sword
If there then be slim pickins'
We'll give you the very dickens

For it's Wannasea pirates we be
The bane of your shores
The scourge of your seas
It's Wannasea pirates we be

we'll waylay your boats
we'll steal all your goats
if we find you've no gold
we'll take what can be sold
leave all what remains
in the most miserable of pains

> For it's Wannasea pirates we be
> The bane of your shores
> The scourge of your seas
> It's Wannasea pirates we be

The band does the song two more times before the crowd is satisfied.

AN OPEN SESSION

Saturday, August 3, 10:36AM. Beth is on the stage of the Southside Primary School along with Cathy Sheffield, who is running as an independent and Jerome Fields, a New Jericho disciple now representing the Fishermen & Wharfworkers Party. Beth is seated behind a table with the other two candidates. Olivia, Angelique, and Abe are seated in the second row of the audience along with Roberta Johnson and Vic Newton. Valerie Smythe is conducting the one and only debate between the Ward 6 council candidates from a row of tables in front of the stage which has been set up for the press. A few more than 100 people are in attendance.

Beth is as comfortable as she is able to be in the 33rd week of her pregnancy. She has two bottles of water in front of her. She is currently just as worried about needing to take a restroom break as she is about the debate.

Olivia, Angelique, and Roberta believe that the Ward 6 council seat is in the bag. Vic Newton isn't quite so certain. Newton has been advising Beth to be non-confrontational.

"Good morning, everyone," Valerie Smythe says into her microphone. "Welcome to Wannasea Ward 6 open session between candidates for a seat on the Island's council. I would remind everyone that each of these candidates has posted position papers on their campaign websites. Additionally, 'The Islander', has articles posted in its political section marked Ward 6 for each of the candidates. To begin today's proceedings, I will remind each candidate that they have committed to making no direct personal attacks on their opponents. We will begin by providing 5 minutes for each candidate to introduce themselves and their main campaign objectives. We will begin with Beth Stolz, the Mountain Centrist Party candidate."

"Welcome everyone," Beth says into her microphone. "I am Beth Stolz. I have lived in Ward 6 my entire life. For the past 8 years, I have operated 'The Place' near the intersection of West Road and Mountain Way. The primary purpose of my candidacy is to assist in bringing progress to our island which benefits all residents in our ward. The first step in this effort will be to modernize the legal code of our Island focusing upon citizenship requirements, marriage, and common property laws plus the shipping code. I will promote the expansion of the educational and healthcare initiatives on this island. I will remain open to my constituents' concerns. Looking out in the crowd, I recognize many of you from the bi-weekly sessions that we have conducted over the past five months. I promise to do my best to bring truth, fairness, and transparency to our island's government as well as healthy prosperity for the residents of Ward 6. I hope that you view my candidacy as your opportunity to have a say in not only the running of Ward 6 but the entire Island. Thank you for coming out today."

"Cathy Sheffield, who is running as independent candidate is next," Valerie Smythe announces.

"As almost all of you know," Cathy Sheffield begins, "I am the current councilperson for Ward 6. I have been your representative for the past 12 years. In those twelve years, I believe that we have seen both Ward 6 and this island advance as part of my stewardship. There have been some mistakes along the way, but I can assure you that I have learned from those mistakes. I believe that our Island is currently on a good course. I see no need to meddle in a legal code which has served this island well for over 100 years. As my husband Charles is always telling me, "If it is not broken, don't fix it". I promise that I will continue to serve your interests faithfully just as I have for the past 6 terms. Thank you for being here today."

"Jerome Fields from the Fishermen's Conservative Party," Ms. Smythe says.

"I am bringing the realm of God to you," Fields practically shouts into his microphone. "I abide by the rules of God, not those of the ungodly, who you see seated upon this stage next to me. God is under attack from the forces of Satan everywhere today. You see those evil forces arrayed before you in the streets, in the restaurants, on the beaches and in the bars of this island. Satanic forces which strive to undo God's teaching and lead you upon the path toward eternal damnation. Forces which must be brought under the dominion of the Almighty Lord. Join with me in God's Army to defeat this evil. I am a charter member of that army. If I am elected, the will of God shall begin to be put in place on our island. The heathens and ungodly are to be driven out. This island will move toward becoming a paradise of Godliness. A vote for me is a vote for God."

"The next segment of our program will be the opportunity for each of the candidates to ask the other candidates two questions," Valerie Smythe announces. "Again, I remind candidates to refrain from personal attacks. Questions and responses should take no longer than three minutes each. We will begin by allowing Mr. Fields to ask two questions of Ms. Stolz. Mr. Fields."

Fields looks over at Beth and keeps his eyes focused on her, "I want to know why an ungodly abomination such as yourself thinks it is appropriate to not only be running for council but to present herself in public in such a condition?"

Valerie Smythe gives Fields an angry look.

"If you are referring to the fact that I am both a lesbian and pregnant," Beth says, "I will say to you that I make no attempt to hide either. I have said that I stand for truth and transparency. The truth is that my partner is another female. I believe that it is obvious to everyone that I am also very pregnant. In the interests of full disclosure, I will tell you that I am pregnant with twins."

"I want to know why a despicable Satanic mongrel such as yourself," Fields replies into his microphone angrily, "is allowed to promote unnatural activities including gay prostitution, lewd musical acts as well as having her personal "Monkey Boy" attack members of good standing in God's Army?"

"Mr. Fields!" Valerie Smythe shouts into her microphone.

"Your question and claims are as absurd as they are false," Beth says vehemently.

"Witness this mongrel abomination of Satan!" Fields shouts into his microphone as he points toward Beth. "God knows that she is a Hoyden. God will punish any who dare to support her. Her words lead you straight to the gates of Hell! Seek salvation, drive this abomination and all like her from this island!"

Valerie Smythe motions to the Island constable who is sitting in the front, before saying angrily. "Mr. Fields, you were instructed how you must conduct yourself before this event. You have failed to do so. I have no other choice than to have you removed."

"These are the wages of sin before you!" Fields yells into the crowd rising from his chair. "God will annihilate all who chose to protect this deplorable creature of Satan."

The constable and another officer in plain clothes come onto the stage and grasp Fields by his arms.

"Beth Stolz," two women call out in unison from the crowd, "you are doomed to eternal damnation. You are beyond salvation. God has witnessed your sinful acts. You are an abomination to his island. The rest of you must repent and fall at the feet of Brother Jerome or face God's justice and wrath!"

"You are wallowing in the sewage which Satan has wrought!" Fields yells trying to point back toward Beth. "You are an evil crone, who is bent upon subverting God's Island to your demented ways. God shall hold you to account for your denial of his will!"

The officers guide Fields, who continues to shout threats, off the stage and out of the auditorium. The two women, who have shouted support for Fields, follow behind them.

Valerie Smythe allows a minute for the audience to settle down before saying, "I am very sorry that you had to witness that disturbance. Both Mr. Fields and his political party were warned several times before this disturbance that such outbursts would not be tolerated. We will now continue this session without a representative from the Fishermen's Conservative Party. Ms. Sheffield, it is your turn to ask two questions of Ms. Stolz."

"Ms.Stolz," Cathy Sheffield begins, "why on earth would you think that you are even remotely qualified to run for Island council?"

Beth holds back her anger before responding, "I have been involved in the politics of this island almost from the time that I learned to talk. My great-great grandmother, Alice Bailey and her husband, Hugo, were instrumental in the downfall of the Reginalds and bringing democracy to this island. Alice Bailey and my great-grandfather, Nathan Stolz, were assassinated because of Island politics. The business which I have grown is controlled by island politics. The children, who my great-grandmother, grandmother and I have brought into our house to protect, are products of this island's politics. I have long promoted educational opportunities and initiatives at Wannasea Extension. I know and have had contact with the majority of the people who live in Ward 6. Over the past months, I have come to learn their concerns and hopes for our island. I have shown that I will not be bullied or cowed by intimidation. I have passion, not only for the future of the Mountain area and Ward 6, but the entire island. I feel this is more than ample qualification for the Ward 6 council seat."

"Ms. Stolz," Cathy Sheffield, "isn't it true that you represent only a very narrow segment of the population of our Ward and not the majority of its voters?"

"Who I represent," Beth replies, "are those like me, who began their education at this very primary school and continued their education on this island. Those like me, who feel that living on an island which has long subscribed to a policy of live-and-let-live, is to their liking. Those like me, who have worked hard to turn a failing business around and make it prosper. Those like me, who grew up without a father or a mother. Those like me, who try to do the best that they can with what they have available. Those like me, who long for fairer laws and better representation. Those like me, who want a better future on this island for our children. Are those the people and voter to which you refer?"

Cathy Sheffield does not respond.

"Ms. Stolz," Valerie Smythe announces, "it is now your turn to ask two questions of Ms. Sheffield."

"I only have one question for Ms. Sheffield," Beth says. "That question is related to the disclosure earlier in the year that Ms. Sheffield had taken illegal campaign contribution from the Sylvester Brothers and others in return for voting to approve their bid on the old government center. My question to you is why did you believe that interests of the Sylvester Brothers, who did not then reside nor have ever resided upon in this island, were more important than the interest of the Ward 6 residents which you were elected to represent?"

"That's yesterday's news," Cathy Sheffield says dismissively. "I admitted to making something of a mistake. I apologized to the voters. That is all behind us. I think the people of this Ward will chose to recognize the good work which I have done for them over the years and opt for me to continue that work."

"The next portion of this proceeding will be questions from the audience," Valerie Smythe announces. As she does, Beth motions to her. She comes over to and stands beside Beth's chair.

"Could we take a short bathroom break?" Beth whispers to Ms. Smythe.

The reporter returns to her table, looks at her watch and announces, "We will now take a short ten-minute recess. We will start back up at 11:30."

Beth rises and walks off the stage. Roberta Johnson and Olivia come up the aisle to meet her.

"I need to go the bathroom," Beth announces in a lowered voice. "Fast."

The pair usher Beth out of the auditorium and to the staff bathroom which is on the other side of the entrance kiosk.

"You did great," Roberta says to Beth as she enters the front stall and locks it.

"That Fields guy was a real show," Olivia says. "I can't imagine why the Fishermen's Party allowed him to be their candidate."

"There are a lot of New Jericho people in the Fishermen's Conservative Party now," Roberta says. "A couple big donors, I'm told."

"Who?" Beth asks from inside the stall.

"The family, who runs the west end marina," Roberta replies, "as well Maggard, who owns the fish processing plant on the south side."

Beth exits the stall and walks to the sink to wash her hands.

"Angelique says she heard," Olivia says, "that Sheffield was trying to be nominated in Ward 6 for the Farmworker's Party. Seems Betty Furness stood in the way of allowing her to run."

"I'm actually amazed that she is running," Roberta remarks. "Takes quite a bit of audacity to do what Sheffield is doing."

"Either that or a complete lack of self-awareness," Olivia says as they walk with Beth back into the auditorium.

"You did great, Kitten," Abe says as he walks up behind her and pats her on the arm. "Are the twins behaving?"

"So far," Beth says with a smile.

She climbs the stairs and goes back to her seat on the stage to await the restart of the session.

"Please take you seats," Valerie Smythe announces, "we will be resuming shortly."

Smythe waits a full minute before continuing, "The final phase of our event will be taking questions from the audience. We ask you to limit your questions to no more than two minutes. If you have a question, please raise your hand. One of the assistants will come to you with a microphone."

"I have a question for Beth Stolz," a middle-aged woman in a flowered summer dress announces.

"Go ahead," Valerie Smythe responds.

"Some of us on the island are beginning to become concerned by the amount of property which you have acquired on the mountain," the lady begins. "It brings back bad memories of when the Reginalds were operating up there. Would you address those concerns?"

"One of the primary considerations in purchasing the old government center property," Beth says, "was to ensure that the Wannasea Historical Society can establish a museum in the Castle. The society now has a 100-year lease on ¾ of the castle. The museum should be opening next February. Additionally, we had a need for expansion of our present business and programs to help children escaping problems in their homes. We are using a 27-acre portion of that acquisition to make that possible. The remainder of the facility will be leased to Island Resort to operate a resort/casino facility which is projected to have 200 full-time staff positions, another 100 part-time and 150 seasonal positions. Our feeling from the start regarding the old government center property is that we wanted to do what could be done to keep the ownership of the property in the hands of Wannasea Islanders. Does that answer your question?"

The lady nods her head and goes back to her seat.

An elderly gentleman from the other side of the aisle asks, "Are you in anyway beholding to Island Resorts politically? There are rumors that business is the main contributor to your campaign."

"We have absolutely no political affiliation with Island Resorts," Beth says. "Roberta, would you mind describing who the donors to my campaign have been?"

Roberta Johnson rises from her seat and says, "There are only 3 donors. Beth, her grandfather, and Ralph Jones. They have contributed approximately $60,000."

"Who is Ralph Jones?" someone from the other side of the audience calls out.

"He is the musician, who is known as Zack Tillerman," Roberta replies.

"Further to this question about Island Resorts," Beth says. "I do recognize that organization is a large part of my current business income stream. I promise you that I shall recuse myself from any Island legislation which may have a direct impact upon them."

No one else comes forth from the audience.

"Any further questions?" Valeria Smythe asks.

She waits a full minute with no one else rising.

"I sincerely thank all of you for your attendance," Valerie Smythe says. "This open session is now closed."

ELECTION DAY

Tuesday, September 3, 7;32PM. Beth sits in the sofa chair of the living room at the house. The TV is tuned to the local news station which is providing coverage of Island voting which just ended two minutes ago. Beth isn't really all that interested in what's being reported on the TV. For the past few weeks, her main focus has been drinking enough water and consuming enough food to satisfy the two beings growing in her womb.

Beth has come to feel that her entire life has now been taken over by forces which she herself had placed in motion months ago. Forces which are now almost completely out of Beth's control. The decision to start a family with Marie led to the twins and her present state. The decision to expand 'The Place' has led to the just recently completed event area, which Abe, Zack, and most of the staff are now referring to as the 'Shell'. The need for more space to house the people who Beth has brought in is on the verge of producing a tiny house village not far from where Beth sits.

Beth takes a sip from her open bottle of water, then reaches for the hotdog and bun covered in mustard which sits on a plate atop the side table. Beth now eats pistachio ice cream by the quart and hot dogs and buns by the package. Prior to pregnancy, Beth couldn't remember having a craving for either. Now filling that craving has become almost her primary purpose for existence.

"They are just starting to get some results," Josh, who is seated on the floor says.

Beth isn't all that much concerned about what the elections results will be. Those results are just one more thing which Beth has put in motion which has spun out of her control. If there actually is a God, Beth has begun to speculate, is this feeling of having put things in motion and then having all those things take on a life of their own, how that God must feel all the time?

Beth takes another bite of the hot dog.

Marie sits on Beth's side of the couch. Marie has now become the rock which Beth rests upon. Marie has taken over almost every element of the running of 'The Place' and the on-going construction efforts. She has also become Beth's main supplier of pistachio ice cream and hot dogs.

Abe sits about 3 feet in front of Beth on a large rolling desk chair which he has brought in from the studio. The chair was just purchased last month to replace the one which had been destroyed in the blaster ball attack. Abe doesn't spend much time in the desk chair or the studio these days. When Abe is not working on his grandmother's journals, he has now become something of an aged prowling tiger, ready to pounce on anything which impedes the progress of Beth's twins into this world. Beyond the journals and pestering the Constabulary to get to the bottom of who was responsible for the attack on the house, Abe's focus has shifted to the on-going work at what he has come to call the 'Tiny House Village'. Twelve days ago, Abe received an $85 million dollar settlement in his lawsuit against the Sylvester Brothers. After taxes, Abe was left with $58 million. He immediately gave Beth $3 million to cover the damage which had been inflicted at 'The Place'. Abe has used $15 million to set up a scholarship fund at Swansea University which will be managed by the Wannasea Historical Society. Last week he had been able to talk Beth into allowing Steve Harmony's crew to begin work on both the Rebecca Stolz Meeting Center and the Jane & Julia Stolz Aquatic Center. Abe had also talked Beth into allowing the continued construction of single and double tiny house units. The plan now is for a total of 60 of each type units in addition to building two large additional restroom/shower areas toward the rear of the new property. All Beth knows regarding the new facilities is that Abe is putting much more money into the facilities than Beth had planned. Beyond having become Beth's primary chauffeur, Abe is also now spending at least two days a week over at Zack & Dave's 'Island Sounds' recording studio.

Beth gets what has become an all too familiar feeling. She puts her hand on Marie's arm.

"I need to go to the bathroom," Beth says.

Marie helps Beth up from the sofa chair. Beth is now no longer able to walk normally. She waddles with Marie holding her arm first into their bedroom, then to the master bath in the rear.

"Looks like Olivia is doing really well in Ward Two," Molly, who is sitting on a chair Zack brought in kitchen, says about the posting of first results in that ward.

"I talked everyone in my family into voting for her," Zack says, who sits a few feet from Molly in another kitchen chair says.

"Still nothing for Ward 6 though," Abe comments.

Zack isn't around the house much anymore. When he comes, it is usually to Abe's in-law suite to talk over some lyrics he would like to have Abe produce. Two weeks ago, Zack's blue VW, covered in holes and dents from the paintball gun attack, had been restored to drivability. He's become the talk of the south end of the island for driving the badly battered vehicle around. Zack spends most of his day now either at the studio in SouthTown or at Southeast Beach. The move has not stopped Zack's popularity from spreading. Last Friday and Saturday, Zack had his first performances at 'The Shell'. Friday had been a sea song and folk event performed with his father and two members of the 'Rummies' as his band. 382 people had purchased tickets. Zack played from 8PM until a quarter past 11. The second night was blues and folk rock focused. 425 people had attended the event with at least another 100 sitting outside the event gates in the patio area listening. Zack had played until 11:45PM on Saturday.

Marie helps Beth across the room and back into the sofa chair.

Toward the end of July, Molly had gone into something of a funk over Zack disappearing from the studio. Although the studio being out of commission had given Zack a valid excuse for not coming to the house, Molly had become convinced that Zack was avoiding her. The only times she was now seeing Zack were primarily when he had a performance. The last week in July, Abe and Beth had decided to see if having Molly take over the event management of the 'Shell' might help get her mind off Zack. For the first two weeks, the addition of the role had not done much to stem Molly's constant litany of "Where is Zack" queries. Two weeks ago, when the early completion of the first two double occupancy units up at the 'tiny house village' were complete, Molly had asked to move from the upstairs dormitory area of the house into the unit closest to Mountain Way. Beth and Marie's initial plan for the bigger units was to have two people move into them. Molly had been insistent that she wanted the larger unit just for herself and agreed to pay the $420 monthly which it will cost to do so. Moving into the little house shifted Molly's attention from Zack for the time being. Decorating and improving the small unit became her new passion, though it remained clear Molly still had not given up on going well beyond her business relationship with Zack. The younger kids, who were left living in the house, had begun referring to Molly as the 'Queen of Tiny Village'. Molly had heard the term a few times and didn't seem to mind. She had also kicked herself into gear in mid-August when the 'Shell' was finally complete. She'd lined up two musical acts from the Mainland for the next week and had been actively pushing Marie to allow scheduling of the event center on Sunday nights. Currently only Wednesday through Saturday use was planned.

"Some numbers are now coming in for Ward 6," Josh says from his seat on the floor.

"They look good for Ms. Stolz," Judith, who is sitting beside Josh says.

Beth isn't all that certain that she is a fan of being called "Ms. Stolz" by Judith and her younger sister, Jenny. It's what people used to call Becca. Marie mentioned to Beth on Sunday that she thinks there is something going on between her brother Josh and Judith. Beth notices how close they are sitting to each other and surmises that Marie is probably right.

In the past month, Beth has acquired 4 new residents. A sixteen- and eighteen-year-old set of brothers, and two sixteen-year-old girls. All are essentially escapees from the new Jericho Temple. The oldest brother had been working at 'The Place' since the beginning of spring through a work program offered by the Wannasea school system. In mid-July after a blow up with his parents over being at 'The Place', the oldest brother moved into the upstairs area over Abe's in-law suite. Three weeks later, his younger brother came. Saanvi and Ray Simmons had brought the girls out, ten days ago. Now that Molly, Annette, and Emily had moved to 'Tiny House Village', there had been room upstairs to accommodate the new girls.

Annette, who is seated between Marie and Jenny on the couch, has begun to be something of a revelation for Marie. Annette, who is 24 years old, has worked at 'The Place' for the better part of 8 years. Six years ago, she moved upstairs due to drug and jail problems which her mother was experiencing. Annette had always been a conscientious and hardworking waitress. Last year Annette had expressed an interest in attending Wannasea Extension. She is now working toward acquiring a degree in Hospitality Management. Marie feels that with proper mentoring, Annette can become a key component for the management of 'Tiny House Village'.

"You've got a 500-vote lead now Beth," Molly says as updated results come on to the screen.

Beth has fallen asleep on the sofa chair. Marie switches off the light on the side table.

"Olivia is up by 350 votes now," Zack says to no one in particular.

The election watching on the TV continues for the next hour and half before Beth's cell phone, which is on the side table rings. Beth, who has been napping wakes as Marie picks up the phone.

'Hello Roberta," Marie says, "Beth will be with you in just a few seconds."

Beth stretches as much as she can, takes a sip from her bottle of water then takes her cell phone from Marie.

"Hi Roberta," Beth says into the phone. "What's up?"

"You've won," Roberta tells Beth. "Congratulations."

"By how many votes?" Beth asks.

"You had 65% of the vote," Roberta says. "Surprisingly, Fields was the nearest to you, he got 2,200 votes or so. Sheffield bombed."

"How did Olivia do?" Beth asks.

"She won by 1200 votes. There will now be two Stolz women on the Island council."

THE ARRIVAL

Monday, September 9, 9:04PM. Beth is in the Wannasea Medical Facility Maternity Ward delivery room #2. She has been here since just a little after 4PM. Marie is in the room seated beside the head of her bed. Forty-five minutes ago, Beth had delivered a 6lb 2oz boy, who they are planning to name Nathan. The second baby has been more reluctant to make its debut. Beth is exhausted. She has reached the point where the pains of delivery have been a lesser concern than her feeling of complete exhaustion.

"Let's give it one more big push," Colleen Hendricks, the primary attending midwife says to Beth.

Vandana Gurnani, a recent graduate midwife P.A, is standing nearby to assist. She is being precepted over the next six weeks by midwife Hendricks.

"Give this whatever you have left," Marie says pressing Beth's hand and trying to help her tighten her traverse abdominals.

"The head is coming," the midwife says, "just a couple more good pushes."

Beth takes a slow very deep breath through her nose. As instructed in the birthing class, she exhales through her mouth trying to relax her buttocks.

"One more series should do it," the midwife says.

Beth summons all the will which she has left. She knows this must be the last push. Beth simply has no more pushes in her. Unable to stop from releasing a huge groan, Beth delivers the second baby out of her womb. Beth has never been this physically exhausted in her life. She is unable to move as she hears the second baby cry.

"It's a girl," midwife Gurnani tells Beth and Marie.

The news of the girl makes Beth smile but does little to relieve Beth of her exhaustion.

"Would you push on Beth's stomach?" midwife Hendricks asks her assistant as she completes separating the umbilical cord.

After a few minutes of cleanup and weight and health checks, midwife Hendricks delivers the girl baby to Beth. The midwife then goes to the small incubation box at the front corner of the room and brings out her brother, who she also carries to the bed.

"I didn't think that it was ever going to be over," Beth says weakly.

"It is now," the midwife says reassuringly, 'and you now have yourself two beautiful little babies."

"We do," Marie says grinning broadly.

"The girl weighed two ounces more than her brother," midwife Hendricks says. "The twins I have delivered usually are not quite as big as these two."

"I'm going to call Abe," Marie says moving toward her purse in the corner of the room.

"We are going to move you into the recovery area in a few minutes," midwife Hendricks instructs.

Marie pulls her cellphone out of her purse and turns it on. She pulls Abe's number from her contacts and taps on it.

Abe has been in the waiting area for the past five hours. Most of his time has been spent pacing nervously back and forth between the two rows of half-filled chairs, the reception desk and the vending area.

"Hello Marie," Abe says after pulling his cellphone from his pocket. "How's it going up there?"

"Beth just delivered the second twin," Marie says, "it's a girl. Beth is completely exhausted. They are moving her to a recovery room over the next 30 minutes. You should be able to come up then."

'Wonderful," Abe says. "Congratulations!"

Abe disconnects connects the call. It suddenly dawns on him that he doesn't have anything to take up to Beth. With 30 minutes until he can go to see her and his new grandchildren, Abe decides that he has time to walk two blocks to the local grocery store, which is just east of the Medical Center. Putting his cell phone into his jacket pocket Abe walks out the front entrance of the Medical Center and turns right. It is a beautiful night. The sky is clear. There is hardly any wind. A good night for not only a walk to the grocery store but the birth of two great-grandchildren.

After helping take the two babies from Beth, who has fallen asleep, and putting them into the incubator. Marie follows the nurse as she wheels the twins down the hall to the nursery for further health checks. She waits outside the 8'X4' window watching as the nurse uses instrumentation to examine each baby. There is only one other baby in the nursery currently. As Marie watches, she pulls her cellphone from her purse. She sends a text to Josh saying, "You are now the uncle of a new boy and girl. Beth and twins are doing fine. You should be able to come see them tomorrow morning'. Then Marie formats a similar text to Zack, Saanvi, Molly, Annette and Sallie asking that they spread the word.

It is another ten minutes until the nurses are complete with the tests on the twins and are rolled out of the nursery toward the recovery room.

"You are very lucky," the nurse tells Marie as they move down the hallway. "Delivery of twins is usually not without problem. I know your partner probably isn't thinking this at the moment, but honestly, the birth of these two could not have gone much smoother."

They enter the room where the midwives have moved Beth. She now has an IV drip going into her arm. Beth is pale and drawn. Her breathing is somewhat shallow. She is now somewhere between sleep and consciousness. For the first time Beth can remember in her life, she misses not having her mother. Since the first baby was delivered Beth has had an inexplicable longing for her mother. A mother, who Beth has not seen for more than twenty-four years. A mother, who had died before turning twenty. Beth had never longed for her mother like this before. She feels Marie's hand on her forehead.

"The babies are doing fine," Marie says. "Abe should be up in a few minutes."

Beth forces herself awake.

"Have you filled out the girl baby's name yet?" Beth asks Marie.

"No," Marie says. "They are Baby Boy Stolz and Baby Girl Stolz at this point. Are we still going to name them Nathan and Rebecca?"

Most of Marie and Beth's baby naming process had focused on boy's names. They thought the odds were good that the twins would both be boys. Nathan was the name chosen for the first twin. If the other had been a boy, it was going to be called Abraham. Rebecca had been their only choice if one of the twins turned out to be a girl."

"How about Nathan Abraham for the boy," Beth says weakly, "but I would like to name the girl Julia Jane if that is alright with you."

"Seems perfect to me," Marie says as the nurse places Julia in Beth's arms.

NEW ROUTINES

Friday, September 27, 10:48AM. Beth stands in the studio beside the cribs of the two twins. Arlette Baptiste, the woman Prisha had recommended to help with their care, stands beside her.

"You are lucky your babies are so well behaved," Arlette says to Beth. "They certainly don't cry much. Gabriel's been crying almost from the time that I brought him home from the Medical Center.

Gabriel is Arlette's ten-month old son, who has fallen asleep on the mat of his playpen, after having spent the morning using his new skill of crawling to explore the studio.

"Honestly," Beth says, "I'm just happy that they are healthy."

Beth has gotten into the routine of adjusting to the babies' schedule. Although Arlette now helps watch the twins from 9AM through 4:30 Wednesday through Sunday, Beth rarely goes down to 'The Place' these days. Prisha having started work in the kitchen the week that the twins were born, means there really isn't all that much for her to do now, except help with the business end of things. Even in that area, Molly, Annette, and Marie make sure that there isn't much of anything which Beth must do except sign things.

Beth's also been surprised by how much help she now has with the twins when Arlette isn't at the house. Judith and Jennifer in particular have become adept at feeding and changing Nate and Julia. Saanvi is now in the habit of coming to visit at least twice a week. Abe is always coming over either taking the twins for a walk in their big pram or holding one in each arm and telling them stories from Alice's journal. Molly and Annette have taken to coming over after events and helping to feed and put the babies back to sleep. Beth is lucky in more than just one way. Even Zack is now in the habit of coming up to the house to see "his babies" before the days of his performances.

Abe and Oliva enter through the sliding glass door. They both wave silent greetings to Arlette and Beth and move to the other side of the cribs.

"They look like little angels," Olivia whispers across the cribs to Beth.

"Where do you want to have our discussion?" Abe whispers to Beth.

Olivia has come up to talk about the Constabulary's findings regarding the attack upon the house which occurred in June.

"Would you mind if we take a walk up to the old government center?" Beth replies.

In the past week, Beth has finally begun to get her stamina back. After spending four days in the Medical Center with the twins, the first two weeks back, even with all the help which she has received, had left her constantly fatigued. Only this Wednesday had she begun to feel something of her old self.

"Okay by me," Olivia whispers back.

"I'm always up for a walk," Abe says moving away from the bassinettes and toward the sliding glass door.

Beth walks around the front of the bassinettes where Six is lying and gently lifts the dog by the collar so that he follows her out the new sliding glass door. They walk across the patio and into the parking lot before Olivia says, "They have finally identified all four of the attackers."

This is news to Abe and Beth. The Constabulary had identified two of the attackers, both males in their late twenties by Defense One's identification of their cell phones, a few days after the attack. The pair were now in the Constabularies holding area without bail charged with attempted murder. Even with the severity of the charges, the Constabulary had indicated to Abe that they were not able to pressure either of the two into revealing the identity of their two companions or admit their connection to New Jericho Temple.

"Seems one of the two identified through their cell phone number is an individual, who tried to attack Zack in March when you and Molly were in Halifax with him," Olivia says. "That individual made the mistake of complaining to the Constabulary about Zack and that incident. Detectives on the Mainland were able to track the second person in the Halifax incident through surveillance tapes and interviewing kitchen workers from the restaurant. The second Halifax attacker is a 19 year old, who currently lives in the New Jericho Temple. "

They walk across Mountain Way to the pathway on the other side of the road.

"Through pressing the 19-year-old," Olivia continues," they uncovered not only that he was part of the attack on your house, but the identity of the fourth attacker and testimony that Jerome Fields played a direct role in planning the attack. The 19-year-old is currently aiding the Constabulary by assisting in the planting of listening devices inside New Jericho Temple and select areas of Ainsley's new compound on the west end."

"So why haven't they arrested all of them now that they have this information?" Abe asks.

"Seems there are things going on inside New Jericho which are much more important to monitor than formally charging the four perpetrators and Brother Jerome," Olivia replies. "They are asking that we not do anything which may jeopardize their on-going investigation. They asked that we, along with the insurance companies back off for the time being."

"Are we in physical danger?" Beth asks.

"I'm told by the Constabulary," Olivia says, "not at this time. Seems the focus of Ainsley's ire has shifted to the Governor and Betty

Furness, for trying to stop people from living in what they refer to as their   church."

"Steve Harmony was telling me that they are trying to build some sort of compound on Round Hill at the west end."

"They are," Olivia says, "but they aren't getting anywhere with it thanks to Betty Furness."

"What is it exactly the Constabulary want us to do?" Beth asks.

"Lay low for the time being," Olivia says. "They will let us know if and when anything changes."

"That will be kind of hard to do when we both are sitting on the island council," Beth says.

"Still a few weeks before we are sworn in," Olivia says. "They ask that neither of us give out any interviews until then."

"Okay," Beth replies. "Does this mean that we are going to have to delay our proposal for changes the island's rules on voting, citizenship, marriage, ship registration?"

"Oddly enough," Oliva says, "no. The New Jericho Temple wants the changes we are proposing for citizenship and voting. Ainsley thinks the citizenship changes will expand their share of the vote?"

"Will it?" Beth asks.

"I don't see how," Olivia says. "I don't believe New Jericho has any idea how many people, who have lived on this island for a long time, are not currently citizens and do not have a right to vote. From what I know, if we get those changes passed, New Jericho will be even more marginalized."

"What about the marriage laws?" Beth says.

"Ainsley thinks if the marriage laws are changed," Olivia says, "it will give him something to yell and scream about which will have the potential to drive voters to him."

They come to the portion of Mountain Way where the new entrance and exit to the 'Tiny House Village' is located.

"Wow," Olivia says, "it's really changed up here. I thought all you guys were doing was putting up that event shell and a few housing units. How many of those little houses do you have over there now?"

"Currently there are a total of 18," Abe says. "When it is all said and done there probably will be 150 of them."

"Is anybody using them yet?" Olivia asks.

"Molly Peters, Josh, Annette and Emily are living there now," Beth says. "We've made a policy that you must be 18 and finish secondary school to move into one of them. The younger kids are kind of bitching about it, though, but at this point, I'm keeping them at the house."

"Is the plan for all the units to be long term rentals?" Olivia asks.

"No," Abe replies, "We are going to keep 1/2 of the units as daily or weekly rentals for the retreat events which we are planning on hosting."

Beth whistles at Six to come back. The dog has drifted a little further ahead of them than Beth likes. Six turns and comes back.

"What kind of retreats?" Olivia asks as they move on toward the old government center.

"The Historical Society is going to begin having 4 or 5 sessions starting next year," Abe says. "I've talked to Swansea University, and they are thinking of maybe doing as many as ten."

"Molly has been working with Extension on retreats as well," Beth says. "They have committed to five, but Molly thinks that will at least double over twelve months."

"Where are the sessions for these retreats going to happen?" Olivia asks.

"There is a 5000 square foot meeting center being built as we speak," Abe replies. "It ought to be finished sometime in November. There is also a good-sized gymnasium and indoor/outdoor pools which won't be finished until February."

"Angelique said you guys were making some big changes up here," Olivia says. "Is it okay to go in and look around on my way out?"

"Sure," Beth says, "if you want, I'll call Annette when we are back at the house and have her give you a little tour."

"That would be great," Oliva says.

They walk in silence for a few minutes over the steep section of the ascent to the old government center parking lot.

"Let's go look at how they are coming with Sam and Sallie's restaurant and the castle," Abe suggests.

They walk toward the old government center building but cannot get close as there are wire fences in place in the construction areas. The castle itself looks to be generally unchanged from Reginald's cold, imposing, somber, original construction.

"How soon is all this supposed to be ready?" Olivia asks. "The Historical Society portion is complete except for a few things on the inside," Abe says. "They are planning on opening the second week of December."

"Sallie says the restaurant will be ready to go by mid-January," Beth says. "The theater is almost done but they won't open until February when the Island Resort's Hotel and Casino are up and running."

"Want to walk over and see how they are doing there?" Abe asks.

"I'm game if you are," Olivia says to Beth.

"I think I'm up to it." Beth says as they begin moving down the now paved roadway to the quarry.

"This is the first time I've been out here since they started construction," Beth says. "I knew they were planning on building right into the quarry but had no idea it would integrate as well as has."

Island Resorts has built their hotel almost seamlessly into what had been the open portion of the quarry. The casino, an almost entirely glass structure is in front of it. Dark granite taken from the quarry has been used to create a variety of statues of characters from Wannasea history and legend as one approaches the broad expanse of the main casino and hotel entrances.

"It's quite impressive," Olivia says.

"It's how our ancestors should have built the castle," Abe says. "That's if they had had any artistic sense."

"The Reginalds did dark and brooding," Beth says. "I don't think this resort fits their style."

CHAOS

Tuesday, October 15, 6:54PM. Beth sits in the island council chamber along with the 6 other newly elected council members. Olivia and Beth are the two representatives from the Mountain Centrist Party. There are three members of the Farmworker's Progressive Party now on the council. Two members of the Fisherman's Conservative Party round out the group of seven. Lieutenant Governor Ron Waller, who will conduct the opening for the 50th session of the council, is standing at a podium beside the raised council member seating section.

Abe, who has come to the council session while Marie watches the twins, is seated in the second row of seats beside Angelique, Roberta Johnson, and Vic Newton. A little more than half of the seating is occupied.

On Sunday, Beth had attended a dinner with Marie as her guest hosted by the Governor at his residence along with the other council members. She had been sworn into office by the Governor in a ceremony just prior to the dinner.

Suddenly a disturbance arises from the outside the doorway leading into the council chamber.

"You cannot bring those signs into this meeting," a voice shouts from outside the doors.

Increasing loud chants of "God's way is the only way" can be heard coming toward the chamber before the oak doors burst open and a long line of protesters lead by Edgar Ainsley carrying a bullhorn enters the chamber.

"Stop these illegal proceedings," Edgar Ainsley shouts through an electronic megaphone. "You are in violation of the Constitution of the Island of Wannasea. None of the people seated as council representative are valid. None have been certified by the Island

Council of Churches which I represent. All must be removed and replaced by the only representatives authorized by God, the members of the Party of New Jericho." "You are out of order sir," the lieutenant governor shouts back at Ainsley. "I call upon you to seat yourself and your group. We will address your compliant in the due course of this council meeting."

"You will address my complaint now," Ainsley says approaching the podium. "This is an illegal council meeting with invalid members of the council. You will either swear in the properly certified individuals or I will be forced to take over this meeting."

Ron Waller backs away from the podium and summons a member of the constabulary, who serves as the sergeant-at-arms for island council meetings. After a brief whispered discussion, the sergeant-at-arms pulls a two-way radio from his belt and says, "Now".

"You are in violation of not only God's law," Ainsley shouts through his bullhorn, "you are in violation of your own written laws."

Approximately twenty island police officers rush through the side entrance to the chamber and position themselves along the walls. They are arrayed against what appear to be almost 100 supporters of Ainsley.

"You will either sit down and be quiet until you are called upon," Waller says loudly from the podium, "or you will be removed."

"I will neither sit down nor be silenced," Ainsley shouts through the bullhorn moving closer to the podium. "I demand to speak with the Governor!"

"I am the Governor's representative," Waller shouts back. "You will either sit down and obey protocols or I will have you and the rest of your group arrested and charged with civil disobedience." "I will not be silenced," Ainsley turns and shouts to his followers. "This man is an affront to God and his laws!"

"This meeting will now be a closed session," the lieutenant governor announces. "Officers, please remove all attendees, who are not council members."

"Those sinful abominations on the stage are not valid council members!" Ainsley cries through the bullhorn. "The rightful council members are these seven members of God's Army."

Ainsley points to the first seven people directly behind him, all of whom had been candidates for council of the various wards from the New Jericho Party.

"Officers," Waller says loudly, "please clear the room."

The Officers and sergeant-at-arms move toward Ainsley and his protesters. As they pass the people, not associated with New Jericho, they inform them that they must leave the chamber as well.

"Have you ever seen anything like this before?" Abe asks Angelique.

Angelique shakes her head negatively as they follow the rest of the milling crowd out the oak doors and into the hallway. Once in the foyer, Angelique takes Abe's arm and guides him down the left hallway away from the main entrance. They duck into an entrance marked "Legal Affairs".

The assembled officers gradually force Ainsley and his followers out of the council chambers through the foyer and into the parking lot.

"God will punish you," Ainsley continues to call out with his bullhorn from the first row of parked cars. "Seat God's chosen council members not the candidates of Satan! God's way is the only way!"

"Any idea what that is all about?" Abe asks Angelique.

"Seems Ainsley or one of his lot dug up an obscure election reference stating that any who run for office must be approved by the Island Council of Churches," Angelique says. "There hasn't been a "Council of Churches" for forty years, so Ainsley appointed himself and ten of his church members to be a "Council of Churches" and filed with the island incorporation office as such."

"Does Ainsley saying the elected council members are invalid have any standing?" Abe asks.

"Perhaps prior to the election occurring," Angelique says. "Once the election has occurred and the results have been validated, it is too late."

Angelique peers around the corner to view the now empty hallway aside from two police office standing in front of the closed entrance to the council chambers. "I suspect the Governor knew this was coming," Angelique says. "That's the only way that many members of the constabulary get into the chamber that fast. It's also a little odd that the council members were sworn in last night at the Governor's dinner. The swearing-in is usually done by the Lieutenant Governor right after he opens the first session."

"Strange days," Abe says shaking his head.

"Strange days indeed," Angelique says as she pulls her cellphone from her jacket pocket and begins preparing a text to her father. Once complete, she says to Abe, "Let's go out and see if the officers will verify that everything is okay inside the chamber."

Abe follows her down the hallway to the chamber entrance.

"I'm afraid you cannot go in Miss Stolz, " the officer in front of the right door says to Angelique. "We have been told that they will not be reopening tonight's session to the public."

"Is everyone in there, okay?" Angelique asks.

"They are all fine," the officer says.

Realizing that the news of Ainsley's invasion of the council session has probably reached the house, Abe pulls out his cellphone and sends a text to Marie that everything is now under control and Beth is fine.

Angelique walks over to the wide stairway to the right of the chamber entrance which leads to the upper floors.

"Mind if we hang out here?" Angelique asks the guards. "We're always happy to have you hanging out with us," the guard by the left door says with smile.

Angelique walks up three steps, turns, and then sits down. Abe follows her actions. Where they are seated is out of the view of Ainsley and his protesters.

"Ainsley is a real nuisance," Abe says.

"I think that it is much more than just being a nuisance at this point," Angelique says. "I'm honestly beginning to believe Ainsley thinks that he can actually take control of this island."

"With less than three hundred active church members?" Abe asks.

"Unfortunately, we seem to be on a path toward finding out," Angelique says with a small grimace before returning to her cellphone.

The next five minutes are spent in relative silence until Angelique asks, "What do you know about Ray Simmons?"

"He wrote that Hanover Herald article about Zack," Abe says. "He's now dating Zack's sister. He seems to be nice enough guy."

"Do you know anything about the dirt that he is digging up on Ainsley?" Angelique asks.

"I've heard that he is working on some kind of article about New Jericho, but beyond that, no."

"He has been talking to Olivia and Dad, a lot the past few weeks," Angelique says. "If what Ray Simmons has told them about Ainsley's actions prior to coming to the island are true, I cannot understand how

Ainsley avoided prosecution on the Mainland. It seems the Mainland's criminal justice system ignored complaints against Ainsley and were more than happy when he moved his church out to our island."

"Isn't your father pretty well plugged into the Judiciary over in Hanover and Halifax?" Abe asks. "Wouldn't he know?"

"Dad isn't quite as plugged in as he used to be," Angelique says, "and everyone that he's talked with over there has said to stay away from the subject."

"What kind of connections does Ainsley have?" Abe asks.

Angelique shrugs her shoulders.

Angelique goes back to her cellphone for the next few minutes before Abe says, "There are four new kids, who came from New Jericho, which Beth and Marie have brought in to live with us over the past month. They are nice kids, but they are extremely tight-lipped and defensive about anything which happened to them at the Temple."

"Do you know if Ray Simmons has talked with them?" Angelique asks.

"I believe that he has," Abe says.

After twenty minutes, the chanting of "God's way is the only way" from the parking lot has ceased.

Abe and Angelique spend two more hours talking mainly about family history, taking occasionally walks down the hallway and using their cellphones. Finally, the chamber doors are pushed open from the inside and the council members begin coming into the foyer. Beth is fourth in line behind Olivia.

Angelique and Abe rise for the steps to greet them. After Abe gives Beth a hug, Beth says, "That was wild."

Abe nods his head as they walk out to the mainly deserted parking lot. After saying "goodnight" to Olivia, Angelique and some of the council members, Abe leads Beth to her VW van.

"Why don't you drive?" Beth says to Abe. "That session has me worn out."

"Were you able to get anything accomplished?" Abe asks.

"We've started a committee on formulating a referendum to change many of the island's rules," Beth says.

"Who was elected Council Chair?" Abe asks.

"Betty Furness," Beth says. "She's on board for getting this referendum rolling as soon as we can."

"How much time did you spend talking about Ainsley?" Abe asks.

"The entire first half hour," Beth says. "Thanks to Ainsley, there will now be only 1 island council session per quarter which is open to the public."

CHANGING PLANS

Thursday, November 16, 8:14PM. Beth is seated in the living room of the house on the sofa chair reviewing an email from Steve Harmony. The email outlines proposed changes to the units being built at 'Tiny House Village' to accommodate a limited number of larger structures. The larger units would contain a full bathroom and kitchenette with oven and stovetop. Harvey email is suggesting that these larger units be built behind the patio area of the Meeting Center to keep them somewhat separated from the single- and double-unit areas. Beth has requested plans for such units with the thought of using them to house homeless mothers with small children.

Having had Arlette come to work twice in the past two months with bruises, Beth and Marie have decided the 'Tiny House Village' needs such structures. Arlette's had told Beth that the first bruising was the result of having slipped and fallen while chasing Gabriel. When two blackened eyes were added to the bruises two weeks later, Arlette admitted that her husband had beaten her. Arlette had then stayed with Gabriel at the house for four days before rejecting Beth's advice to seek counsel from the Island's Family Services and returning to her husband.

The two episodes had caused the request for Harmony to develop a plan for larger structures able to serve as a refuge for in-danger women with children. After learning of their need, Steve Harmony discussed a variety of options with them. Beth and Marie had settled on changing out 10 of the single units for what will eventually be 8 larger 600 square foot units to house those such as Arlette, who are in need. Beth is in the process of finalizing the materials to be used for the bathrooms in these units. After completing her selections, Beth emails them to Steve Harmony.

Beth had just put the twins to sleep in their cribs located in Marie's old bedroom at 8PM after giving them their bottles. Since the Twins' arrival, Beth's normal practice had become to lay down on the bed in their room after she put them to sleep until Marie came back from work at 'The Place'. She's decided tonight to end that practice, believing that checking every 10 minutes to see that the babies are okay is neither good for the Twins nor herself.

Beth shifts to reviewing her emails related to the Island Council. Two weeks ago, the council had approved having an island referendum on changes to the legal code. The referendum will occur on Jan. 14th. Olivia, Betty Furness, and Beth have taken it upon themselves to be the primary supporters of the changes. Beyond receiving approval for the referendum, the past five island council meetings have been one Ainsley driven circus after another. When a closed session occurs, Ainsley shows up with what he terms "God's approved council members" and tries to have them seated. The one open-to-the-public session which the island council had tried to conduct in the last week of October turned into another fiasco. Ten of Ainsley's followers were arrested and charged with public disturbance after chaining themselves to theater-style seats in the front of the Council Chamber. The council had been lucky to have forty minutes to deal with actual business during that meeting as even after Ainsley and those arrested were removed, more Ainsley followers came into the chamber and disrupted the proceedings with shouts and threats. Despite the Governor issuing a new policy on council session behavior and having conducted two private council sessions at his residence, council members are frustrated that valid concerns of their constituents are not being heard. Beth has taken to having a 90-minute open session at 'The Place' on Monday evenings, the day before normally scheduled council meetings. Beth has been encouraging Ward 6 residents to attend via both the Mountain Party website and her Ward 6 email list. The result has been a flood of new emails into her inbox. Fortunately, neither Ainsley nor his followers have shown up to disrupt the Ward 6 sessions at 'The Place'.

The front door of the house swings open and Marie's brother Josh comes into the living room.

"Looking for Judith?" Beth asks.

"No," Josh, who has just completed his last class of the evening at Wannasea Extension says. "I'm kind of hoping that I might have a few minutes to talk with you before Judith gets here."

"Sure," Beth says, her curiosity rising, "what would you like to talk about?"

Josh walks to the couch and sits down on the side closest to Beth.

"I'm really getting worried about Randy," Josh says referring to his younger brother, who lives with his mother at the New Jericho Temple.

"Have you talked to Marie about it?" Beth asks.

Josh shakes his head, then says, 'I'm worried that Marie will get angry, go down to New Jericho and things will only get worse for Randy."

"Okay," Beth says hesitantly, "why don't you tell me what it is exactly that has you concerned about Randy."

"Randy is telling me about all sorts of weird things which are going on down there. Randy and other kids are being forced to do things which they don't want to do. Randy says that he is going to be forced to drop out of his last year of secondary school come the first of the year. Prophet Ainsley is opening a New Jericho School out on the west end and anyone belonging to the Temple has to go there and basically be home schooled."

Beth closes her laptop and puts it on the side table.

"Do you know what these weird things are and if any of them might be illegal?" Beth asks shifting in the chair so that she is looking directly at Josh.

"Randy won't talk about them," Josh says. "Other than to tell me that they are just getting weirder and more disgusting."

"Does Randy want to leave the Temple?" Beth says. "If he does, he can stay with us. I'm pretty sure Prisha and Sallie can find a job for him at 'The Place'."

"I don't think Randy is ready to do that yet," Josh says. "He's worried about my mom. She now gives the Temple everything she makes. She won't say a word against Ainsley. Anything Ainsley does is fine with her."

"Have you asked Randy to come out here to live with you?" Beth asks.

"I have, but Randy still thinks that he can talk some sense into my mom and get her out of there."

"Have you talked to your mom?" Beth asks.

"She won't even look at me much less talk," Josh says. "The three times that I've seen her this past year, she has yelled at me and told me that Marie and I are dead not only in her eye's but in God's eyes."

"That's rough," Beth says reaching over and patting Josh on the arm. "All that I can suggest is to keep reminding Randy that he's welcome here and that if anything harmful or illegal is happening, he needs to go to the Constabulary."

"I'm pretty sure Randy wouldn't go to the Constabulary, no matter what happens," Josh says.

"Then keep telling him that he can come to you about anything which happens," Beth says rising from the sofa chair. "Whatever it is, I'll help you work it out. You want something to drink?" "I wouldn't mind a can of Coke," Josh replies.

Beth goes into the kitchen. Walks to the drawer on the other side of the sink and pulls out a 3"X5" memo pad and pen. She then goes to the refrigerator for a can of coke and a bottle of water, before returning to the living room. She hands the can of Coke over to Josh before sitting back down on the sofa chair. She sets her bottle of water on the side table and picks up her cellphone. After finding Jack Druce's number in her contacts, Beth writes it down with his name on the top page of the memo pad. Beth tears off the top page and hands it to Josh.

"Please give his name and number to Randy," Beth says. "If there is anything which Ralph believes is illegal or potentially harmful, tell him to call it. I will make sure that Jack is aware of Randy's situation."

Josh takes the paper, folds it and puts it into his wallet.

"Have you or Randy talked anyone else except you about his concerns over New Jericho Temple?" Beth asks as she hands Josh the can of Coke.

"Randy met with a fellow named Ray Simmons once," Josh says. "But I think Randy has told him even less than he has told me. Randy also talked to that Smythe lady from the island newspaper."

"Valerie Smythe?" Beth asks her curiosity raised.

"Yes," Josh replies. "Randy says that she is really nice. I have no idea what he has told her about the Temple."

Josh takes a sip from his can of Coke, then says, "Please promise me that you won't mention this conversation to Marie."

"I won't talk with Marie about it," Beth replies, "but you need to promise me that that the minute you believe that things are beginning to get worse, you will let me know."

"I promise."

Beth puts the memo pad and pen on top of her laptop and picks up the bottle of water. She takes a long sip before saying to Josh, "I think that just being there for Randy is what he needs right now. Hopefully if something dangerous begins happening, he will talk to you about it."

"I hope so too," Josh replies.

A POWDER KEG

Saturday, December 7, 10:22AM. Beth is helping Arlette put the twins down for their morning nap after their feeding. She hears her cell phone, which is on the side table near the sofa chair in the living room ring. She gently places Julia in her crib, then fast walks into the living room to grab her phone. She notices the caller is Olivia.

"Hey Olivia," Beth says into her cell phone, "what's up?"

"Have you seen the news?" Olivia says excitedly.

"No," Beth says, "I've been tending the twins since a little after 6 this morning."

"Turn on the Island News Channel," Olivia says, "Angelique and I will be out to see you in just a little bit."

"I'm kind of a mess," Beth says.

"Don't worry about that," Olivia says, "we just need to talk. See you in ten minutes."

The call disconnects from Beth's cell phone.

Beth takes the television and satellite remote from the coffee table. She turns on the tv and mutes the sound, then uses the guide to select WWIN, the island's news channel. The chyron at the bottom of the screen announces, "PROPHET AINSLEY AND SIX SENIOR MEMBERS OF NEW JERICHO TEMPLE INDICTED ON 35 COUNTS".

Beth switches off the television, picks up her cell phone and laptop from the side table by the sofa and walks into the kitchen, where Arlette is making coffee.

"I am going over to Abe's" Beth whispers to Arlette. "If you need anything just knock on Abe's door or text me."

Beth exits the sliding glass door which leads out of the kitchen area and walks across the patio to Abe's in-law suite. Abe is seated at his kitchen table writing in a green journal. Beth knocks on the glass. Abe rises, unlocks the door, and pulls it back.

"What brings you over here?" Abe asks Beth as she comes in through the sliding door.

"You've got to come see this," Beth says walking past Abe and going into the living room area of Abe's in-law suite where his seldom used television resides.

After fiddling with the inputs, Beth manages to bring up WWIN on the screen.

"Ainsley has allegedly been engaged in trafficking minors for the purposes of sex and extortion," the tv announcer says. "Ainsley and senior church members are being detained in the Island Constabulary Holding Facility without bail."

As Abe sits down on the couch, Beth places her laptop on his coffee table. Beth then texts Olivia to let her know that she is in Abe's in-law suite.

For the next five minutes Beth and Abe listen to the television announcers describe the arrests at New Jericho Temple at 7AM this morning. The news channel flashes a video of what appears to be dozens of Ainsley's supporters now outside of the holding facility demanding Ainsley's immediate release. When the channel switches to the weather report, Beth mutes the sound.

"Olivia and Angelique are coming," Beth says.

"When did you find out about this?" Abe asks as he walks into the kitchen and fills up his electric water kettle.

"About two minutes before you did," Beth replies. "Olivia called me and told me to turn on the news channel."

Beth joins Abe in the kitchen helping to prepare a tea tray which Beth carries into the living room area and sets down on Abe's coffee table.

"Let's hope this is the end of Ainsley," Abe says from the kitchen.

A knock comes from the sliding glass door. Abe walks around the kitchen counter and slides the door open allowing Angelique and Olivia to enter. They are carrying newspapers.

"Let's sit over in the living room so we can see the television," Beth says to her cousins.

Angelique hands Beth a copy of the Hanover Herald, whose bold headline says, "The Walls of New Jericho Come Tumbling Down". Olivia gives Abe a copy of 'The Islander' which has the same headline. Immediately below is the first half-page of a story by Ray Simmons and Valerie Smythe which outlines the history of Ainsley's New Jericho Temple, sexual abuse and trafficking as well as links in the highest circles of Mainland government.

Olivia lays down a copy of Halifax Times which contains the same headline. In addition to the story filling the first half of the front page. Simmons and Smythe's story continues on the next two full pages in each newspaper.

As Abe and Beth read through the story, Olivia and Angelique pour tea and sit down on Abe's couch. The gist of the story is that during the five years when Edgar Ainsley operated his church in an area just north of Halifax, he had begun a process of indoctrinating select 12–16-year-old church members both male and female to serve as "Spiritual Guides". These spiritual guides were trained in performing sexual services designed to bring the rich and powerful into the arms of New Jericho Temple. One of the first individuals the guides managed to entrap was the longtime head of the Mainland's Domestic Intelligence division. Ainsley's sexual outreach had expanded to entrap a prince, two other royals, three members of the House of Lords, MPs, and various other foreign and domestic government representatives. Two years back, when three children selected to become spiritual guides had gone to their parents and then local authorities, the Head of Domestic Intelligence had been key in having the charges dropped in return for the New Jericho Temple leaving the Mainland. Ainsley had then moved both his church and his |Spiritual Guide" operation to Wannasea Island. Ainsley's spiritual guide business has only grown since the Temple's arrival on the island with the Head of Intelligence assisting in the spread of its services and collection of recordings associated with powerful figures.

"Seems Simmons and Smythe have solved the riddle of how Ainsley got away with what he did over on the Mainland," Olivia says. "What their story doesn't say is how serious Ainsley's ambition to take over this island is."

"How could Ainsley take over the island with only two hundred members or so?" Abe asks.

"Keep in mind that the only thing which this island really has protecting it is a police force of about 100 officers and the goodwill of the Mainland Military," Angelique says. "Considering Ainsley has at least another two or three hundred highly committed followers on the Mainland and all sorts of incriminating materials of people in high places, I'd suggest Wannasea Island may well still be at serious risk."

"I spoke with Ron Waller earlier this morning," Olivia says, "he indicates that Ainsley has been bringing weapons and explosives on to the island. The Constabulary hasn't been able to track down more than a little of what Ainsley has allegedly been able to bring in."

"Is the Mainland going to do anything to help us?" Beth asks.

Wannasea Island is a protectorate of the Mainland. The island, though having local autonomy, is dependent upon the Mainland to provide security and protection. Currently there are no Mainland bases or forces on the island other than 8 Mainland security officers, who work on a day-to-day basis with the Constabulary primarily on customs and importation issues.

"The Governor is working frantically to have the Mainland send some type of force out here," Olivia says. "That is part of the reason that we have come out to talk with you. The Governor would like to use the facilities up at the old government center. The parking lot, the inner courtyard of the castle and your parking lot for your retreat area. The estimate is that it will be needed for 9-12 weeks. The Governor hopes the Mainland will send at least 500 troops."

"I'm okay with that but will need to clear it with my lessees," Beth says.

"You can speak with them," Olivia says, "but you cannot mention anything about arms or explosives."

"We won't" Beth says.

"I will call up Steve DeJean and arrange things with the Historical Society," Abe says.

"I will take care of Island Resorts and Sallie," Beth says. "We could also give them our Mobile Kitchen if that will help."

"Let me call Ron Waller," Angelique says as she walks toward the kitchen to place her call.

Abe goes into his bedroom to call the Wannasea Historical Society as Beth walks out the front door. Beth leaves a message for Jay Cuthbert before calling Sallie. Beth remains vague with Sallie about the reason that there will be a delay in the start of her lease, but Sallie doesn't seem terribly upset by it.

"I'm waiting for a call back from Island Resorts," Beth says, "but Sallie is okay with a few weeks delay in opening."

Olivia immediately dials Ron Waller and lets him know aside from Island Resorts' approval; the old government center area can be used as temporary troop placement.

Abe comes out of the bedroom and goes to his desk where he sits down.

"The Historical Society is going to delay their grand opening until mid-March," Abe says. "Steve DeJean will do whatever he can to assist when troops get here."

"There is going to be a special council session at the Governor's Residence at 5PM tonight," Olivia says to Beth. "The purpose of the meeting will be discussing the situation with New Jericho and possibly deciding to offer to permanently host troops from the Mainland on the island."

Abe grimaces, "This island has long tried to avoid having a Mainland military presence here Too many islanders see having troops station here as an incursion on Wannasea's limited sovereignty."

"We are all aware," Olivia says, "but maybe the threat of having someone like Ainsley trying to take over the island by force will change attitudes."

"Still will likely be a hard sell," Abe comments.

"Do you know if any actions have been taken over on the Mainland about those associated with Ainsley?" Beth asks.

"I know that Head of the Domestic Intelligence Service plus two of his aides are now in custody," Angelique replies. "They are claiming that all their actions with Ainsley are covered under their charter as a domestic surveillance entity. Not sure how far they can get with that defense."

"What about all those people who Ainsley supposedly recorded?" Beth asks.

"Like last time, they are hoping that this will go away fast without anything being revealed about their own dealings with Ainsley," Angelique replies.

"Is that possible?" Abe asks.

"Seems unlikely with what Simmons and Smythe have disclosed," Angelique says, "but stranger things have happened."

Abe's cell phone rings. It is Hugh calling.

"It's Hugh," Abe says, "I'm going to take it."

"Remember nothing about the weapons or explosives," Olivia reminds Abe as he rises from his desk chair and goes out the front door.

"How much risk do you think the island now has from Ainsley?" Beth asks.

"Not as much as it would be if Ainsley was actually able to have pulled off some type of assault," Olivia says. "What we don't know is how crazy Ainsley's followers are likely to get now that Ainsley is in custody."

"Do you know why Simmons and Smythe came out with this story now?" Beth asks.

"The rumor going around is they have been sitting on their report since the end of last month at the request of the Constabulary," Angelique says. "Somehow higher ups in the Mainland got wind of it early last week, so they had no choice but to release."

"There is also the element that Ainsley is supposedly planning to launch his attack on Dec.23 at the last council meeting of this calendar year," Angelique says.

"Do you think we are in physical danger?" Beth asks.

"Ainsley's followers with automatic weapons in the council chamber," Olivia says. "I don't like our odds in that scenario."

Beth receives an incoming call from Jay Cuthbert on her cellphone. She answers it and begins explaining the situation. Cuthbert tells Beth that as they currently have no plans to open either of their venues before the first week in March, his only worry would be making certain construction workers can access the casino. Beth passes that question on to Olivia.

"Let's have Ron Waller talk with him," Olivia suggests, "so that we aren't in the middle of something we can't control."

Beth informs Cuthbert that Ron Waller will call him to work out his concerns. By the time she hung up, Olivia has texted Waller and gotten him to call Cuthbert.

Abe comes back in from the patio and returns to his desk chair.

"Hugh knew more than I did," Abe says. "Seems the Mainland is sending a troop ship out here with 300 Marines on it. 250 of those troops will be coming to the old government center tomorrow."

"Did Hugh know about the weapons and explosives?' Angelique asks.

"He did," Abe replies. "There are at least 75 AK-47 type weapons and 10,000 rounds of ammunition plus four cases of various sizes of military grade explosives now floating around this island in the hands of Ainsley's people."

OCCUPATION

Tuesday, December 10, 9:14AM. Beth and Marie are seated at the patio table closest to the parking area of the house. The twins are with them in their pram. Zack is leaning over the pram trying to make the babies smile.

"These guys are too serious," Zack says before sitting down on the chair at end of the patio table.

"Being a baby is serious business," Marie tells Zack. "It's a lot of hard work training your parents to respond immediately to your every whim."

"Guess it is," Zack says. "Would you guys mind if I use "the Shell" next Monday and Tuesday nights to have free concerts for the troops?"

Yesterday, 125 Mainland Marines had set up camp at or near the parking lot of the 'Tiny House Village'. There are another 85 Marines and two helicopters in the parking lot of the old government center. In addition to the physical troop presence on the island, the Mainland has positioned an Albion-class transport off the South Islands as well as 30 troops bivouacked at the new government facility plus another 25 at the Constabulary.

"Did you ask Molly about it?" Marie asks. "Molly is the event planner now."

"She said I need approval from you guys," Zack says.

"I'm all for it," Marie says.

"That's a terrific idea Zack," Beth says. "We are even willing to throw in free coffee and drinks."

Zack pulls out his cell phone and sends a text to Molly letting her know that he has gotten approval for the performances.

"How is that new studio of yours working out?" Marie asks Zack.

"Great," Zack says. "We've finally got everything set up. We did two recordings of island groups yesterday. You guys ought to come out and look at it when you have a chance."

"Abe says that you are working on some new songs," Beth says.

"We are," Zack says. "I'm trying to get Abe to help me pull a new blues album together centered around the people, who I knew in Iraq. It's been a hard slog so far. We keep getting distracted by what's going on here on the island."

"Along with everyone else," Beth says, "but it does seem to be getting better. Olivia told me this morning that there are only about ten Temple of Jericho protesters at the holding facility now."

"Might have something to do with a squad of Marines being there all the time now," Zack says.

"Probably does," Beth says, "Marines are also now camped out in the shopping center where the New Jericho Temple is located."

"It's pretty quiet on the rest of the island though," Zack says.

"Are you going to get rid of your Bug?" Marie asks, hoping to move the subject away from AInsley.

Zack continues to drive around the VW Beetle which was shot up during the blaster ball attack. It is currently parked beside Beth's VW Caddy in the parking area.

"Absolutely not," Zack says. "I've come to realize that my Bug makes a perfect statement about who I am and how I approach life."

"I take it then that you aren't planning on taking up dating anytime soon?" Marie says.

"To love me," Zack says with mock gravity, "you need to love my Beetle."

Beth and Marie laugh.

"Saanvi and Ray are getting pretty serious," Zack says. "I think Ray is going to propose to her before Christmas."

"You okay with that?" Beth asks.

"Sure," Zacks says returning to seriousness. "Saanvi deserves to be happy, and I think Ray makes her happy."

"He's certainly sent shockwaves through here and the Mainland with his New Jericho article," Marie says.

"Without Ray's article, do you think Ainsley's arrest would have generated as much interest as it has?" Zack asks.

"Probably not," Beth replies. "At a minimum, those who were made part of Ainsley's 'Spiritual Guide' recruitment would probably once again stay out of the public's view."

"Abe says there are some very high-ranking people being interviewed by the police over on the Mainland now," Zack says.

"There should be," Marie says. "I'm also thinking that any parent of a minor, who allowed Ainsley to use their children as his 'Spiritual Guides', should not only be interviewed but should be charged."

Abe comes out the sliding glass door of his in-law suite and exchanges greetings with everyone. He walks over to the pram and investigates the twins, who have now drifted off to sleep.

"I swear they are getting bigger by the day," Abe says.

"Three months old now Grandpa," Beth says. "They won't stay babies forever."

Abe pats Zack on the shoulder as he walks to the table and takes an empty seat beside Beth.

"Hugh asked if you want to have a surveillance system put in at the "Tiny House Village' once things settle down?" Abe says.

"With the possibility of irate spouses wandering around when we get the family facilities finished, it's almost a necessity," Beth says.

Julia awakens and lets out a sharp cry.

"Want me to take them for a walk?" Zack asks.

"Let me check to see if they are still dry," Marie responds. "Then I'll go with you if you go out by the lakes."

"Deal," Zack says.

Marie rises and checks the twins' diapers. Finding that they are dry, Marie motions for Zack to come follow her as she pushes the pram toward the parking area as Six follows at her heels.

"Odd that I have begun to find it kind of comforting to have all these Marines milling about up here," Abe says. " Even if it will set back the completion of the Meeting Center by a few weeks."

"Small price to pay for safety," Beth comments. "Seems Ainsley's followers have settled down somewhat."

"I think they ought to take Ainsley and the others over to the Mainland," Abe says.

"So does the Governor," Beth replies, "but nothing can be done to indict them until an investigation and charges can be filed on the Mainland. Seeing as how some of those charges involve the Mainland Domestic Security Division, that is unlikely to happen before early next year."

"Any progress on tracking down Ainsley's guns and explosives?" Abe asks.

"Not so far," Beth says, "The Constabulary is working on it 24 hours a day."

"Let's hope however it works out, we've seen and heard the last from Ainsley," Abe says.

After a few moments of silence, Beth says, "When I went to the first island council session, I started asking myself how crazy I was for agreeing to be a candidate for council. Beyond wanting to change some archaic laws, I really didn't have any reason for being there."

"You are still feeling that way?" Abe asks.

"I won't say that the thought still doesn't cross my mind," Beth admits. "I've also begun to discover that if I continue to listen to my constituents and keep the island's best interests in mind, I actually may be able do some good for this island."

Abe smiles broadly.

"I been doing a little thinking," Beth says. "I've decided to take some on-line courses at the Extension which should allow me to combine my existing credits together to get a degree in general studies at the end of the next term."

"That's wonderful," Abe says.

"I'm thinking that if I can pull that off," Beth says. "I'm going to look into getting into a program to earn a master's degree in public administration."

GONE IN SECONDS

Friday, December 13, 12:21PM. Beth is seated at a conference table in the Stolz law office in the village of Wannasea. Olivia and Betty Furness are with her. The trio are working on plans for publicizing the coming vote to change the island's legal system.

"I'd suggest that we stick with passing out flyers and newspaper advertisements until Christmas is over,' Betty Furness suggests. "Hardly anyone is going to give any thought to the referendum until Christmas has passed."

"Particularly as long as the island continues to have Edgar Ainsley hanging over our head," Olivia says.

"Will we start scheduling radio and television advertisements on Dec. 26?" Beth asks.

"Sounds about right," Betty Furness.

"What do you think about sending out an email notification to registered voters?" Beth asks. "I think we could make the notification like the normal voting reminders which we do before elections."

"Sounds good to me," Betty Furness says. "Olivia are you okay with that?"

"Sure," Olivia says. "Let's put one together to send early next week. Then we'll do another one on Jan. 2 as well as one early on the day before the referendum."

Beth's cell phone rings. She reaches in her purse and pulls it out. Noticing that the call is from Marie, Beth says, "I need to take this."

Beth rises from the conference table and accepts Marie's call.

"Hi Marie" Beth says as she turns away from the conference table and walks toward the hallway. "What's up?"

"Somebody has taken our babies," Marie says in a panicked voice.

"What?" Beth says incredulously.

"Somebody has taken off with our babies," Marie says. "Arlette came back from taking them for a walk about forty minutes ago. The twins were asleep, so she left them in the pram outside of the kitchen door to bring Gabriel into the kitchen to feed him. After feeding Gabriel, she went back out to the patio. The pram and the twins were gone."

Arlette had made it a routine to take the twins for a walk in the pram around 11AM on warm, clear days. She would put the twins in the pram, then place her baby Gabriel in a front-outward baby carrier slung around her torso. Arlette would then take all three babies for a walk. Usually on path around the lakes since the Marines had come.

"Is she sure Abe or Zack didn't take them for a walk?" Beth asks, trying to force herself to be calm.

"Abe and Zack were down at the recording studio in SouthTown," Marie says. "They are both now headed to the house."

"Did Abe call Defense One to see if they might have something on their surveillance system?" Beth asks.

"He's doing that on the way over," Marie says.

"Have you called the Constabulary?" Beth asks.

"Not yet."

"I'll be there in a few minutes," Beth says moving back into the conference room and grabbing up her purse.

Beth disconnects the call.

"I've got to go," Beth says in breathless voice. "Someone may have taken off with our babies."

"I'm coming with you," Olivia says rising from the table to join Beth.

"Please let me know when you find out what's going on," Betty Furness tells Beth as the pair disappear down the hallway.

Beth calls John Druce as she walks beside Olivia through the lobby of the law office and into the parking area.

"I'll drive," Olivia says motioning toward her BMW.

"Sorry to bother you John," Beth says into the speaker over her cell phone, "but it is possible that someone may have kidnapped my two babies."

Beth slides into the passenger seat as she explains to John Druce what Marie had told her. Druce tells her that he is coming to her house.

Olivia races through the streets of downtown Wannasea and turns up Mountain Way as Beth tries calling Abe, whose phone is busy. Beth then calls Zack.

"We are headed to your house," Zack tells Beth the second that her call is connected. "Abe is on his phone with Defense One. They have identified that someone made off with the pram less than three minutes after Arlette went into the kitchen."

"Okay," Beth says, not really being okay with the information which Zack has given her. "We will see you at the house."

Olivia does not bother to stop for the stop sign at the intersection of West Road and Mountain Way. She quickly swings her car right into the entrance for the place, then adeptly negotiates her vehicle up the driveway and into the parking area behind the house. As soon as the car is parked, the pair jump out of the vehicle and race across the patio and into the kitchen area of the house.

"I've called Jack Druce," Beth says. "He should be up here in a few minutes."

"Why would somebody take our babies?" Marie asks.

Beth thinks she knows why. All those reasons start and end with Edgar Ainsley.

Gabriel is still in his highchair. All the frantic activity has caused him to be unusually quiet.

"Let's get this guy cleaned up," Beth says walking to his highchair and pulling the now almost 15-month-old Gabriel from it.

Beth takes the child to the sink and uses warm water to rinse off his face.

Gabriel's mother is seated at the kitchen table, her head in her hands weeping.

Jack Druce knocks on the sliding door of the kitchen.

'Let me take him," Marie says to Beth as she pulls Gabriel from Beth's arms. "I'll take him into the studio."

Beth motions for Jack Druce to come inside as she walks up behind Arlette and gently pats her on the back. "This isn't your fault," Beth says to Arlette. "Can you tell Mr. Druce exactly what happened?"

Arlette raises her head as Jack Druce sits down in the chair beside her.

"Take your time," Jack Druce says as Arlette begins to compose herself. "Once you are ready, I would like for you to tell me as clearly as possible what you remember from the time that you took the babies for the walk. Particularly if you happened to pass or see any other people on the way."

Arlette takes a few moments to compose herself before saying, "We only passed two people along the way. Two ladies both wearing hooded sweatshirts seated on the bench at the upper lake."

"Did you recognize them?" Jack Druce asks gently.

"I didn't really pay much attention to them," Arlette says. "They both had on dark sweatshirts. Their hoods made it hard to see their faces. I didn't think anything of it at the time."

Abe and then Zack come in through the sliding glass door.

'Defense One is passing the audio and video off to the Constabulary," Abe says as he enters.

"Why don't we go into the living room?" Beth says to Abe, Zack, and Olivia. "That way Mr. Druce and Arlette can talk a little more easily."

Beth leads them through the wide portico entranceway from the kitchen and into the living room.

"So far," Abe says, "Defense One has not been able to do anything to identify who took off with the pram. The person did not have an active cell phone. The individual was obscured by the hood of their sweatshirt. It appears that person must have followed Arlette and the babies back from their walk. Within thirty seconds of Arlette going into the kitchen, the pram was grabbed, headed across the patio, through the parking lot, over the little rise and out on to Mountain Way. The cameras were only able to follow as far as the intersection of West Road. At that point, the pram was still being pushed toward the town."

"Arlette said she saw two ladies in hooded sweatshirts seated on a bench along the lake trail," Olivia says. "My guess would be those ladies were watching Arlette for a chance to snatch the Twins."

DEMANDS

Friday, December 13, 4:05PM. After Abe had received a copy of the Defense One video of the taking of the twins in their pram. Marie, Beth, Zack, and Abe have spent most of the past two hours trying to determine if they recognize the person dressed in very baggy, dark grey sweatpants and an overly large dark green sweatshirt with the hoodie pulled up, who had made off with the pram. It is extremely difficult to determine if the person is male or female, let alone any other recognizable features. Olivia had left around 2:30PM to see if there was anything she may be able to find out in town. Jack Druce, who has been in and out of the living room, is now in the kitchen talking to the head of the Constabulary's Investigative Division. Arlette, who continues to be traumatized over the disappearance of the twins, is now asleep in Marie's old bedroom with Gabriel.

"Olivia says that Constabulary has now restricted everyone inside the New Jericho Temple," Beth says as she reviews the text from her cousin. "The plan is to interview all of them in addition to scouring the place for anything related to the abduction."

Jack Druce comes into the living room, "Your pram has been brought into the Constabulary by two twelve-year-old boys. "

"With the Twins?" Marie interrupts excitedly.

"No," Jack Druce continues. "What was in the pram was a note which says that Prophet Ainsley plus the other six Brothers must be released from jail immediately as well as all the Marines off of Wannasea Island by 5PM tomorrow or the babies will never be seen again."

Marie screams. Despite herself, Beth begins to sob.

"Ainsley," Abe shouts, "is an evil bastard!"

"At least we can be fairly certain now that it is Ainsley's people, who have kidnapped your twins," Jack Druce says. "That at least gives us something to work on."

"What about the two kids, who brought the tram into the Constabulary?" Abe asks.

"They had just gotten out of the school up the hill from the Constabulary," Jack Druce says. "A man approached them with the pram and gave them each a $50 bill to deliver it to the desk sergeant inside the Constabulary. Aside from the man wearing sunglass and a black hoodie, the kids can't remember anything else other than being told that if they didn't deliver the pram to the Constabulary immediately, he'd know about it and track them down. He then showed them some type of handgun."

"New Jericho planned this," Abe says. "I'm going to call Defense One and have them review camera footage from her at the house to see if there have been any suspicious people lurking about in the past week."

"Already been done," Jack Druce tells Abe. "In the past ten days, there has not been an instance of anyone observing the house. Odds are that they were doing their observing on the trailways and basing their plan on the Arlette's routines."

The front doorbell rings.

"Let me get it," Jack Druce says walking toward the entrance door of the house.

A young boy around ten stands at the doorway holding out a small manilla envelope. Jack Druce reaches into his pocket and pulls out his constabulary identification.

"You are going to need to come inside," Druce instructs the young man. "How did you come to be delivering this envelop?" The youngster tells much the same story as the twelve-year olds have at the Constabulary. Jack Druce pulls out a pair of disposal vinyl gloves which he puts on before taking the envelop from the lad and carefully opening it.

"Same message as at the Constabulary," Druce says, before telling the boy. "You will need to come with me to talk with an investigator."

Druce and the boy walk through the living room and into the kitchen before going out the sliding glass door.

Beth's cell phone rings with a call from Olivia.

"The Governor just received a list of demands," Olivia tells Beth. "He wants to have a full council session at his residence at 7PM."

Beth informs Olivia of the demands also being delivered to the house and the Constabulary.

"I don't know if I should leave here," Beth says. "The instant there is any chance that the Twins are being brought back I want to be here for it."

"I really think that you can do more for the Twins by coming to the Council meeting, " Olivia says. "If you want, I'll come out and pick you up."

"Let me think it over," Beth says. "I will call you back by 5:30."

Beth disconnects Olivia's call and informs Marie, Zack, and Abe about the unscheduled Island Council session.

"I really think that you ought to go," Abe tells Beth. "You'll have the chance to represent the twins' interests in any decision which the Governor decides to make."

"Aside from worrying," Marie says, "Abe and I can take care of things here. Why don't you go to the council session?"

"Let me go out and ask Jack Druce what he thinks," Beth tells them.

"If you decide to go to the council meeting," Zack says. "I can drive you down there and wait for you."

Beth walks out of the living room area and into the kitchen. Jack Druce isn't there. She goes through the sliding glass door and out onto the patio. There are four Marines standing guard and three plain clothesmen examining things on the patio."

"Is Jack Druce out here?" Beth asks.

"He's over in the CVR," the plainclothesman closest to Beth replies. "Let me take you to him."

The detective guides Beth around the patio on the side closest to Abe's in-law suite then out into the parking area where a Fuchs CVR is parked.

"Lieutenant Druce," the plainclothesman says after knocking on the vehicle's door, "Ms. Stolz would like to speak with you."

Jack Druce climbs out of the vehicle. Beth explains Olivia's call and the 7PM Council meeting.

"You really should go," Druce advises. "At this point, this area is the last place where Ainsley's people are going to show up."

"Zack says he can drive me to it," Beth says.

"Not that I don't think Ralph is completely capable of protecting you," Druce says, "but until this is resolved you are going to always have at least two Marines with you. They will be escorting you to the council session. Just let me know what time you want to leave your house."

CONSEQUENCES

Saturday, December 14, 8:58AM. Everyone at the house has spent a mostly sleepless night. Abe is dozing at the far end of the couch. Marie has gone into the bedroom bathroom to shower. Beth is seated in the sofa chair with cell phone in hand reviewing messages. The Governor has scheduled another council meeting for noon. Council members have been asked to come up with a plan which will engage whoever is behind the demands which were received yesterday.

Josh, Marie's brother, rings the doorbell, then immediately comes through the front door trailed by his younger brother, Randy.

"Beth," Josh says somewhat breathlessly, "Randy has something that he needs to tell you."

Beth rises from her chair and walks toward the two youths.

"What is it, Randy?" Beth asks softly.

"I think my mother may have taken your babies," Randy says with downcast eyes.

"Why do you think that?" Beth asks with urgency rising in her voice.

"Last night she called me around 10PM," Randy said. "I heard a baby crying in the background. There is only 1 baby in the New Jericho Temple and my mom wasn't in the building."

Beth opens her cellphone and selects the video which Abe has sent of the twins' abduction. Beth shows the video to Randy.

"That's mom," Randy says. "That's the sweatshirt that she was wearing yesterday morning when I saw her before I left for school."

"You need to come with me Randy," Beth says. Then turning to Josh, tells him "Please stay here at the house with Marie but don't tell her what Randy has told us just yet. Make sure you keep your cell phone handy. Tell Marie that she needs to stay here and keep her phone with her at all times."

"Okay," Josh says as walks to the opposite end of the couch from Abe and sits down. "Where are you guys going?"

"I don't know yet," Beth says, "but I will let you know as soon as I have news."

Beth leads Randy out of the living room, through the kitchen and out on to the patio. Jack Druce is seated at the far patio table with two Marine officers. Beth guides Randy to the table.

"Jack," Beth says, "this is Marie's youngest brother Randy, who I have told you about. He has something very important to tell you regarding the Twins."

Jack Druce shakes Randy's hand then listens to the teenager's description of his telephone conversation with his mother last night.

"I've shown him the video from Defense One," Beth says. "Randy believes that it is his mother, who took the pram."

"Would you two come with down to the Constabulary?" Jack asks without really waiting for the pair to voice agreement.

"I'll contact you as soon as we have something on possible location," Druce tells the two Marines before rising and walking toward the parking lot.

Druce issues a loud whistle toward a police officer, who is lounging on the backside of the studio bathroom.

"Phil, I need you to drive us down to the Constabulary," Jack instructs the young policeman as he heads toward his vehicle in the parking lot.

"Can I have you mother's cell phone number?" Druce asks Randy.

Randy reads the number out from his cell phone. Druce reads it back to verify as they climb into the vehicle.

"Text me that number as we ride," Druce instructs Randy.

The four climb into Druce's vehicle and begin heading toward town. As they clear the lower part of the driveway, Druce calls the Head of the Investigative Division of the Constabulary.

"We have a probable identification of the abductor," Druce tells the official on the other end. "I'm going to text the contact information for that person to you."

Druce disconnects that call, pulls up the text which Randy has just sent him and forwards it to the person to whom he has just spoken.

"Was your mother with anybody else when you last saw her yesterday?" Jack Druce asks Randy.

"She was with Mrs. White when I left for school," Randy says. "They looked like they were going out for a walk."

"Do you know this Mrs. White's first name?" Druce asks.

"I believe that it is Hilda," Randy says. "Mom doesn't usually hang out with her. Hilda's one of the New Jericho people, who came over with Ainsley from the Mainland."

Druce texts the information which Randy has just provided to the head of the investigative division. As they enter the village of Wannasea, the young police officer turns on his siren and the flashing blue lights. In less than six minutes, they are parked at the entrance to the constabulary. Three tents are set up on the left entrance to the parking lot. At least ten Marines can be seen milling about near them.

"Let's go in," Druce says as he pulls open the passenger side door.

He leads Beth and Randy through the entrance to the Constabulary. Nods to the Desk Sergeant and two officers standing at the front desk before veering down the right hallway toward the entrance to the Investigative Division.

There are three constables of various ranks standing behind a command center, where an individual with Captain's insignia is studying a display.

"I think we've located her," the captain announces. "Brady, you take a vehicle out there and do a quick surveillance. We also need one of our patrol boats to do some quick surveillance from the waterside. Those observations must be done as inconspicuously as possible."

Two of the constables back away from the command center and head out the rear door.

"Can you hold down the command center, Jack?" the captain announces. "I need to go speak with the Chief."

"Sure," Jack says sitting down at the now vacated chair which the captain had just occupied. "Why don't you two grab a couple chairs and sit here beside me?"

Randy and Beth pull over two chairs from the back wall.

"Do you happen to remember if the lady, who was with your mother yesterday morning, was wearing a dark grey sweatshirt?" Druce asks.

"I think she was," Randy says.

"Would this be her?" Druce says pulling up a photo of two women from a surveillance camera taken yesterday morning at 9:20 at the New Jericho temple. Druce points to the woman in the dark sweatshirt.
"That's her and mom," Randy says.

Druce spends the next ten minutes typing in instructions and reviewing various alerts which pop up on the right-hand screen.

"There are vending machines near the back entrance," Druce tells Randy and Beth. "Why don't you two go down and grab something. I'll have someone come get you when we need you to come back in here."

Beth doesn't want anything to drink or eat but recognizes that what Jack Druce is saying is not really a suggestion, it is an instruction.

"The Desk Sergeant will get someone to help you find the machines," Druce says.

Beth and Randy walk out the way they came in.

"Jack Druce said you might be able to lead us to the vending machines," Beth says to the officer at the desk.

"Sure thing Ms. Stolz," the officer says rising. "Bill, please show them where the vending machines are located."

A policeman to the right of the Desk Sergeant rises and guides Beth and Randy through the center hallway to an area in front of the rear entrance which contains vending machines.

"Get whatever you would like?" Beth says pulling a 10 bill from the purse which had been slung over her shoulder.

"You sure you don't want something?" Randy asks as he begins to survey the machines.

Beth shakes her head. Beth has been averse to vending machine food from the time that she was ten. At this moment, her stomach is telling her that she is averse to all food and drink. Beth sits down on one of the five empty chairs across from the vending machines. Randy returns with a meat pie which he has heated in the nearby microwave and a Pepsi Vanilla Café. Randy takes the seat next to Beth.

"I don't think that I can go back to New Jericho now," Randy tells Beth as he takes a sip from his drink.

"Would you want to?" Beth asks.

"I haven't wanted to be at New Jericho since Mom drug me there," Randy says. "I thought she'd eventually come to her senses but if anything, she has become even more attached to that craziness that's going down there."

"Let's hope that New Jericho is finished," Beth says without a great deal of conviction.

"Will you still let me stay at 'The Place' now that mom has kidnapped your babies?" Randy asks.

"Of course," Beth says. "You are always welcome to stay with us. I asked Josh last week to tell you that."

"He did," Randy said, "but I thought what mom has done might change things."

Beth leans over and hugs Randy's around the back of his shoulders.

"You are family Randy," Beth says. "Don't forget that. Your sister is my life-partner. Those two babies your mom took are not only her grandchildren, but they are also your niece and nephew."

"I haven't even gotten to see them yet," Randy laments.

"Let's hope that changes today," Beth says.

"I don't get why anyone wants to follow Ainsley," Randy says. "He's a creep."

"Evidently Ainsley is also a very good salesperson," Beth says. "How else can you explain being able to offer what is nothing but promises in return for taking over someone's life? There aren't too many salespeople who can do that."

"I think my mom was built to be taken over by someone like Ainsley," Randy says. "It's kind of the way my dad was, but Ainsley is my dad on steroids."

"You are probably on to something," Beth says. Then after a few moments of silence, while Randy chews on his pastie, asks. "What are your school plans?"

"I would really like to finish up at Wannasea Secondary," Randy says between bites. "I'm hoping to get into the construction trades after I'm finished."

"What kind of construction?" Beth asks.

"Houses, shops, that sort of thing," Randy says, "but I'm worried no one will hire me after this New Jericho stuff."

"I think it's much too early to worry about that," Beth says. "I think finishing up your secondary schooling and finding some stability in your personal life are more than enough to deal with now."

"Probably so," Randy says finishing off the rest of his meat pie.

Randy rises from his seat, goes back to the vending machine, and purchases a packet of Ding Dongs.

"What do you know about this "Spiritual Guide" thing at New Jericho," Beth asks.

"Not much," Randy said. "I've listened to some of the younger kids at New Jericho complaining about it. I was too old when mom took me down there for the elders to be interested in getting me involved in it."

Randy returns to the seat and opens the cellophane package. He wolves down one of the small cakes in what are essentially two bites.

Phil, the young police officer who had driven them to the Constabulary, comes down the hallway.

"Lieutenant Druce would like you to come back into the command center," the policeman tells them.

Randy eats his second Hostess cake and rapidly finishes his drink before rising. He drops off the wrapping and drink can in their various receptacles before following Beth and the police officer back up the hallway, around the corner and back into the command center.

Jack Druce is still operating the console. The captain is seated beside him in another desk chair.

"We have identified where your babies are being held," Jack Druce says pointing to the screen on the right which shows a typical Wannasea seaside property complete with white walls and two-story structure. "It's a villa out on the southwest corner of the island. Have you ever been out there, Randy?"

Randy looks at the screen, then shakes his head. "I've heard the younger kids talk about something which they called a 'safe house' out that way, but I've never been there."

"Both your mother and Hilda White are currently in that villa," Druce says. "It's probably safe to assume the babies are with them."

"How many other people are there?" Beth asks.

"We know there are at least three others," the captain says. "We are working with the Marines to try to identify if there are any others."

"The plan is to make the people in that villa believe that our primary focus is at the New Jericho Temple," Jack Druce says. "In two minutes, we are going to force everyone out of the Temple building and into a temporary holding area. The Marines are then going to perform a room-to-room search of the temple. We don't expect to find anything. We are, however, hoping someone at New Jericho contacts someone at that villa." "We will be making a big show of it," the captain says. "We will have both Marine helicopters flying overhead. All the people currently inside New Jericho Temple will be put into a steel-wire holding facility which the Marines just finished building. In addition to hoping there is communication to the villa. This will also give the Marines a chance to take over the two homes on either side and do a little more surveillance."

"Why don't you guys take a seat at the back wall," Jack Druce says. "You should be able to get an idea of what is going on by watching the big screens up front. The one on the left shows New Jericho Temple. The one of the right shows three views of the villa." "I want to make certain that as soon as any contact is made with babies," Beth says. "I will be taken to them."

"We cannot promise that Ms. Stolz," the Captain says, "but I will assure you that the moment it is reasonably safe, we will reunite you with your babies."

Beth and Randy take seats against the rear wall as more people come into the center. Three take up positions at the command console. One is the Chief Constable, who walks to where Beth and Randy are seated.

"Mind if I sit down with you?" the Chief, who is a Wannasea school contemporary of Abe, says as he takes the chair beside Beth.

They watch the left screen as people stream out of the New Jericho building and are herded into the steel wire enclosure. Once no more people are coming from the building, 2/3rds of the Marines at that location enter the building.

"Helicopters in route," comes from a speaker on the console.

"Roger that, Sky Hawk," the officer to the left of Jack Druce says into a microphone. "We will update when arrival at Primary Location is required."

Ten minutes pass with a flurry of activity. The Helicopters are both hovering in place near new Jericho's building.

"Contact to Primary Location has been detected," Jack Druce calls out. "Forwarding phone information to Marine Command at New Jericho."

A series of transcribed phone information and words appear on the screen to the left of Druce.

Five more minutes pass before the left screen shows two marines pulling a man from the wired-in area into their command tent.

Jack Druce turns toward the captain, who gives him a nod.

"Proceed with diversion," Druce says into the microphone in front of him.

The right screen shows a standard island police vehicle pull up in front of the villa.

"This will be the diversion," the Chief says to Beth. "Those two officers are extremely competent."

They watch the right screen as the officers exit their vehicle and proceed to the gate of the villa. They ring the bell to the gate for a full three minutes before a man dressed in flowered print shirt, shorts and sandals comes through the gate.

"We've heard reports of unusual activity here from your neighbors," the police officer on the right tells the man in shorts.

"There is nothing going on here," the man in shorts says. "You can hear for yourself that everything is quiet."

"I'm afraid that we are going to need to come inside and see for ourselves," the second officer tells him.

"Three individuals on the move at Primary front," comes from a speaker in the command console. "All are armed with L85 class weapons."

The right screen is now split into two segments. The left segment shows the front gate area. The right segment shows the gate and the villa.

"Do you have a search warrant?" the man in shorts says. "I cannot let you on this property without one."

"We do," the second officer tells the man, as he pulls documents from inside his jacket and hands it to the man.

"Give me a second," the man in shorts says as he moves back toward the gate.

"Ben," the man in shorts calls out, "they have a search warrant."

"Search warrant or not," a voice yells from behind the gate, "those godless demons are not to be let in here."

The man in the shorts runs behind the gate and slams it shut. Almost immediately the barrel of an assault rifle is poked out between the iron grating.

"One more armed individual coming from the front of Primary residence," the speaker says.

The two police officers at the gate move to the side and pin themselves against the wall.

"Sky Hawk," the officer to the left of Jack Druce says into his microphone, "proceed to primary."

On the left screen a Husky APV roars into view and pulls up behind the police vehicle. As a Marines exit the vehicle on the street side and begin moving toward the gate, a burst of automatic gun fire comes from the weapon poking through the gate. Almost immediately that gunfire is followed by two quick shots.

"Gunman at Primary Gate taken down," comes from the speaker.

"Proceed with rear assault,' Jack Druce announces through his microphone on his headset.

Suddenly the left screen, which had been on the activity at New Jericho Temple, switches to the rear of the property. Eight Marines can be seen coming from the dock area. They advance across the small lawn to the rear entrance of the villa. The sound of helicopters circling above can be heard.

"Drop your weapons and there will be no further bloodshed," is announced from a speaker in the front of APV. "You are now surrounded. If your weapons are not dropped in 30 seconds, we have orders to open fire."

"All in Primary Front have either dropped weapons or are incapacitated," comes from the console speaker.

They watch the right screen as the Marines break open the sliding glass door at the rear of the villa and rapidly enter.

"One individual incapacitated inside Primary," comes from the speaker, followed in twenty seconds by, "Two individuals detained. Abductees have been recovered. Medical officer examining."

Jack Druce turns toward Beth and says, "Your babies are now safe,"

Beth has been absolutely paralyzed during this entire sequence of events. Her mind has been unable to believe what her eyes have been seeing, much less understanding that all the activity centers around the Twins.

"I don't know how to thank you, " Beth says earnestly.

"You don't need to," the Chief says patting her on the arm. "It's our job."

"Gunman at front gate is deceased," comes through the speaker. "All others now in custody. Search of premises on-going."

"How soon can I get my babies?" Beth asks.

"Phil will take you right out there," Jack Druce says, "The Corpsmen will take great care of them until then."

"I'm coming with you," Randy says.

Beth pulls her cellphone from her purse and calls Marie.

"They are safe," Beth says into her cellphone the moment Marie answers.

"Thank goodness," Marie says then only half-in-gest adds, "I'm so damned mad at you for not bringing me along that I cannot see straight."

"I'll bring the Twins back to the house as soon as I can," Beth says. "I'm on my way to get them now."

Beth follows the officer and Randy out to the police vehicle parked in front of the building. Beth climbs in the back seat as Randy climbs in the passenger side. Phil turns on the flashing blue lights and siren. In six minutes, they arrive at the villa.

Two corpsmen, one male and one female, are standing in front of the APV holding the two babies when they arrive. Beth jumps from the vehicle and first takes Nate from the male Marine's arms gives him a hug then hands him gently to Randy. Beth then picks up Julia and hugs her tightly. Beth has never been so glad to hold anything in her entire life.

"Thank you," Beth calls out to the nearby Marines and Constabulary officers. "Thank you. Thank you,"

NEXT MOVES

Wednesday, January 8, 6:48PM. Beth is seated with Saanvi, Ray Simmons, and Abe at Abe's table at the far righthand corner of the stage. Marie is up at the house tending the Twins. The same day that the twins had been recovered, Ray Simmons had proposed to Saanvi. She accepted and is now planning to have her wedding at 'The Place' on Sunday, April 12th.

"Do you know what's going to happen to Marie's mother yet?" Saanvi asks.

"Preliminary charges have been filed against her," Beth says. "Marie wants the book thrown at her but I'm trying to talk her into backing off a little. I'm certain that she did not know what was going to result from snatching the Twins. She is Marie's mother, after all."

"I'm just glad that they moved Ainsley and those twelve others over to the Mainland," Abe says. "The island really isn't capable of holding someone like him for long."

On the Saturday of the safe return of the Twins, the Marines had discovered that the hull of the yacht docked at the New Jericho 'safe house' contained the weapons and explosives which they had been trying to track down. Once verifying that New Jericho was fully disarmed, the Marines packed up and left the mountain on Dec.22. A week later, Ainsley and the others were transferred to the Swansea district jail. A contingent of 20 Marines are still at the Constabulary. Two patrol boats and another 30 Marines are out at South Island.

"Do you think that the Governor is going to approve having Mainland troops stationed on the Island permanently?" Ray Simmons asks.

Beth knows that is what the Governor wants to do but the Governor hasn't yet figured out how to proceed without creating disruption which will overshadow next week's referendum on changing the Island's legal code.

"I've heard he's thinking about it,' Beth says noncommittally.

"Mom really enjoys working out here again," Saanvi comments apropos of nothing anyone else has said.

Beth is glad that Saanvi has shifted the subject.

Since the first of the year, Prisha has taken over the running of the kitchen. Sallie will still be around for another few weeks to assist until "Sam & Sallies" is approved by the inspectors and turned over to Sam & Sallie.

"You mom has also helped us get things going up at the Meeting Center," Abe comments. "Without your mom, I think Annette would be just treading water."

"Are you going to do some type of formal opening for your 'Tiny House Village'," Saanvi asks.

"We prefer to call it 'the Mountain Retreat'," Beths says as she looks directly at Abe, "but for some reason that designation hasn't quite caught on."

"Whatever you call it," Ray Simmons says, "it looks pretty neat to me. Saanvi and I took a walk up there before we came in 'The Place'. It seems to be close to being finished."

"There are still five more structures in the Family Area to be completed," Beth relates. "There are also about forty more tiny houses Steve Harmony needs to get finished and the Aquatic Center hasn't really been started yet. We are hoping that perhaps by mid-May, we can do a formal opening."

"Aren't some people living up there now?" Saanvi asks.

"Just a few of the people who are working here," Beth replies.

Currently Molly, Annette and Emily reside in double units. Josh and Alfie live in single units. Arlette and Gabriel moved into a family unit this past Monday.

"Do you know the date that things are going to be opening at the old government center?" Ray Simmons asks.

"Sallie's restaurant should open on February 7th,' Beth relates. "I'm told Quarry Hotel and Casino are going to have their grand opening on March 15. Abe is the expert on the Historical Society plans."

Beyond continuing to work with Zack on developing new songs, Abe now spends a good deal of time up at the Castle. Abe has promised to provide his grandmother's journals to the Society at the end of the month. Abe has held off providing the journals until after the referendum. Abe wants to take no chances that Alice Bailey's role as a partner to assassination will cause a distraction in the looming referendum.

"March 1st is going to be the Historical Societies formal opening," Abe says. "There will be a few tours and sessions before then for dignitaries which will start in mid-February."

"I hear that you will be conducting weekly sessions on Island History," Ray says.

"Every Wednesday at 1PM hopefully," Abe says. "The focus will be the period from 1850-1950."

"Zack has been telling me that you are soon going to have some interesting revelations about the beginnings of democracy on the Island," Ray says, "I would like to do an article on it, if you will let me."

Ray Simmons has recently written two more widely distributed articles about the New Jericho Temple, its rise, and its downfall.

Beth gives her grandfather a what-have-you-been-talking-about-that-you-shouldn't-be look. Abe realizes that he has been a little too forthcoming with Zack about what's contained in his grandmother's journals. The problem is that Abe is having increasing difficulty trying to refrain himself from talking about the contents of the journals.

"If you can wait until the last week of the month," Abe says, "I'll help you all that I can."

"I'm tied up until the end up the month with Ainsley stories," Ray says, "but if you can do the first part of February, I would really like to work on it with you."

"That will be good for me," Abe replies. "What do think the ramifications from New Jericho's fall are going to be over on the Mainland?"

"There are a lot of high placed people quaking in their shoes," Ray Simmons says. "Ainsley has been threatening to have everything which he's recorded released unless prosecution against him is stopped.

"Haven't the authorities tracked down Ainsley's recordings," Beth said. "I was under the impression that they have possession everything from New Jericho."

"The recordings which they have come from the Head of Domestic Intelligence," Ray Simmons says. "Reportedly, Ainsley has a large stash of recordings hidden somewhere which he says can bring down the entire Mainland establishment."

"They haven't been able to get any of Ainsley's people to talk?" Abe asks.

"I'm not sure that the New Jericho followers in custody have full knowledge of Ainsley's "Spiritual Guide" program," Simmons says. "Considering the ones who do, have already given over most of their worldly possessions and their future to Ainsley, what really is left to pressure them into talking?"

"Do you think Ainsley's followers who aren't in custody are a danger?" Beth asks.

Ray Simmons shrugs his shoulders, "Only time will tell."

Zack, his father and two members of the 'RumRunners' file into the bar from the rear entrance carrying their instruments. Dave, the sound guy, has been setting up the audio equipment for the past ten minutes. Zack is on tap to perform a set of sea and folk songs. 'The Place' is almost at full capacity, though Abe notices a table in the center of dining room area which only has one young woman sitting at it.

"When are we going to start getting serious about this wedding?" Beth says with a big smile.

"I don't want anything big," Saanvi says. "I'm hoping that we can fit the whole ceremony in here. Kind of like what Marie and you did last year."

"That's not what I'm hearing Prisha wants," Beth says. "Your mom is talking about needing to use 'The Shell'."

"Time will tell," Saavi says with a laugh.

Zack nods to Abe, as he turns around toward the band to make certain that they are ready. Abe rises from his chair, picks up the wireless microphone from the table, then heads to a position in front of the stage.

"Welcome ladies and gentlemen," Abe says into the microphone after switching it on. "Tonight, we will have an evening of folk and sea songs from Zack Tillerman and Company. You are encouraged to sing along to the stanzas. I sincerely hope that you will enjoy the performance."

Zack and the band break into 'The Place' which most of the audience seems to know. They sing along loudly and cheer when Zack follows it up with 'Wannasea Pirates'. Toward the end of the second song, three young women come through the front entrance and go to the table with the empty chairs.

Abe notices that Zack is now peering hard into the crowd. Zack repeats the last refrain of the song three more times moving ever closer to the front of the stage. When the song ends, rather than breaking into the next song, Zack sets down his guitar and says into the microphone, "I need to take a short break. I'll be right back. The band will provide you with some sea shanties until then."

Zack practically leaps from the stage and races toward the table where the three young women had just seated themselves. As he does, a lanky young woman with quite striking features quickly rises from the table and tries to make her way out the front entrance. Zack catches her by the elbow three feet before reaching the door. Words are exchanged for a moment before Zack and the young woman disappear out the front entrance.

"What on earth is that all about?" Beth asks, turning toward Abe.

"I'm not 100% certain," Abe replies, 'but I think that I may have a pretty good idea."

FOR MORE ABOUT BOOKS FROM NG RIPPEL:

https://www.amazon.com/author/ngrippel